A RASH OF MURDERS LEADS UNAMBITIOUS SMALL TOWN LAWYER HAMISH O'HALLORAN TO EMBARK ON A DANGEROUS INVESTIGATION ON HIS OWN LEADING TO PERIL AND EVEN ROMANCE.

When Patrolman Wayland North finds a homeless man rifling the already empty pockets of a corpse in an alley, luckless lawyer Hamish O'Halloran is appointed to represent him. The strange saga that follows portrays the squalid underbelly of the idyllic little town of Pine Ridge, North Carolina as two more murdered corpses are discovered. O'Halloran becomes dangerously involved as Detectives Crouse and Frank X. Farrell work with little evidence to connect the murders and uncover the nefarious secrets of Mother Nature's, a restaurant/bar cum brothel, whose subliminal connection to the murders is exposed. A satirical parody rife with vignettes of pitiable and pathetic courtroom characters as O'Halloran plies his trade, this highly amusing story, characterized by pathos and bathos, is a delightful follow-up to the first Hamish O'Halloran mystery Just Add Water.

"...vivid characters...fast paced and often hilarious tale of murder and mayhem...Once you start reading it you will not want to put it down or stop laughing."—*Thomas Keith (District Attorney (ret) Forsyth County, NC (Winston-Salem).*

"... the emphasis is on unique and shady characters. You feel like you are very familiar with the town of Pine Ridge and the strange denizens who make it come alive and intriguing."—*Joseph L.S. Terrell, Author of the Outer Banks-set Harrison Weaver Mystery Series.*

STRANGE GOINGS ON AT MOTHER NATURE'S

David R. Tanis

Moonshine Cove Publishing, LLC
Abbeville, South Carolina U.S.A.

FIRST MOONSHINE COVE EDITION APRIL 2016

ISBN: 978-1-937327-87-3
Library of Congress Control Number: 2016904326
Copyright © 2016 by David R. Tanis

About The Author

After service with the U.S. Army's Green Berets, Tanis was a company commander in combat in Viet Nam when his career in the military was brought to an abrupt end by a North Viet Namese mortar round landing next to his right foot, amputating his legs.  Thereafter, he attended graduate school to try to compensate for a poor academic record, a consequence of the distraction of a basketball scholarship at Lehigh University. Graduating from Wake Forest University Law School, he began his career by prosecuting criminal cases, followed by thirty years as a trial lawyer, with a stint as District Court Judge. District Court was a fertile field for many of the humorous anecdotes he includes in his novels. Writing, then, is his third career.

He has served as Chairman of the North Carolina Vietnam Veterans Leadership Program appointed by President Reagan, the Governor's Advocacy Council for Person's with Disabilities, appointed by Governor James Martin, co-founder of the Triad Viet Nam Veterans and has served on various community boards, and church councils.

A member of the North Carolina Writers Network and Hampton Roads Writers, he won a short story contest sponsored by the North Carolina State Bar, published in their Journal. He has also had two short stories published in *O-Dark-Thirty,* a journal of the Veterans Writing Project. JUST ADD WATER, his first published novel, was the first in series featuring small town lawyer Hamish O'Halloran.

He is married to Stefanie Weidinger, a retired instructor in the Department of German and Russian at Wake Forest University, has two adult children, and resides on North Carolina's northern Outer Banks. The author's website is:

http://www.davidrtanis.com/main.html

To my son, Stephen Tanis, aviation marketing guru extraordinaire.

Also by David R. Tanis

Just Add Water

From the sublime to the ridiculous is only one step. From raillery to insult is even less.

—Bernard Le Bovier de Fontenelle
1657-1757) French Author

STRANGE GOINGS ON AT
MOTHER NATURE'S

Chapter 1

Officer Wayland North was just a little bit fearful of the dark but would never publicly admit it in a million years. He carefully looked around the deserted streets of the little North Carolina town, worried that something might be happening but nothing ever did. He was on foot patrol, alone in the pitch blackness of the wee hours. Nothing moved, there wasn't a sound, and the late summer Southern air was so thick with mist he felt as if he needed gills to breathe. He sucked in a deep breath, struggling to get any oxygen out of the moisture saturated night atmosphere. Looking around for a sign of anything out of place, the patrolman stared along the main drag at the row of eerie streetlights, giving off nothing more than a diffused glow, devoid of color. It reminded him of a London Street in a Jack the Ripper movie he had once seen, and he gave an involuntary shudder as a pang of fear tingled his spine.

He had been demoted for roughing up a low-life perp just a week before. Excessive force, the Lieutenant had said. North never liked the Lieutenant, a namby-pamby college boy, with horned rimmed glasses. How could any self-respecting cop enthusiastically work for such a by-the-book type nerd anyway? He was seriously considering quitting the Pine Ridge police force and transferring over to the fire department.

The demotion was only part of the problem for North. In his inflated self-image, he had imagined he was well on his way to receiving that promotion to detective he always wanted, when that wimp lieutenant set his plans back, perhaps interminably, just for knocking around that worthless piece of crap drug user. Now his feet hurt as he walked the fourth hour of this crummy beat in this dead town. He probably had blisters. He knew it was a punishment tour, so he just had to deal with walking the beat on the graveyard shift, until he could prove himself, do something heroic, like saving a child from a burning building or singlehandedly taking down a gang of bank robbers. The idea that policemen were not supposed to be judges, and should not sentence and inflict punishment on individuals they considered violators of the law, had eluded him. That was solely up to the courts. Without due process, the guarantee in the Fifth and Fourteenth Amendments to the Constitution, we would inevitably devolve into a police state. The nerdy lieutenant well understood this concept, however, it was lost on Way North.

Experiencing some incipient anger along with the underlying fear of the dark, Patrolman North was feeling sorry for himself, big time. In his mind, he was the victim of crass injustice as he wandered the empty streets of the little village in the middle of the night. Nothing ever happened in the boring little burg. Sure it was an attractive, even idyllic town, with all the pansy filled flower boxes along the street in the downtown area, and the beautiful pink, red, purple and magenta azaleas and rhododendrons festooned around the Victorian and carpenter Gothic houses on the tree lined avenues in the spring. The trees, stately elms and spreading live oaks, tinseled with Spanish moss, provided shade and a respite from the often oppressive summer heat. If Pine Ridge had been in New England, Norman Rockwell would have painted it. But this was almost autumn. The pansies were gone, killed by the summer heat, the flowering plants were past their glory, a few washed out, withered remnants of flowers clinging to the stalks, and the beginning of the torrent of leaves lying like dead fish in the curbs.

North felt he deserved to be comfortably riding around in a Ford Taurus cruiser, eating a donut, sipping some coffee from the local confectionery which proudly catered to the local constabulary —gratis. Instead, he was walking this boring beat, checking doorknobs on businesses on this eerie night. This was the absolute pits.

He was virtually in the middle of Pine Ridge's block long downtown, as he approached the alley between Shapiro's Haberdashery and Suggins' Hardware store, an alley that was wide enough for a delivery truck to be able to back up to the loading dock which served both stores. North froze when he heard a slight rustling sound emanating from deep within the pitch black alley, the metallic sensation of fear coursing through his loins. With no small degree of trepidation, hopefully wishing the noise just came from a stray cat out mousing around, he shined his MF Tactical Cree LED flashlight into the alley. This foot and a half long tool could also be used as a club if need be, for self-defense only, according to the book, as interpreted by that dweeb Lieutenant. Thinking about the strung out meth addict he had bopped with it, maybe a couple of times too many, a brief smile crossed North's face, until the beam of light settled on a skinny black man rifling through the pants pockets of a body sprawled in the alley.

"Freeze scumbag. Don't move an inch or I'll unload this .357 on ya," North yelled with as much authority in his shaking voice as he could muster.

"Uh oh," the skinny black man said. "I din't do nothing.' I jis' foun' this guy here. Wanned a see if he awright. He ain't."

The guy not only froze, he stopped breathing as North hyper-cautiously approached him, the well blued personal Smith & Wesson Model 627 short barreled .357 magnum pointed right between the suspect's panicked, exophthalmic, wide open eyes. It suddenly dawned on North that he had a problem. He had the flashlight in one hand and the .357 in the other. He needed a third hand to be able to take out his plastic Zip ties and cuff the perp. For a split second he didn't know what to do, but then, sticking the gun into the man's face, he lay the flashlight down and retrieved his Zip ties from the back of his belt with his free hand. There was just enough ambient light so that North could see that the shaking perp did not break contact with the pistol snuggled firmly into his eye socket.

After the skinny black man was cuffed and splayed on the ground, motionless, except for the heaving in his chest, since he had started breathing again and was trying to catch up on any oxygen he might have missed, North determined the body was in fact dead and immediately called it in. In less than five minutes, for Pine Ridge was a pretty small town, the ambulance with a pair of EMTs were there. After checking for vital signs and declaring that the body was in fact a dead one, the extraordinarily obese EMT, whose short arms barely reached his belt buckle, announced, "The coroner's on his way in." He said this nonchalantly as he was putting his medical equipment back in the ambulance. The driver, a tall, solidly built woman with the short white sidewall haircut of a seasoned Marine, just beginning to go gray, stood there and said nothing.

North went over to the shaking man who was still lying face down on the oil and filth stained cement alley floor. "Looks like the hot seat for you, jerkoff. You are going to get the needle." The guy started crying hysterically, slobbering all over the ground, wheezing out his denials and pleas.

In a few more minutes, the duty sergeant, the four-eyed Lieutenant, and a detective named Crouse arrived on the scene. After being told to search the suspect, and put him in the sergeant's police cruiser, North, a mere patrolman, was quickly rendered a supernumerary. Seething, North stood there watching the Lieutenant and the detective investigate. *"That should be me investigating this crime scene,"* he thought, almost out loud. It was beginning to dawn on him that when he searched the suspect and found absolutely nothing on him, no ID, nothing from the body, not a coin or even a dime bag of weed, that there was a problem with his case.

Detective Crouse was not a big man, perhaps 5'11" but lean and solidly built. He looked more like a Marine Corps drill sergeant, with his white sidewall haircut, than the lone detective in a small county Sheriff's department. He came over toward North who immediately tensed up. "Did you take anything from the body, Wayland?" Crouse asked, polite and all too calm.

"Not me. That's a crime scene and I didn't touch a thing except to take this asshole into custody," he said, motioning toward the backseat of the cruiser with his thumb.

"Hmmm. What did you find on him?"

North was slowly beginning to realize he wasn't ready for prime time yet, at least not as a real detective, as he responded uncertainly. "Uh, not a damn thing, Detective Crouse. I don't even know his name, yet."

"Nothing, huh? Okay. Don't say anything to him or ask him any questions. I will properly interrogate him when we get him downtown later. Wait a minute, get him out of the cruiser and let me have a look at him."

North smirked. This dick was stupid. They were already downtown. The station wasn't more than a block away. Did he think he was in some big city somewhere? But North did as he was ordered. The detective shined a flashlight all over the quaking suspect, looking closely at various parts of the suspect's body and clothing, his furrowed face inches from the suspect's skin, totally unnerving the sweating man.

"Okay, son," he said with just a hint of condescension, "we are arresting you for attempted robbery at this time. There may be more charges later. Don't talk to anyone until you have spoken to a lawyer who will be appointed for you. Just keep your mouth shut for right now."

North was astounded. This was nothing like the standard Miranda rights waiver he would have given the suspect, the one that was printed on the laminated card he always had to carry. The detective's charge totally pre-empted what North was thinking about doing, but then he realized, it would be the Sarge who would be driving the perp to the station in his cruiser, and not him. Maybe the detective didn't want the sergeant to mess up the arrest with an un-Mirandized confession, aided by a little strong arm, a little intimidation. North had to think about this ploy, but right now he thought the detective was just stupid, by clueing in the defendant.

The patrolman still had a beat to walk, and the Lieutenant had been eyeing him with suspicion, trying to figure out if North had been lollygagging. He had already checked for powdered sugar on his uniform in the event North had scored a donut somewhere. When the scene was cleared, the others going about their business, leaving North alone, he sighed, now seriously thinking about transferring to the neighboring County Sheriff's department, or maybe even going back on active duty in the Army.

An hour later, Detective Crouse was sweating the perp in the box at the Police Department. The box was a small windowless room, not more than eighty square feet, with a metal table, two straight back metal chairs, and no other furniture. Bolted to the wall high in one corner near the door was a camera, dubbed Big Brother by the cops. It was pointed at the center of the table, watching the goings on, recording everything to make sure the cops used proper procedure, and recording whatever the suspect said. After a few minutes of softball questions people being interrogated often relaxed and forgot about the camera. The 150-watt bulb made the room brighter than it ordinarily should have been, and certainly more uncomfortable. It was much easier to hide, and to prevaricate, in a darkened room, the theory went.

Before Crouse entered the room, he could hear the suspect loudly sobbing. The crying continued even after the detective entered and plopped down on the metal folding chair, heavily, for effect. Crouse gave him the look for a few minutes, wondering about the grown man crying like that. Either this guy was one of the greatest actors of all times or he was truly frightened out of his wits.

He sighed, introduced himself, read the suspect his rights, and simply said, "If you don't want a lawyer, why don't you talk to me."

Amidst the tears, slobbering, and gasping for breath, the perp told him everything. He was one of those smooth skinned blacks whose actual age was a mystery. He claimed to be homeless. He told the detective his name was Antoine al Aqwon. He knew it was a Muslim name but he was Southern Baptist, he claimed. His father was in jail and his mother hung out in a crack house most of the time. He had been homeless after being released from jail on a trespass charge at the McDonald's last month, where he had gone in the hope of getting something to eat. He was in the alley searching for a morsel to assuage his hunger, he said, when a truck started to back into the alley. He hid behind a big plastic bag full of what he suspected was refuse. He heard a thump and then the van pulled off in a big hurry. All he could tell the increasingly skeptical Crouse, was that he glimpsed a light colored panel truck with nothing in the way of signage to identify it, but couldn't tell the make or model, or even the color. Antoine didn't remember any identifying marks, dents or damage or even if it had a license plate. When the panel truck sped off, and he was sure he was alone, he went to investigate and stumbled upon the body. He just figured the guy might have a dollar or two and then Antoine could go to the all night Waffle Haven restaurant for a bite to eat, but the body didn't have anything; no wallet, keys, coins, not even a watch or wedding ring, nothing.

Just then, a CSI tech with horn rimmed glasses came into the room and turned the lights off without a word. Antoine let out a little shriek when the blue light appeared, but the tech soon turned the lights back on and said. "Nope. No gunshot residue," and left. There was a little blood on Antoine's pants but they both knew it had to have come from the body. What was most interesting to the detective was that there just wasn't a hint of evidence to disprove Antoine's story. In the back of the detective's mind, though, a slight electric buzz gave off a warning. He just couldn't figure out what it meant. But he had this experience before and knew the buzz was important.

In a few minutes, they were at the magistrate's office. Antoine was booked on the charge of attempted robbery from a corpse. Crouse knew the charge probably wouldn't stick since there wasn't really a complainant, but he wanted to keep the defendant around for a while, and his soft spot figured the kid could use a little fattening up. Geez, he was so emaciated he looked like a refugee from Bangladesh. After booking the suspect, he was marched off to the county jail to await the next step in the process which was supposed to occur the following morning.

It didn't. A whole day and night passed before Antoine was brought before a judge. At first appearances, Antoine stood shaking before Judge Sam Hill, who snickered a little when the next name on the attorney appointed list was announced by the clerk. It was Hamish O'Halloran. Nevertheless, with a bit of a flourish, he grandly appointed O'Halloran to represent Antoine and set the court date for the detective's regularly scheduled monthly court appearance, three weeks into the future. He set the bond at $500 but it might as well have been a million unless an angel appeared to post it, and that was highly unlikely. Southern Baptists with Muslim names, it seemed, did not have a direct line to the almighty. The bail bondsmen who had been hanging around trolling for clients quickly vanished. None of them, it seemed, wanted to take a chance on this one. The smart betting was that this defendant wouldn't show for his court hearing if he was released on bond, but would head for the hills as soon as he was sprung from custody.

When O'Halloran received the notice of appointment, he reluctantly went over to the Pine Ridge jail, across the street from the Courthouse. Directly behind the Courthouse was a row of commercial establishments fronting the road, including the popular local restaurant, The Courthouse Coffee, which changed its name every day at precisely eleven o'clock to The Legal Lunch. Gus, the chain smoking proprietor, naturally his name would be Gus, had a rotating sign of which he was very proud. It worked by simply pressing a button. The food in the restaurant was, well, food.

Edible, but just barely. It was a popular spot because it was the only place in town where you could get a cup and a bite to eat.

The little jail, two doors down from the restaurant, housed about a dozen inmates most of whom were in there waiting for trial. A few were serving short sentences. O'Halloran was a serious claustrophobic and absolutely hated meeting clients in the jail, any jail, from the puny little Pine Ridge holding facility to the state of the art confinement facility in the much bigger nearby city of Greeneburg. Most of the prisoners in the holding facility were perennial losers, regulars, some of whom just wanted a warm place to bed down and get free meals. Three hots and a cot, they called it. But every so often there were a couple of really bad dudes sprinkled in, or maybe some genuine looney toons, which made even the regulars nervous.

There were only four individual cells, and one big room full of double bunks, about half a dozen in all, housing up to a dozen men. The cells were full, naturally, and Antoine was placed in the big room, in what the jailers called genpop, for general population, where the least crazy, strung out, suicidal and violent defendants were kept. If any of the prisoners were convicted, and got a sentence of more than six months they were sent out to one of the state's prison facilities. If less than six months, they were taken to the county jail or out to the Farm to serve their time. The Farm was just that — a facility where inmates got their first taste of agriculture, and a pretty comfortable way of serving their sentences, that is, if they enjoyed the out of doors, getting their hands dirty, and sweltering in the hot, oppressive, North Carolina sun.

O'Halloran met Antoine in a very small anteroom, just big enough for two chairs and a table the size of a TV-dinner tray. O'Halloran was already set up in the tiny room when they brought Antoine in, shackled in leg irons, looking around like a rabbit in a fox den.

"I'm your court appointed lawyer, Antoine," he said, handing him a coffee stained business card. It didn't matter because Antoine just glanced at the card and put it down. The realization dawned on O'Halloran that Antoine perhaps couldn't read. "Look Antoine, my name is O'Halloran. I'm a lawyer. I have been appointed to represent you in court on this charge of attempted robbery. Tell me what happened. What really happened."

O'Halloran was not your typical lawyer. Oh, he started out that way, all full of *'save the world'* zeal, feed the hungry, and help for the downtrodden, all that kind of feel good altruism. But after twenty-five years, most of it spent in District Court where the really petty stuff was tried, he was just a burned out, tired, old street lawyer. And he looked it. O'Halloran was what one might euphemistically call sartorially challenged. It was the first thing one noticed about him. He looked like he crawled out from the basement of a Goodwill Store. His clothes were perennially mismatched, and wrinkled. He usually wore a colored shirt, like gold, avocado green, and sometimes a maroonish purple one, that were leftovers from the style challenged fads of the 70s. He probably didn't own an iron. One might be able to deduce correctly that he frequented the local thrift shops, even the Salvation Army store. He often wore khaki pants, which hadn't been pressed in years even if they were of the Permanent Press sort that was always hyped in men's clothing stores. He would have preferred something more comfortable but he opted for khakis because he had been chewed out by a judge once, for wearing an old pair of jeans to court. For purposes of formality and to show respect to the Court, he wore a sport coat, an amorphous gray one, badly in need of pressing, starch, or something to give it shape.

He was almost irreverent, having long ago figured out that District Court was merely a processing center for low life ne'er do wells, an unending stream of them. It was often the poor man's alternate dispute resolution forum, turning petty neighborhood squabbles into kiss and make up sessions before they became full-fledged feuds. Sometimes, when he really had to dress up, he wore a wrinkled seersucker suit, yellowing around the neck and cuffs, with faded blue stripes. But his real problem was that everything about his dress was always wrong. His shoelaces were often untied, the shoes scruffy, not having been polished since he had been admitted to the bar decades ago, and his socks were more often than not different colors. He was either color blind or didn't stop to check if they matched. You could almost bet his fly would be open, or a shirttail hanging out. He usually sported a colorful tie with some cartoon character, like the Tasmanian Devil or Santa Claus emblazoned on it, but the thin end always seemed to be noticeably longer than the wide end, and the four-in-hand knot was invariably off center — considerably. He was more likely to be arrested on suspicion of being a vagrant than picked for the cover of GQ.

Physically, O'Halloran was tall and a little stooped, kind of Lincolnesque. He was rather angular and looked almost disjointed except for his small pot belly, and he wore his pee gray hair in a ponytail despite the fact that he was nearly bald, or at least well on the way to getting there. "High forehead" he liked to say. "Sign of intelligence," he would add.

So you can imagine the reaction of Antoine al Aqwon when he saw O'Halloran sitting there, but you would be wrong, dead wrong. Antoine was delighted to have someone who actually seemed to be there for him, even if his lawyer was paid by the very state that was prosecuting him; even though he was a slovenly mess, with the oratorical skills of a deaf mute. But O'Halloran was Antoine al Aqwon's very own lawyer, so he exuded nothing but admiration and esteem for the old attorney.

O'Halloran asked him about the facts, but in typical O'Halloran fashion he forgot to inquire about the basics, you know, stuff like social security number, date of birth, home address and contact information. After talking with Antoine, O'Halloran wandered over to District Court to see his friend Billy Brown, the aging Assistant District Attorney, whose prodigious memory put the entire courthouse crowd in awe. Billy remembered everything about every miscreant whoever darkened the doors of the District Court in Pine Ridge. It was simply an astounding feat of mnemonics. But Billy was a few months or maybe years short of the retirement, which he dreamed of as being the perfect solution to his dreary job and daily contact with the crud of the earth, at least the crud that constituted the Pine Ridge soil.

Billy was just wrapping up a morning of boring, mind numbing and mundane administrative matters such as appointing attorneys for indigent defendants, continuances, and misdemeanor guilty pleas. He noticed O'Halloran as he sat down in the back of the Court room, and nodded to him. When the lunch recess was called, O'Halloran approached his friend. "Billy, I just got appointed to represent some really skinny guy named Antoine al Aqwon on an attempted robbery from a dead body. Neither had anything on him, and so far as I can tell there is no ID on the corpse. Are you actually going to go through with this thing?"

"Haven't seen the report yet, Ham, but based on what you say, no, I'll can it in District Court. That is, unless the guy had something to do with the body being dead."

"Hmm. Hadn't thought of that." Ham mused. "Okay. See you later."

Chapter 2

Built around the turn of the century, the Pine Ridge Courthouse was a rather simple two story affair architecturally, with just enough corbels and niceties to look important. Lowly District Court, located in the basement of the building, was a large plain room with wormy chestnut wooden paneling, and portraits of Judges long forgotten. The ignominy of complete oblivion having been spared these men because of these almost cartoonish portraits, still nobody knew who they were. Or cared. The much more formal, and exalted Superior Court on the second floor was richly endowed with Art Deco carvings and architectural devices and adornments. It actually did inspire a little awe. So did Judge Harley Martin, an imperial and learned Judge, who was practiced in the art of inspiring awe, as he made experienced attorneys and prosecutors alike quake in their proverbial boots.

The District Court Judges dealt with all manner of domestic squabbles, from downright evil control freaks criminally dominating their meek spouses, to the dreaded domestic violence cases where inarticulate husbands, frustrated in their inability to communicate their point to their often mouthy, constantly interrupting and overbearing significant others, felt they had no choice but to resort to base violence. These Judges dealt with social misfits whose family arguments escalated to the point where the only recourse they had to any civilized dispute resolution was the District Courts. There, the Judges handled cross-warrants where neighbors, feuding over such pettiness as a barking dog, charged each other with trespassing, assaults and communicating threats, most of it stretching the definition of any crime at the unwitting urging of a bored magistrate who issued the warrants just to save the peace, and get the squabbling parties out of his office, sight and earshot. These judges dealt with a vast range of misdemeanor offenses, too, from the pathetic and pitiful, to crimes of downright inventive and repulsive moral turpitude. Society's troglodytes desperately fighting to survive, might sneak a package of fat laden ground beef from the grocery store and stick it down their pants, or even eat a bar of candy to keep away starvation before going to the checkout. Occasionally, it was someone of high standing, like the wealthy dentist's wife, arrogantly shoplifting a pair of chi-chi chic sun glasses as if it were her God given right.

These courts were inundated with tattooed teens who, wandering the streets without any direction at all, were easily caught by zealous cops, whose favorite charges were possession of a bag of pot, or worse, a rock of crack or cocaine pipe. The District Courts were full of aimless youth without jobs or ambition, dull witted pot smokers, pathetic, concentration-camp skinny meth addicts, youths decorated with silly indelible tattoos on their fingers or skinny arms where biceps should have been, pounds of tasteless bling, and goofy baseball caps worn sideways, their beltless jeans hanging precariously at mid-thigh, as they postured, parading their imaginary virility and toughness. Then there were society's real outcasts — cross dressers and runaways charged with soliciting prostitution, homeless alcoholics, mentally challenged or impaired folks wandering the streets or malls, and much more. If one could imagine the absolute worst in society, sooner or later it appeared before the District Court Judges. More than occasionally, that absolute worst was even worse than a normal court watcher could even imagine, which is why there was a troupe of elderly folks, mostly old men, who would daily find the best seats in the Court room. Watching a morning of District Court was amusement that would make even Jerry Springer blush. This was unscripted, unexpected, spontaneous entertainment, at its most lurid resulting in scenes that were often truly hilarious.

District Court was not so much the rule of law as it was the rule of the personality cult of the Judges. There, the law was what the judges said it was, not necessarily in accord with the actual law as it was set out in the statutes. If somebody didn't like a judge's ruling, no matter how correct or how wacky, they could always appeal to Superior Court. The judges were an interesting lot. They were all regular church goers, not so much because of their strong religious beliefs but so they could actually see and be with the decent and honorable segment of the local citizenry. In this way, they could wash off the taint of evil and the social depravity and weirdness that permeated the District Courts.

There were three regular District Court Judges elected by the citizenry, or at least that's what it was supposed to be. Most of the citizenry didn't vote and most of those that did, didn't have the faintest idea of who to vote for among the judicial candidates or even why. Often, it was the catchy name of the judge, or the fact that the local newspaper gave their endorsement that was enough for a win. Being a judge was a precarious existence, for one never knew when someone named Andrew Jackson or John Elway would run for judge. You only had to be a lawyer. It didn't matter if the candidate failed the bar six times, or suffered from narcolepsy. Predicting judicial races was risky business.

So there was really no rhyme nor reason why these three District Court judges were the ones that were elected. But each of them was a character. Yes indeed, they sure were characters.

L. Rita Axelrod was the Chief Judge. She was a fixture, having been re-elected four times, and going on her eighteenth year on the bench. Some thought it was the fact that her name began with an A and therefore was the first name on the ballot that was the key to her electoral successes. Some candidates had even thought of changing their name to Abbott just to get the coveted first spot on the ballot. But truth be told, L. Rita was actually a very good judge. She was a smart, conservative Republican which was something of an oxymoron because she was black. Dark black. Dark blue black. But boy, did she mean business. She had gone to the famously conservative University of Chicago at a time when blacks enrolled there were quite rare. In fact, there weren't any other blacks. The esteemed Chief District Court Judge had majored in economics and then attended the much more liberal law school at Catholic University in D.C. She was affectionately, or maybe not so affectionately, referred to as the "Ax" or sometimes, when she was in one of her moods, as "the Battle Ax." Woe be it to the young black man who appeared before her for some crime that she considered demeaning to her race. It was even reported that some young tough, an extortionist of lunch money at his high school, had fainted dead away when confronted by the glaring "Ax" who had made him stand before the bench with no attorney to protect him, no desk to lean on or hide behind, no Momma to save him.

Then there was Judge Sam Hill. He was the only male judge in District Court, yet somehow seemed to get the vast majority of the testy domestic cases. Sam was a veteran and started Court each day with the Pledge of Allegiance. Almost nobody knew the words anymore, so there was a cacophony of mumbles as those in the courtroom pretended to follow along. Then the Judge would ask for a moment of silence while he said a silent prayer. So did most of the miscreants who were new and not familiar with Court. They fervently prayed to God even if they didn't believe. It just seemed like an awfully good idea at the time, to pray for mercy in this terrifying, frightening Hall of Justice.

The third judge was Tara Elmo. At over six feet tall and a good two hundred pounds Judge Elmo was intimidating. Her huge shoulders looked like she had a curtain rod in them, but it was just a swimmer's physique. She had been an Olympic swimmer once, and believed everyone should have the focus and dedication that activity required. She was therefore not kind to slackers. It seemed she considered just about everyone who came before her to be a slacker. Of course, that was generally the case. Disciplined, driven people with direction seldom found themselves in District Court. Judge Elmo demanded punctuality and perfection. That was why O'Halloran was just about her least favorite of Pine Ridge's lawyers. For some odd reason, Judge Elmo usually handled the cases involving juveniles and the dreaded Department of Social Services, Pine Ridge County's equivalent of the Gestapo.

Hamish O'Halloran was used to the District Court judges and they were used to him. Not impressed by him, or awed by his ability, just used to him. They just knew what to expect and whatever that was, it was the bare minimum. He was never a challenge to the judges, not to their legal knowledge, common sense, or their wisdom. Judge Sam Hill was happy with that, Elmo hated it, and L. Rita just accepted it.

Now Superior Court was another matter. The resident Superior Court Judge was Harley Martin. He was tough, demanding, and invariably impatient. That impatience was especially heaped upon unprepared lawyers, and defense lawyers who equivocated, puffed their client's alleged or imagined attributes, and especially, for those that were stupid enough to actually lie. God help the poor defense lawyer Judge Martin caught in a lie. There were stories of the graveyard being littered with the bones of defense lawyers who lied to Judge Harley Martin.

The day after O'Halloran had the misfortune to meet the pathetic Antoine al Aqwon, he had to appear in Superior Court to represent a client O'Halloran was convinced was one of those rare persons with absolutely no redeeming social value. None. Zip. Nada. The legal system was totally unprepared to deal with this lot, but fortunately there just weren't that many of them — in the whole world. In his twenty-five years of practicing law, O'Halloran had come across maybe half a dozen. Scoundrels was a euphemism for them; scumbag was a term in the vernacular of the law enforcement officers, but there just wasn't a term on the proper side of the English language for people like that, and O'Halloran had a young one to try to represent. But as he appeared before the eminent jurist his mind was still troubled by the pathetic Antoine, as he tried to figure out just who and what may have been the body whose pants Antoine had been caught rifling.

"Mr. O'Halloran," Judge Harley Martin raised his bushy black eyebrows, which contrasted starkly with his snow white hair, in an implicit request for a response from the taciturn old lawyer. Well maybe O'Halloran wasn't really old, you couldn't actually tell what his age was. He was balding, but what little hair remained on the top and sides was pulled back in a tight ponytail, as neat as he could manage it because this was, after all, Superior Court. What hair he did have was an unappealing shade of gray with a few yellowish strands mixed in. It had just a hint of being unwashed, and maybe a week or two past when he really needed a trim.

Hamish O'Halloran had been a fixture in the courts of Pine Ridge for a generation. He certainly wasn't what one would call a brilliant lawyer, uninspired was more like it. But he was a regular, so it came as something of a surprise when Judge Martin had to prompt him. It kind of looked like O'Halloran had been daydreaming, not a particularly surprising occurrence.

"Do you have anything to say on behalf of the defendant?"

Hamish looked down at the unkempt young man, who stared back, cocky, even arrogant. There wasn't a hint of trepidation in his dull witted eyes. As a sign of his utter disrespect toward the world, he wore a t-shirt adorned with an overabundance of bling. The black t-shirt advertised some gangsta rapper and showed two blazing guns superimposed on, believe it or not, a large marijuana leaf. Hamish didn't know who the young man was trying to impress but it certainly wasn't Judge Harley Martin who was just about seething under his breath, waiting to get at this malcontent. O'Halloran, and just about everybody else in the Courtroom, could tell that the Judge was metaphorically rubbing his hands in glee at the anticipation of getting a hold of this ne'er-do-well and declaring some sentence of epic and devious proportions.

Hamish sighed. He was so tired of drugs and thugs. That's all there was to represent any more. God was he tired. Tired and disillusioned.

"No, your Honor. He's guilty. He has no job, no education. He has quit everything he ever tried, and has now even stopped trying. He lives off his grandmother's Social Security check, and any pot he can sell. He has no future, but worst of all, he doesn't give a rap about anything. Put him away, Judge."

The onlookers in the Courtroom gasped. The defendant's cocksure attitude disappeared in a flash and was replaced by a seething anger. He turned to his lawyer and gave him a push. "Come on man. You gotta say sum'pin.' You set me up, man, you honky shyster."

O'Halloran did not respond, nor even glance in the direction of his hapless client. He just looked at the judge with a blank expression on his face. But Judge Martin recognized impending disaster and threw O'Halloran a line.

"What do you have to say for yourself, young man?" He was sorely tempted to use the word, "son" but felt it would be considered too patronizing. Martin couldn't believe himself. He was giving in to the unwritten speech restrictions of political correctness, but he just couldn't risk creating grounds for appeal based on judicial partiality or worse, ineffective assistance of counsel.

The Defendant stood there facing Judge Martin, experiencing true fear for probably the first time in his life. He was turning red with embarrassment, well actually, more like mahogany. He didn't know what to say. Even when he wasn't under this kind of pressure he could barely articulate a thought. Unbelievably, tears began to well in the corners of his eyes. What was this? Was it...? Yes. It was panic! Pure unadulterated panic. Hoo boy. Wait till the gang in the hood heard about this.

He blurted out something along with a bunch of spittle and snot, and then started bawling, begging.

"Please jerdge, I be's changed. Please...?" And that was it. This tough son of the streets, this posturing, pathetic pissant, in an instant, was transformed into a sobbing, bawling, sniveling wreck.

Even the hard old judge was moved by the spectacle as he levied the sentence. It was a tough sentence, but it still was probation. The kid had to get his high school equivalency, which meant he had to learn how to read. He had to get a job and had to abide by a curfew to be enforced by his grandmother, who he had to live with and obey. And drug tests, oh my, the drug tests! His urine would be virtually public. But he was happy because he wasn't going to jail, and his virtual inability to look past his nose would haunt him later as he violated each and every provision of his probation.

When the simpering Defendant had been sentenced and was trotting out of the court room on the heels of a visibly perturbed veteran probation officer, a true prophet of doom, because he was absolutely convinced it was a waste of time and the Defendant would be back in Court in a couple of days on a probation violation, Judge Martin glared out from under his bushy black eyebrows at the unconcerned lawyer, who was still standing idly in his place. After a few long seconds, he said quietly, "Join me in my chambers, Mr. O'Halloran."

O'Halloran knew what was coming but he was long past caring. He simply followed the scowling Judge into his chambers and quietly shut the door behind him. Judge Martin was standing, propping himself up solidly with both hands on his desk as he looked across it intently. "What was that all about, Hamish?"

O'Halloran was relieved that there wasn't any tirade, so he just sat down in the worn leather couch that had been a fixture in the Judge's office since the time of Nero, and looked it. He didn't wait to be invited, he just sat. He looked straight at the judge unwaveringly and sighed, but he didn't apologize. "I'm tired, Judge, I'm just plain tired. I'm tired of this endless parade of punks. I'm tired of drugs and thugs. I'm tired of lying lawyers trying to make a silk purse out of a sow's ear. Judge, you yourself know that.... that.... scumbag of a Defendant is utterly worthless, just as I do. What did you want me to say? 'Oh, Judge, he won't ever do it again. He'll be good, Judge, he'll go straight, I just know he will. Give him another chance. Please Judge, Oh! Please, don't make his momma cry.' That punk wasn't worthy of a single positive statement. In his 19 years he has accomplished absolutely nothing. I wasn't about to lie for him, Judge. Not to you, I wasn't. No sir, you would see through the smoke and mirrors in a minute and it would be my reputation, what little is left of it, that would be going up with the smoke."

Judge Martin couldn't help but smile, but he tried mighty hard to suppress it, so it ended up more like a smirk with the corners of his mouth turned up. He slowly sat back and breathed a heavy sigh. "Of course, you're right. Our society continues to breed that kind of human detritus. His father's probably in jail, his mother is most likely trying to keep up with the five younger ones, all from different fathers, and desperately trying to eke out a living, and he's just a lost soul. But Hamish, we've still got to play the game. We have to make it look like there is some semblance of due process. You're his lawyer. There must have been something you could have said on his behalf."

"What is that, Judge? Should I have said it was only pot he was caught selling, not crack or crystal meth?"

"Okay! Okay! I get your point and you're right of course. But please don't make a mockery of my court or the judicial system for that matter. You could have said something good. Maybe, his grandmother loves him."

"She doesn't, Judge. She's scared to death of him. That's why she gives him her Social Security check and eats pinto beans she gets with food stamps and WIC. She hates him, Judge. Everybody does. Everybody who knows him actually wanted him to go to jail. But of course, that is something I really couldn't say in open court, now, could I?"

Judge Harley Martin, that paragon of judicious toughness, just pushed back and sank down in his chair. He shook his head slowly. Not saying a thing at first, after a minute or so, he just motioned to the door. Hamish got the hint, got up and started to leave. In a last ditch effort, Judge Martin said quietly, "Take a vacation, Ham. Go somewhere. Go fishing. You need a break." As the lawyer walked out of the courthouse it was as if a huge weight had been lifted from his shoulders.

Naturally, like a homing pigeon, he headed over to The Court House Coffee. It wasn't 11:00 a.m. yet so it was still The Court House Coffee. After that Gus would happily push the button to change the sign and it would become The Legal Lunch. He walked in and saw his old friend, Mr. Sparrow, reading the morning paper at his usual booth in the back. Hamish went over and sat down. "Don't you ever work?" he said to his prim old friend, a venerable example of the last vestige of the Southern Gentleman lawyer.

"That sure was a lot of words for you, Hamish. Judge Martin just chew you out?"

Hamish was amazed. Sparrow must have some sort of listening device. He had walked straight out of the judge's chambers, directly to The Court House Coffee, and yet ol' man Sparrow already knew about what had happened. If scientists could figure out the physics of Court house gossip it would constitute a massive paradigm shift.

"Well, now. I really don't know, come to think about it. But it sure felt good to let that worthless punk hang out there in the breeze."

"Well it's not goin' to feel so good when the defendant turns you in to the State Bar, now is it?" he said, nonchalantly turning the page of his newspaper.

Chapter 3

O'Halloran was in District Court for the Antoine al Aqwon case. He hadn't talked to the prosecutor about his client since Billy Brown told him he'd dismiss the case unless the kid had something to do with the death of the person whose pants he had his hand in. Brown saw O'Halloran when he entered the courtroom and made a hand gesture indicating his lawyer friend had to wait a bit.

After about an hour of dealing with administrative matters such as continuances, appointing lawyers to represent indigents, motions for psychiatric evaluations, Brown called for a recess to buy a little time to get his docket in order. The bailiff made the announcement in a voice worthy of a Baptist preacher at a tent revival, baritone notes echoing from the courtroom walls. O'Halloran sidled up to the DA's bench and waited until Brown was finished fumbling around with the court jackets, the little tan envelopes that had the paperwork for each District Court case. They would be put into large manila folders if the case was appealed or otherwise sent to Superior Court. "Decide about al Aqwon's case yet, Billy?"

"That murdering bastard?" Brown surprised O'Halloran with the epithet but then he realized Brown was kidding, or maybe O'Halloran just hoped he was. Generally, Brown had a weird sense of humor, and O'Halloran, well, he was virtually bereft of a sense of humor. Not much laughing going on at the breakfast table with these two. Brown did chuckle at his friend's discomfort, but then he said, "Let me call Crouse, find out what he's got."

O'Halloran took a choice seat in the jury box and opened up the morning newspaper to the crossword puzzle, while

Brown went off to get in touch with Detective Crouse. The Courtroom was virtually empty, since everyone else had run off to smoke cigarettes, empty their bladders, and otherwise escape the courtroom walls for fear they would start closing in on them.

In about twenty minutes, long past the ten-minute recess the bailiff had called for, people started filtering back in. Among the first was Judge Axelrod who asked no-one in particular where Brown was. Just then the prosecutor rushed in, panting a little bit.

"Sorry Judge. I was on the phone with a detective." The first thing he did was to call out the name of the defendant, Antoine al Aqwon. O'Halloran peevishly got up and approached the defense table. Peeved, because Antoine was nowhere in sight, presumably still languishing in the fetid humors of the holding cell, a bad omen.

Brown announced to the Judge, "Your Honor, the State moves to continue this case because the Detective hasn't conclusively determined the Defendant's role in the murder of John Doe, the unidentified corpse the Defendant was found near."

Brown was laconic and always used as few words as possible. He felt no need to explain further. Judge Axelrod looked at O'Halloran expectantly.

"I, uh… object, your Honor. I, uh… we're ready to go."

Brown was quick to respond. "Judge, I promised Mr. O'Halloran, here, I would dismiss the attempted robbery charge if we determined that the defendant had nothing to do with John Doe's death. We are still looking into it."

"Seems like a pretty good offer, Mr. O'Halloran. You still object to the continuance for, let's say, a couple of weeks?"

"Uh. No, your Honor. I can live with that, but maybe I'd like you to reconsider his bail." Judge Axelrod had done his negotiating for him and instead of a month's continuance to Detective Crouse's next Court date, it was only two weeks. The Judge looked at Brown and he just nodded.

"All right then, continue the case for two weeks. I'll address the bond issue at the end of court today. You don't have to come back, Mr. O'Halloran. I'll just enter an order *pro forma*. Do we need to subpoena Detective Crouse, Mr. Brown, or can you make sure he is here?"

Brown merely nodded again and that was it. O'Halloran walked off toward the holding cell to tell Antoine.

The kid was fat and sassy. Up close and personal in the glaring lights of the holding cell he didn't look so young and naïve, plus he hadn't shaved in a couple of days. He had put on at least ten pounds since his arrest and was just plain chatty. "Oh, thank you, Mr. O'Harran. Thank you for bein' there for me. I don' mind stayin' in here for a couple more weeks. See, I put on a little weight." He pointed to his expanded midriff. "See you in a cupla weeks."

As he was walking off, O'Halloran was more than ever convinced of this guy's innocence. No way it was he who offed Doe. He just couldn't be that complacent about his lot if he was guilty of killing the corpse. But O'Halloran was still really intrigued. Who could the dead guy be, and why was he there in the alley? He would call Crouse in a few days and get caught up on the investigation. Crouse was not one of the sandbaggers peppered throughout law enforcement circles, afraid to tell a defense attorney the time of day. Surely, Crouse would tell O'Halloran what was up.

The next day, just before noon, O'Halloran made a telephone call. "Detective Crouse? Hamish O'Halloran here. What can you tell me about the dead guy and Antoine al Aqwon's involvement?" Hamish was always straightforward. A little too much, usually, but Crouse was not in a mood to talk about the weather, so it worked out.

"That skinny fella? He's just a doofus tryin' to pick a dead man's pocket. Lucky for him it had already been picked clean. That dead guy is not going to file a complaint anyway. The kid's good to go. We haven't been able to identify the stiff and there is no evidence which would even hint at your client's involvement in killing him. No weapon, no blood where it shouldn't be, no GSR, nothing. I'm going to suggest to Brown that he let him go. But keep him close, Mr. O, just in case we need him for something."

"I don't even have an address for him, Detective Crouse. He's just a homeless man. I got no contact info at all on him. Not even a next-of-kin."

"Okay. Then tell him to just stick around. Tell him what bridge to sleep under, or what shelter to go to. I think he'll listen to you. He's all right though. Just a goofy guy, seems like. It's a little weird, though. Most guys like him would be scared to death to stick his hand in a dead man's pocket. That would even give me the heebie-jeebies."

Chapter 4

Later that morning, either lost in thought or his brain idling in neutral, O'Halloran shuffled along the tree lined Main Street to his simple, century old house at the end of town. It was only a few blocks from the Courthouse, just to give you an idea of how big Pine Ridge was. He lived in a clapboard farmhouse built around the turn of the last century when carpenters used hand saws and horseshoe nails and the studs were true two by fours and solid as a rock. The lumber the house was built of wasn't this fast growing, over fertilized so-called white pine that is a close kin to the balsa wood the kids used to make model airplanes.

The white siding had morphed to an artistic gray with age, but the house was still neat if far short of pristine. There was a plain, faded old sign, not professionally done, next to the front door that advertised, "H. O'Halloran, Lawyer." The house was empty. The house was almost always empty. The only person who ever ventured into the house besides Hamish was Mizz Shan Tilly Rice, the ancient housekeeper who came in on Thursdays to straighten up, dust a little bit, do some laundry and leave her renowned "buttermirk" pie, something O'Halloran cherished.

O'Halloran would go to the grocery store once a week and buy several large cans of cheap commercial ravioli. Occasionally he'd buy a head of lettuce, a couple of Roma tomatoes, or a few oranges to keep the scurvy at bay. He didn't have a dishwasher, but it didn't take much effort to wash a plate and fork, especially since most times he just rinsed them. He would spend the evenings reading a little, sometimes a bible, but he was never seen entering foot in any church. The bible always confused, but intrigued him. He didn't understand what all the religious hoopla was about, but he did have vague memories of being in a Catholic church somewhere and smelling the acrid stench of burning incense. For some reason, he had a lingering fear of churches.

That evening he was reading a vapid murder mystery that had been all hyped up in the newspapers and was supposed to have won all sorts of awards. He was not half way through it and was convinced he knew the ending and who done it. Must have been written by the editor's brother-in-law. Oh well, he started it, and therefore he felt an obligation to finish it. Naturally, after he had figured out the plot, he fell asleep with the book in his lap.

About midnight, he heard the dogs barking. He looked out of the kitchen window but it was dark as a tar pit so he turned on the outdoor flood lights which made the dogs even more excited. The lit up backyard, surrounded by a six foot cyclone fence, leached of color, reminded him of a concentration camp scene from an old World War II movie. The two mutts were pacing back and forth along the fence, and Caesar, the massive German shepherd, was pulling so hard on his chain Hamish thought the tree stump it was attached to would pull plumb out of the ground. He looked around but didn't see anything unusual or out of place, and after a while the dogs settled down, probably all tuckered out. *Must have been a coon.*

About 6:00 the next morning, as was his custom, O'Halloran woke and got out of bed. After he showered, shaved and made his cup of tasteless instant coffee, he went outside to investigate. The sun was just peeking over the trees to the east, giving him enough light to take a good look around. The dogs, as usual, were happy to see him, jumping up and slobbering all over him with delight. Even the rather stoic Caesar showed a lot more emotion than normal.

Casually looking around as he scratched the huge beast behind his ear, O'Halloran noticed the door to his shed was ajar. He unhooked the chain from the tree stump and with some trepidation, slowly walked over to the shed, almost being towed by the massive dog.

Caesar immediately lunged into the shed, sniffing everything with the enthusiasm he normally reserved for a piece of raw beef. Nobody was inside, but O'Halloran immediately noticed his lawn mower was missing. It was a very old one with the paint and decals worn off so no one could tell what make it was. Probably worth a good twenty dollars, because it did run. But in the event something more valuable had been taken, and not being happy at all about his property being violated, O'Halloran called the cops. When 7:30 rolled around and no-one had come by, he headed over to the Courthouse Coffee for breakfast. For O'Halloran, habits became unbreakable laws, and breakfast appearance at the greasy spoon was one of them.

It was a routine, boring day in District Court, and he was through with his non-support case and the second degree trespass case by noon. They had been easy pleas, appointed to both by the state, and he figured the minimum fee of $75 each would be granted. That thought caused him to smile, the fee would just about cover the electric bill.

When he got home there was a folded note stuck in his door. An officer named Hank Platt, who he recognized as a reserve rookie, informed O'Halloran he needed to give Platt a call. O'Halloran called and got Platt's cell phone, so he dutifully left a message. A few hours later, while O'Halloran was in the backyard feeding and watering the dogs, Platt called again and left a message, "Go to the magistrate's office and take a warrant out against Robert Boone. The magistrate has the information." Figuring he and Platt would play telephone tag for a week, O'Halloran went to the magistrate's office.

"Robert Boone, huh? Stealing a lawn mower. That guy is one for *Ripley's 'Believe It Or Not.* Okay, O'Halloran, I got some preprinted warrants. Just fill in your name and address and the make and value of the lawn mower." The magistrate's name was Anderson, a tired old ex-cop who had wangled this sinecure, and would be there until he was too old to walk. He already had corns the size of golf balls from his years walking the beat. But what astounded O'Halloran was the fact that the warrants were preprinted. He looked up at Anderson questioningly.

"Boone's a regular, Hamish. Must've stolen thirty lawn mowers just this week. That's all he takes. Cops'll find yours among the hundreds he has littering his yard. Crazy as a loon is Boone."

After taking out the warrant, he walked home. He was still shaking his head at the idea of a town lawn mower thief, when O'Halloran was surprised to see a figure sitting on the stoop to his house. It was Antoine. "What are you doing here?" he asked, none too pleasantly.

In the inarticulate argot of the homeless, Antoine complained of the loss of television and three hots and a cot He lapsed into deep thought for a few minutes as O'Halloran just stood there gaping at his client. "What I goin' do, Missa O'Harran? I gots no place to go."

And so Antoine al Aqwon swept out the shed behind O'Halloran's house and shook out the fleas, dead bugs, and accumulated dust on the big old dog bed, and set up the shed as his own bedroom, while O'Halloran tried to figure out what to do with him. It was still Indian summer in Pine Ridge, so the lack of electricity in the shed wouldn't be that big a hindrance, for a while. At least it was dry. During his stay, Antoine helped out quite a bit, cleaning up the somewhat ramshackle property, washing the porch steps and hosing down the porch where the pollen and mildew had accumulated.

He followed O'Halloran around like a lost puppy, waiting outside The Legal Lunch while O'Halloran ate and visited with his colleagues, or enjoyed a cup of coffee. Antoine seemed to love to go into Court, sitting in the back of the Courtroom unobtrusively, watching O'Halloran ply his trade, in constant amazement, as he took in the whole scene which seemed to be a totally alien world to him. Interestingly, O'Halloran had a little more spring in his step and his Courtroom performance improved markedly. It got to be quite a joke in Pine Ridge, about O'Halloran and his shadow.

After a week of this discomfort, at least for O'Halloran, he found himself in District Court in a new role, that of victim. It was Robert Boone's day in Court. The town lawn mower thief appeared with his own Court appointed lawyer, a competent but incredibly young looking woman named Tammy Barnhill. She appeared to be no more than fourteen but had to be at least mid-twenties unless she was a child prodigy and gone to law school right after high school. When his case was called, she rose and addressed the Judge. "Uh, Judge Axelrod. Um. I need to be recused from representing this, uh, Defendant."

"And why is that Miz Barnhill? I don't usually let appointed lawyers out of their duty to represent defendants they have been duly appointed to represent."

"Uh, your Honor….," sweat was beginning to bead up on the young lawyer's face. "I need to be recused because, uh, I think Mr. Boone stole my lawn mower."

Officer Platt, who was also sitting in Court, waiting to testify, slowly stood up. "Uh, Judge, Mr. Boone stole my lawnmower, too."

Judge Axelrod added red to her black black color, "Awright. I grant everybody's motion. I guess I have to recuse myself since I've heard these unsworn accusations against Mr. Boone, and it sure has got to taint my ability to be impartial. But if any one of you tells him where I live I'll find you in contempt of Court in a heartbeat." She turned to Billy Brown, the ADA. "He get your lawn mower too, Mr. Brown?"

"Not yet, your Honor."

"Good. Draw up an order sending him to Dorothea Dix Hospital for a mental evaluation. Lordy, not a lawn mower safe in this county with Robert Boone on the loose."

Chapter 5

North was warming his hand on a cup of ultra-hot McDonald's coffee, the kind the Arizona woman sued the fast food chain over. He was walking his beat, having been once again relegated to the wee hours for a minor infraction, this time making a misspelling on an incident report. Boy was that lieutenant a nerd. He must have been beaten up daily by the jock clique when he was in high school.

North was exhaling and watching his breath with a morbid curiosity. This was North Carolina in September. It was never supposed to be so cold you could see your breath. He was thinking about trying to get a job in Georgia, or maybe even South Florida when he noticed what looked like a bag of clothes in the gutter. He cautiously approached, fearing somebody had abandoned a litter of kittens. Cautiously, because he hated cats, they caused cat scratch fever and there was a story about cats presaging death. North froze when he saw steam rising from the lump. He bent over to examine the stinky bag. There was an awful stench around it, which seemed to emanate from the inside of the bag. He grimaced and turned away, trying to get a breath of uncontaminated air, when a snort-like sound startled him. He peeled back the green plastic, and there he was, the town drunk, Lemmie Tubbs, shivering in his unconsciousness.

"Hey Lemmie, wake up," said North, as he vigorously shook the drunk, trying to rouse him from his stupor.

"Come on, man, snap out of it. If you freeze to death I'll have to write an incident report."

Lemmie Tubbs slowly seemed to come to, but it was clear he had no idea what was happening. He coughed up some phlegm, snorted, and then passed out again. North was impelled to cover him back up with the rags under which the drunk was nestled, and go about his beat, but he really couldn't stand the thought of the Lieutenant critiquing his incident report, so he called for the EMTs.

In ten minutes they were there, no sirens or fanfare, the ambulance just quietly pulled up. The short armed one, Mickey Mendenhall, walked up to the body with a tarp or some sort of blue plastic sheet on his shoulder. Without a word, he heaved the comatose man on to the sheet on his shoulder, dumped him in the back of the bus, and was gone.

North was perplexed. He wondered about the plastic, but then realized that Mendenhall didn't want Lemmie's stench to ruin his lunch. Apparently they were accustomed to this sort of thing down at the EMT bay.

After an uneventful shift, North was back at the PD ready to go home after reporting to the duty sergeant, when he ran into the Lieutenant. "Where do you think you're going, Patrolman North? Don't leave until you write up an incident report on that ambulance case last night."

North wanted to take those glasses off the lieutenant and whip him good, but he was already on thin enough ice with the PD, and he so wanted to become a detective. He just sighed and went to a desk and grabbed the incident report form and a cup of coffee. He filled out the heading and then realized he had no idea of what to write. He didn't know a thing about Lemmie, or whether he even survived the night. He sighed and drove over to the hospital to make inquiries. He wasn't going to get home until noon.

North didn't know where they had taken Lemmie Tubbs. He went to the Greeneburg hospital, a half hour drive away, and only thought about trying to find him by telephone after he pulled into the emergency bay. A security guard quickly shooed him off. He found a parking place in the main lot and had to walk what seemed like a mile to the hospital reception area. Even though he was still in uniform he was given a number and had to wait another half hour before his number was called.

There was a row of booths, each with a laconic hospital worker on the other side of a counter with a computer.

"Full name and social security number." The seriously obese clerk had an ear bud in her ear, and appeared to be listening to some noise which passed for music, while she spoke.

"I'm a policeman from over in Pine Ridge, and I am trying to find Lemmie Tubbs, who was brought here by the EMTs a while ago.

"When?"

"A while ago. Maybe three, four hours."

"We ain't got no one named Lemmie. You got another name?

It took him a good twenty minutes but North finally determined that Tubbs was still in the ER. The clerk had gotten absolutely beastly with him and called security when North insisted on seeing someone named Lemmie Tubbs, who she was positive was not there. The security guard was an octogenarian who had been a cop once in a former life and had a modicum of intelligence, and at least some compassion. With his help, North was taken to the ER where he was confronted by an orderly.

"Tubbs, Lemuel Junior, please." He had gotten the name with the help of the security guard. The hospital staff was absolutely flummoxed if the name was presented in any other order, such as Lemmie Tubbs, Junior, which is why it took an hour to find him.

Tubbs was dressed in a hospital gown which obscenely displayed every part of the filthy drunk except his shoulders and feet which were swathed in absolutely smelly, filthy socks. He was splayed out like a discarded sweatshirt, and snored and wheezed loudly. A large brash nurse, who acted like she owned the place, quickly intercepted them. "I got this, Clyde. Thanks," she said, shooing the security guard on his way.

"I'm following up on this matter. I have to write an incident report."

"Well you sure as hell ain't going to interview him, now or even anytime today. He's dead drunk. Blood alcohol content of .26. Looks like he hasn't had a bath in a year. What else do you need to know?"

"Well maybe his home address, whether he had been robbed, stuff like that."

"Cain't help you there, son. He didn't have any wallet, ID, or anything else on him except a card from the mission. We called and they gave us his name. No permanent address. No next of kin. No medical history. No nothing. Good luck on writing your report. Unless he strokes out, he will be like this for hours. If there's nothing else, you might as well get out of here. All we are going to do is check every once in a while to make sure he is still breathing." She said all this as she was politely, but firmly escorting the addled officer out of the ER.

North found himself standing on the curb outside of the hospital looking at his breath, thinking about just what he was going to say to his Lieutenant. It wasn't very poetic and there were a lot of words you won't find in Webster's New Collegiate Dictionary. Finally, after hunting for his car in the parking lot for an hour, and steaming after having to pay the ten dollar parking fee out of his own pocket, he went home. The hell with the lieutenant and his incident report.

Chapter 6

O'Halloran was sitting at his kitchen table wondering what to do, an activity he engaged in more often than he would like to admit. He mused on the fact that he might be getting old and just a little bit dotty. The thought of senility frightened him, which was one of the reasons he assiduously completed his daily crossword puzzles in pen. But Alzheimer's...just the mention of that possibility drove him to a state of near panic. His mind was really all he had, and he knew he hadn't exercised it near as much as he should have. He worried that his mental acuity was decaying. Damned ADD. He had to concentrate on being focused, an oxymoron, he knew, but still, that was the panacea for senility.

He thought it was probably too early to fix something to eat, but on the other hand, he was really hungry. This dilemma bothered him, for he certainly did not want to eat before it was time. Habit was the rule in O'Halloran's existence; a rule that was almost absolute. He was scratching his head, while Antoine watched him, incomprehension causing a curious expression to grace his face, when the lawyer's cell phone rang. He fumbled with it for a minute before answering. "Hamish O'Halloran here." Did I forget to tell you O'Halloran loved alliteration, especially with the letter H?

It was Detective Crouse. "We found out who the Doe is." It took O'Halloran a minute to realize that Crouse was talking about the unidentified dead guy they found in the alley, and not a female deer. Pine Ridge was often plagued with herds of deer that invaded the town and wandered the streets in mobs just after dark, grazing on the pansies growing in the town's flower boxes, the Indian hawthorns, evergreen pittosporum leaves, and any other decorative plants that offered tender shoots. The Town Council was seriously considering passing an ordinance allowing hunting in the downtown area, as a temporary measure. Of course, PETA was irate, and was getting ready to file a law suit in the event such a drastic action was taken by the council. But the citizenry was more than concerned. There wasn't a flower garden in town untouched by the deer, and the Ladies Garden Club was up in arms. Literally, for the Second Amendment was really important in Pine Ridge. One member actually suggested the importation of a pair of red wolves, to try to curb the menace. Boy, did this cause some rabid discussion.

Anyway, Crouse told him the corpse belonged to a traveling salesman named Leonard Lethbridge, who was supposed to be working in the Boise area for the week. His wife hadn't heard from him, but she wasn't worried, because she, well, she was having a fling with the pool guy, and wasn't in much of a hurry for the dearly departed to return any time soon. She let on to the Detective that her husband had a reputation as a ladies' man and that had caused her no end of consternation, that is, until she linked up with Armand. Sure. Anyway, Leonard liked to purchase the services of a lovely for the night, at least so she thought, but Leora Lethbridge did not know of any particular house of pleasure he liked to frequent.

After he hung up, O'Halloran forgot he was hungry until Antoine reminded him. He liked the canned ravioli too, and was salivating just thinking about it. Absent-mindedly, Ham heated up a 16 ounce can of the Chef's finest gourmet ravioli while he thought about the demised Mr. Lethbridge. He had never been to a brothel and did not know the first thing about them. He knew of none in Pine Ridge which was pretty much of a Southern Baptist town, so he naively thought there weren't any such establishments in the idyllic little village. Maybe Greeneburg, the big city a half hour drive to the east, might have one, though.

Ham chopped up a half head of lettuce, a couple of tomatoes and, doused them with Russian dressing. Antoine dug in like he hadn't eaten all day, which was a fact, and had polished off his meal before O'Halloran had finished chewing his first bite. O'Halloran, kind of thinking out loud, said, "Say Antoine, do you know of any brothels around here, maybe in Greeneburg?"

"Huh? What you mean Mr. O'Harran?"

"Oh. A brothel, Antoine. A whorehouse. A place to buy sex for the night."

"Oh yeah, I gotcha now. Yeah. I used to work in one dem places over by Greeneburg way, cleanin' up. Got fired. Mother Nature tol' de manager I was too slow an' kep' wastin' time lookin' at them beautiful women."

"Mother Nature?"

"Yeah. Dat's what ev'y body calls her when she wa'nt lookin', but she din't like it none. Had to call her Ma'am all the time."

O'Halloran kept thinking about Lethbridge and his reputed affectation for members of the oldest profession, but soon got bored when he had no idea what to do with that information.

He went out to feed the dogs. It always calmed him down, being with the dogs. Caesar was usually quite staid as if he was the philosopher of the bunch, the calm and confident leader. The mutts were always jumping about and slobbering whenever Hamish came out there, like little kids about to get some ice cream. He stayed outside until it was dark while Antoine cleaned up in the kitchen.

When O'Halloran came back in, he announced he was tired and was going to bed, so Antoine said, "Sho 'nuff," and went outside to the shed. While he was lying in bed O'Halloran forgot about Mother Nature and the brothel and concentrated on what he was going to do with Antoine, for this was getting to be a serious problem. He knew the man couldn't live in the shed forever, especially with winter coming on. It just wasn't right. Plus people were beginning to talk and there were all sorts of unsavory rumors. That's the way Pine Ridge was.

Chapter 7

The cell phone rang at exactly 6:00 a.m. Two seconds later O'Halloran's alarm clock went off, the two discordant tunes uniting to create a cacophony which totally addled O'Halloran's sleep befuddled brain. He picked up the alarm clock and put it to his ear. "Ow, that hurts," he said aloud as he painfully realized his mistake when the shrill, intermittent siren of the alarm clock went off again. He tossed the silenced alarm clock on his bed and fumbled for the cell phone. Finally, pushing the talk button, he said, "Uh, who is this?"

"Mr. O'Halloran, this is Detective Crouse. Do you know where your boy is?"

O'Halloran's mind was still in that twilight zone between sleep and wake. He was confused because he knew he did not have any children, and his response was an almost predictable, "Huh?"

"Wake up man. Where is Antoine?"

"Oh, I don't know, I just woke up."

"Well, go find out. I'll wait."

O'Halloran stumbled about, finally finding his bedroom slippers, which he put on the wrong feet, and donning his bathrobe, he staggered toward the kitchen door. The autumn North Carolina morning was cool and damp. A slight mist, almost like a morning fog, made the yard look like a scene from an old Transylvanian horror flick. Dew covered everything and his slippers were soaking wet by the time he got to the shed. He peeked in. Antoine was curled up on the big dog bed in the fetal position, dry and warm, snoring loudly, sleeping like a baby. Hamish decided to let him be, and went back into the house. Absentmindedly, he put on some water for the coffee. Then he remembered Detective Crouse when he heard a muffled voice from his bathrobe, and pulled the cell phone out of his pocket. "Detective, he's still asleep in the shed."

"Okay. Make sure the two of you don't go anywhere. I'm on the way."

When Hamish had collected his senses enough to ask the Detective what it was all about, the phone was dead.

The coffee was crummy, as usual. Hamish hated instant coffee, but was too cheap to buy regular, and make even a half a pot in the morning. He was thinking about splurging and changing his instant habit if he got a decent fee, when the doorbell rang.

O'Halloran was surprised to see the Detective standing there, but he shouldn't have been. His earlier call had been a mere courtesy to make sure O'Halloran was awake and up. He was only a few blocks away when he made the call.

They went out to the shed and checked on Antoine who had not moved since Hamish had last looked in on him.

"He always sleep here in this shed like this?"

"Uh, sure, why? He's homeless, remember. He seems to like it in there. It's like a fox's den for him. Safe and secure"

Crouse just shook his head as they walked back into the kitchen. "You got any coffee, Ham?"

Crouse hated instant too, so they settled for a cup of hot tea, something O'Halloran was more of a connoisseur about. "Let me tell you why I'm here, Mr. O'Halloran," Crouse said as he appreciatively sipped the golden brew, neat. Hamish had already noticed that the detective reverted back to the formal address when he was about to get deadly serious, so for a second he was just a bit worried. "Last night about 3:00 a.m. we found another body. This one was in a vacant lot, and like old Lethbridge, his pockets were picked clean and there was not a bit of evidence around as to his ID. Also, he had been shot in the head, just like Lethbridge. We found him out in the county not too far from Lefty's. I'm going to see the little twerp right after I leave here. Lookin' at Antoine, sleepin' there, all innocent appearing, like a babe in the manger, there's no way he could have gotten out there by Lefty's and committed the crime. In my opinion, your boy is clean, on this one."

O'Halloran had been to Lefty's a few times in the past. It was a huge, barn-like structure, in a field with not a building anywhere near it, which posed as a hamburger joint and bikers' bar. Most of the clientele were Hell's Angels, Outlaws, sometimes some Pagans, and cops, a lot of cops. Law enforcement of every ilk liked to go in there just to make the bikers nervous, but it turned out they had a lot in common and got along famously. Lefty, on the other hand, was always edgy as a cat in a dog pound. He seemed perennially on the verge of a heart attack, stuttering wildly when confronted, but he made a fortune on his bar so he just abided his nervousness. He was a small, slender fellow with wire-rimmed glasses. Lefty was a not so secret homosexual, and everybody knew it, but his patrons didn't care and just loved the fact you could get a real, half pound lean beef burger, dripping with an extra slice of melted cheddar, mustard, chili, and slaw, and of course, cholesterol laden grease, cooked any way you wanted including blood red rare. He sold thousands of them every month at six bucks a pop. Naturally, the absolutely best go-with was a tankard of beer. Lefty's was the go to place for the he-men of Pine Ridge. And, like moths to a flame, a few wannabes, ex-97 pound weaklings, who spent a couple of months lifting in the gym, popping steroids and carbs, couldn't resist the animal magnetism of the real macho men.

Detective Crouse left to go detect, leaving O'Halloran to ponder the meaning of life and get ready for a dreary day in District Court. By 7:30 he was at the Court House Coffee, his shadow dutifully waiting outside, squatting with his back up against the wall, or wandering about, voluntarily policing up apparently non-biodegradable cigarette butts which had accumulated in the gutter. By the time Doris had brought his usual, O'Halloran had been joined by the District Court prosecutor, Billy Brown, and the esteemed Mr. Sparrow.

"I hear they found another body in Pine Ridge, this one out by Lefty's."

Brown already knew about it. "No ID, nothing on him. Shot in the back of the head, execution style."

Mr. Sparrow just said, "Hmmmm."

This was followed by silence as Hamish slurped his tepid brew, and Sparrow and Brown held out their cups as Doris sloshed some coffee in them. She was adept, was Doris, for even though the coffee slopped higher than the edge of the cups it settled down without spilling a drop. The usual small talk ensued; how one of the older girls in the clerk's office had gotten knocked up, the alleged affair the good looking Superior Court judge from Greeneburg, the one with the beard, was having with his court reporter, things like that.

Just after nine, they broke for Court, Brown first, because he had to at least take a look at what he had to prosecute that day. Brown was an amazing under-achiever. He could call the docket before court, organize the order of the hundreds of cases he would call in his mind, and get through the docket in about half the time it would take the other prosecutors. The District Court Judges loved him for it, but his friends always wondered what he could have accomplished in some other field where his prodigious memory would be better prized. He always demurred, saying that it was only in the District

Court sphere that his memory worked that way. O'Halloran and Sparrow just wondered.

Sparrow headed to the Clerk's office to work out a solution to a tricky estate problem with the aged, bespectacled Assistant Clerk, the one who wore her steel gray hair wound tightly in a braided bun, who headed the estates division. She knew more about estate law than most, if not all, lawyers in the state. O'Halloran had one of his typically knotty indigent cases waiting for him in District Court. He sat down in the plush jury box and took out his crossword puzzle. Court was called to order and a new Judge appeared. A well respected lawyer with a terrific sense of humor had been appointed to fill a newly created judgeship to ease the docket over-crowding, especially in domestic court. Judge Harvey Howell had been a banker and then gone to law school while in his early forties. Instead of going into corporate law, which everyone who knew him anticipated, perhaps guided by an incipient prurient bent, he gravitated to the kind of sordid stuff District Court presented.

Brown quickly proceeded through the administrative matters, continuances, motions, a few softball guilty pleas, and before you knew it, it was 10:45, so Brown asked for the morning recess. Defendants, lawyers, and all sorts of folk who claimed to be interested in some case or another were lined up at the DA's table as Brown was informed of changes of pleas, the dire need for someone's case to be called so they could get back to work, a dentist appointment they had to make, stuff like that. Dentist appointment and Court on the same day? Poor soul.

Anyway, Brown just had enough time to run to the bathroom before court resumed and was pulling up the zipper on his fly as he hustled back into the Courtroom. The first case he called was a probable cause hearing for a heist from a jewelry store. He called the Defendant to come up, "Isaiah Bonheur." A well-dressed man sauntered up and sat down next to the already seated defense lawyer. The lawyer was one of those snooty guys who deigned to darken the doors of the hick Pine Ridge District Court every so often. O'Halloran looked up and noticed the well-dressed man was slumped in the chair next to the young, balding, high priced lawyer from Greeneburg named Goldberg. Brown called the guy from the jewelry store, a slight, well-groomed man in his fifties who was a little persnickety. With an aplomb which came from years of the practice of selling expensive jewelry, and maybe a gig or two on the local stage, the guy identified himself as Mr. Oliver, a senior sales agent at the store, and testified he had worked there for fifteen years. The defendant had asked to see a tray of rings, and when Mr. Oliver unlocked the glass case and pulled it out to show him, the accused forcibly grabbed the tray out of his hands and ran out of the store. The value of what was stolen was $24,000. He was about to itemize each ring, when the Judge stopped him. "This is only a probable cause hearing, Mr. Oliver. That's good enough."

Brown smiled at the new Judge's show of his procedural knowledge, and dedication to brevity and time conservation. He then asked Oliver to identify the thief. Without any hesitation at all, Mr. Oliver stood up, and pointed to a man wearing jeans and a scruffy T-shirt, idly sitting in the corner on the front row behind the defense table. The courtroom audience let out a collective gasp, and Brown started sputtering. Brown didn't know how to resurrect this mess, so he said, "Are you sure? Mr. Oliver, are you absolutely certain the man in the corner is the perpetrator?"

"Oh yes, I'm sure. I've been robbed a number of times and I never forget a face. That is the man who stole the jewels, sitting over there in the corner. Not the man in the coat and tie seated next to Mr. Goldberg, who, I must admit, he does favor."

Without the identification of the man at the defense table as the perpetrator, Brown heaved an audible sigh, and caved. "State rests, your honor." He just knew he had lost, but he had to get on with the docket which was particularly lengthy that day. The full moon must be out, he thought. The criminals were coming out of the woodwork as they always did when the werewolves howled.

Goldberg from Greeneburg, had no questions and immediately rested. Judge Howell looked at the defendant and then looked at the man in the corner. He noticed the distinct similarity, too. "Harry," he said to the bailiff. "Check out the picture IDs of the man identified by Mr. Oliver and also the man sitting next to the defense lawyer there. Goldberg was put out because the judge had obviously forgotten his name.

Harry, the bailiff, went up to the guy in the corner and asked for his wallet. The guy at the defense table slumped further down. When Harry walked up to him the audience froze, spellbound. Not a peep, not even a cough from them. They were entranced as they watched bailiff Harry ruffle through his wallet. A few seconds later, Harry turned and faced the judge. "The guy here at the defense table is named Ivan Bonheur, Judge. The guy in the corner is Isaiah Bonheur."

A burst of oohs and aahs erupted from the audience. "I thought so," said Judge Howell. "Bind Mr. Isaiah Bonheur over to Superior Court for trial and revoke his bond. Let a Superior Court Judge decide if he should be let out on bond before trial. Mr. Goldberg from Greeneburg, if you ever pull a stunt like that in my court again, I will find you in contempt and jail you so fast under such a high bond you will have to mortgage your mansion to get out of jail." He held up his hand to silence him when Goldberg tried to offer an apology. "Next case, Mr. Brown."

Chapter 8

If there was ever an anti-climax, O'Halloran provided it for the audience, still expecting some sort of sordid and unique entertainment from the court proceedings. He pled his hapless client guilty to simple assault. The kid, a twenty-one-year-old tongue-tied, unemployed laborer, who did not have a penny to give his seven months pregnant girlfriend, had pushed her aside in frustration when he couldn't phrase his feeble excuse. He got 30 days suspended, on condition he get a job, pay the girl $200.00 within two months and not assault her again. She was happy in anticipation of receiving $200.00; he was happy in escaping jail time, and neither had the foresight to realize what the future had in store for them." We grow too soon old and too late smart," the old Pennsylvania Dutch expression, adopted by wise old Ben Franklin, goes.

Finished with court, O'Halloran trudged home to fill out his meager fee request, and take a nap. He skipped the Legal Lunch today, because he just wasn't hungry, at least not for the slop they usually served.

Like a loyal canine companion, Antoine was waiting for him on his porch, casually sitting in an old wooden rocking chair that had some serious mildew spotting on it and sorely needed a coat of paint. The mildew probably was the only thing gluing the paint to the rotting chair. "Say, Missa O'Harran, you got anything to eat? Ize hongry." They went in and O'Halloran fixed a rather pathetic baloney and cheese sandwich, one slice of each, on Wonder bread, no less. By the time Hamish had retrieved a lone, brownish leaf of lettuce from the refrigerator, Antoine had scarfed his sandwich down, and sat there looking at his benefactor, still virtually drooling.

"I'm tired Antoine. I'm going to take a nap for a while. You don't have to stick around here if you don't want to."

Within seconds after lying down on the couch and closing his eyes, O'Halloran was in dreamland. Oddly, his dream was a vivid Technicolor dream about Lefty's Southern style burgers with all the fixins including a healthy extra slice of melted cheddar. Odd, because Hamish seldom ate hamburgers and very seldom darkened the doors of Lefty's. There was some incipient feeling of cannibalism, when he did eat a hamburger, but in his dream he had an absolute craving for the allegedly unhealthy food.

He woke with a start and realized he'd been asleep for a couple of hours. Ignoring Antoine dozing in his shed, O'Halloran quickly went to his car and was on his way out of town to Lefty's.

It was almost five when he got there, the evening dinner crowd just starting to arrive. He noticed at least half a dozen Harleys parked outside, and even a couple of choppers. There were also a number of gray Ford Taurus sedans sprinkled among them, the universal ride of the detective. Upon walking into the joint, it took O'Halloran a few seconds for his eyes to get adjusted to the dark, but when he could finally see enough to make his way, he headed toward the end of the bar where there were fewer ominous looking, brash, bearded bikers.

Motorcyclists seemed to love noise. The louder their bikes were, the better. Once, long ago, against his better judgment, Hamish had once attended a NASCAR race when they were still being held at Wilkesboro, and blew out an eardrum. It seemed the magnified cacophony of all the modified cars was aimed right where he was seated. The restaurant/bar theme was distinctly vehicular. In addition to the motorcycles in the parking lot, the walls held all sorts of sports, racing, and biker paraphernalia, and of course, the ubiquitous beer signs.

The end of the bar was also the darkest part of the room where there were fewer neon beer signs providing glaring light. Dark was good, he thought. Dim light hid all sorts of ugliness, from the vivid scars and jail tats of the patrons, to the tired lines and smeared makeup of the biker babes and waitresses. He settled in, and the bartender, a rather buxom women in her late forties who looked like she could handle herself in a fight, sashayed up to him. She asked in a seductively husky voice, "What'll you have, handsome?" O'Halloran looked at her closely. Makeup was slathered on her face like mud on a plasterer's wall. When she noticed his interest, she said, "You can call me Honey, Babe. Anytime," O'Halloran blushed a deep crimson or maybe it was the reflection from the red in the Sam Adams beer sign. He knew he was anything but handsome, but still, a compliment like that was always a welcome stroke to his dormant ego. "Uh, I'll have a Lefty's heart stopper and a large diet Coke, please."

"Huh?" said the barkeep, until she realized he was serious. A diet Coke with a 3,000 calorie burger? She rescued herself with a, "You want Lefty's special hot mustard, red onions and Tabasco sauce with that?"

O'Halloran thought a bit, and felt he couldn't back down, not in front of this fine woman. "Sure, put it on the side." His honor and stomach were thereby saved by that clever bon mot, as he watched the mature woman with a curvaceous, almost caricature like physique, march off. She was soon back with a Coke the size of a gallon jug. He took a big sip through a less than manly straw she had wisely laid down next to the glass, still frothy with brown foam.

"Psst, lawyer man. C'mere." The sound came from a booth swathed in darkness in the back of the room. O'Halloran looked around and could barely make out a few bearded bikers, some clean shaven men he recognized as cops, and a delicate couple flitting about who must be friends of Lefty's. He picked up his extra, extra large Coke with two hands and wandered over to the vicinity where the hiss came from. A man in a booth flicked a Bic, and O'Halloran recognized his friend, Detective Farrell, a Greeneburg detective who had once saved his butt from the clutches of a demented drug dealer bent on murder and mayhem. "Sit down," he said.

O'Halloran did as he was told, for he was not used to disobeying rough people who were carrying.

"Fancy meeting you here in this genteel establishment, Detective." One of the gay guys floated by just then, his slippered feet barely touching the ground. They both watched him for a minute and then O'Halloran continued. "Oh, I get it. You're a gay guy, too, right Detective?"

"Funny as a crutch, Ham. Listen, the reason I wanted to talk to you was about that guy you took in, that Antoine guy, who used to work at Mother Nature's."

"How do you know about that, Farrell?"

"I'm a detective, remember? I know things. Word gets around. Anyway, that last stiff that turned up was in the same condition, same wounds and all, as the one whose pants your good buddy had his hands in. I want to have a sit down with him."

"What's this about Mother Nature, Detective Farrell? Clue me in a little. Tell me about her place."

"It's a first rate brothel situated right on the county line. Whenever she gets raided, the girls always end up on the side of the house, where the raiders have no jurisdiction. The last time we stormed her place, all the girls were in rooms on the

Pine Ridge County side. Somehow, they knew we were coming and just skedaddled down the hall. We found some johns but they all claimed they were just spending the night in this hotel, and since there were no girls in their rooms we had to let them all go."

"Why do they call her Mother Nature, Detective?"

Farrell paused a bit, seeming to collect his thoughts. "Well, a long time ago, we arrested a guy for vagrancy. It seems he had gotten beat up pretty bad at the brothel she ran at the time in Greeneburg, a place called Pretty Polly's. The interior décor in that joint was kind of a jungle motif. She had lots of live plants, palms and ferns and stuff, and a few parrots and macaws flying around, along with some real tiny, pretty black and yellow birds called bananaquits. They flitted all over the place like mosquitoes. It was an interesting operation with all that tropical décor. Even had that musty, jungle floor odor, and an inch or so of sand on the floor. Anyway, anybody who crossed her, such as stiffing the girls or having bad credit, would end up suffering a good beating. Nobody ever complained on her, though. I guess they were really afraid of what she might do if they did. But it went around the community that it was not nice to fool Mother Nature, like that old margarine ad in the 70s, you remember that?"

"Sounds like a real piece of work. Did you ever find out who did the beating?"

"No, the victim was pretty close mouthed about it and after a bit, the trouble at Pretty Polly's stopped, probably because nobody dared mess with her girls or their bar tab anymore. Some of our high school administrators could learn a lesson there, eh?"

"So when did she open this new joint on the county line, what's it called?"

"Mother Nature's, of course."

The buxom barkeep came back and saw Hamish sitting in the darkened booth. "Hey handsome, you're order's here." She plopped it down on the bar forcing him to get up and trudge the five yards to the bar to retrieve the heart stopper. *She must have eyes like an owl to be able to see me over here,* he thought, not realizing that, like the excellent bartender she was, she never missed a single thing among her customers, and had watched him closely as he settled in the dark booth across from the detective.

Farrell stared at the burger the size of a hubcap, grease, cheddar, chili, and ketchup dripping from it like blood and viscera from a gut shot bullet wound. "You're not going to eat that whole thing, are you?" He made a grimace.

"Probably not. You want it when I'm through?"

"Cut it in half, Ham. I'll think about it if you don't barf it up or go into cardiac arrest."

"Very funny, Farrell." Ham chewed and savored, swallowed, chewed and savored. But that's all it took to lose the rest of his appetite. It tasted really good, gourmet in fact, if one can actually say that about a rare hamburger with a straight face, but that little bit caused him to be stuffed. He pushed over the uneaten half. After a few minutes silence while Farrell took a rather obscene bite and chewed laboriously. Ham asked, "What's her actual name, this Mother Nature?"

It took Farrell longer than Ham expected to actually finish chewing the massive bite he had taken. He wiped his face with a couple of paper towels Honey had conveniently and wisely placed on the table as she passed by, and belched. Not a pretty sight, thought O'Halloran.

"Alberta Joralemon," was all he said, lapsing into deep thought, or maybe his brain just shut off so his digestive system could start to process the arduous task ahead of it.

His reverie was interrupted when an argument broke out between a biker and one of Lefty's flighty pals. Someone got pushed into one of the tables and there was shouting and a high pitched shriek, like a girl. Couldn't tell if it was the biker or the limp-wrist who shrieked. Farrell and a couple of other cops were over there in a flash, restoring order, making the pair kiss and make up, so to speak. Apparently, the slight one had taken a swig of the biker's beer without permission, setting off the furor of righteous indignation.

When he came back to the booth, O'Halloran asked Farrell, "What happened to Pretty Polly's, Detective?"

"Board of Health shut her down. They sent an undercover in and when a bananaquit shit in his Shirley Temple, he went apoplectic and shut the place down on the spot. Too bad. It was actually a really interesting night spot. She kept an orderly house, so to speak. I heard, once, she disarmed a guy with a two by four. Apparently, he was pretty drunk and had a nasty habit of firing his forty-four to show how tough he was. She took a swing with the board like it was a baseball bat and knocked the gun flying. Broke the guy's wrist. Didn't have any trouble after that."

After a period of prolonged silence, Hamish broached the subject that had been on his mind since he first sat in the booth. "So, Detective Farrell, why did you want to talk to me tonight?"

"I want to talk to your boy, O'Halloran. Maybe sweat the old broad at the same time. There's too many coincidences about these murders, and Antoine is the connection to Mother Nature's. Can you bring him down to the station?"

"Look, he's not my boy. I have no control over what he does, where he goes. I just represented him on the attempted larceny from the corpse, that's all. Why don't you just go pick him up?"

"He trusts you, doesn't he? I think he'd be more likely to talk if you brought him in."

"What, to the police station in Greeneburg? You will have this Mother Nature there? The two of them together at the police station?"

"Hmmm. Maybe you have a point. Alberta would certainly be ready to call her lawyer if we brought her there. How about Pine Ridge? I'll get my cousin to do the interrogation."

"Your cousin?"

As if it had been a pre-planned cue all along, a man sat down next to O'Halloran, a man all too familiar to him. "Officer Crouse? You're Detective Farrell's cousin?"

"Nephew actually, but also a cousin. My mother is his sister, but my grandfather on my father's side is also his grandfather."

O'Halloran just shook his head as the two smiled at him, kind of oddly. "I don't want to know about some West Virginia genealogy. But this explains everything." He did not elaborate which only served to confuse the two, as O'Halloran smiled back at them, wryly, with a sort of Mona Lisa grin.

Chapter 9

Two days later O'Halloran walked to the police station accompanied by a clueless Antoine. "Why we goin' in here, Missa O'Harran?"

"A detective wants to talk to you about Mother Nature's. There was another murder which you could not possibly have been involved in so they want to find out if you know some things about her place. You don't have a problem with that, do you?"

Antoine thought about it for a minute. "Guess not, Missa O'Harran, but I, ya know, I'm a li'l bit skeered. You know what dey say about Mother Nature. She won' be dere will she?"

"No. I don't think so. Officer Crouse just wants a sit down with you. He will inform you of your rights but since you are not under arrest, you can get up and leave anytime. I will be watching from another room if I am not actually in there with you. You can ask me any questions you have at any time."

But it didn't go like that. Crouse met them at the reception desk and cheerily babbled on about such mundane things as the weather and how the Braves were doing as they followed him down a hall, but it wasn't an interrogation room they settled into. It was the lieutenant's office. "You want a coke or coffee, Antoine?"

The kid brightened up. "Coke would be jus' fine, Off''cer. Yeah. Dat be nice."

Crouse left and came back in a few minutes with a can of cold soda. He put a stained and crazed mug of hot black coffee in front of O'Halloran, and started in without preamble. "Antoine, the reason you're here is we are trying to find out about Mother Nature's involvement in these two murders, and maybe some of her employees. This has nothing to do with you so I'm not reading you any rights and you are free to stop the interview at any time and get up and leave, you understand?"

"Yeah, I t'ink so. Is it awright for Missa O'Harran to stay here wi' me?"

"Sure. We are pretty casual here. What can you tell me about Mother Nature's operation out there on county line?"

Antoine thought about that for a minute or two. "Well it be a pretty nice place. Got lotsa beeyoutifull wimmen runnin' aroun', some almos' half naked. Not really, but dem clothes be nothin' more den a bikini suit, know what I means?"

"What was your job there? What did you do?"

"Oh, mos'ly just cleaned up, sweep de floors, clean de bat'rooms, take de dishes off'n de tables, stuff like dat."

"What about keeping order in there? Keeping things under control. They got any big tough guys who work there? Tell me about them, Antoine?"

"Well, Okay. Dere's dis guy, Fred. He look like he all pumped up, know what I means? He be de bouncer. Never seen him rough anybody up but he sure look like he could. Den dere's a tall skinny guy. He look like he eat coal for breakfas'. Mean dude. I seen him knock a guy out wid his elbow oncet. Guy was causin' sum kinda ruckus. Fred trows him out inna parking lot. Skinny guy goes outside, I guess ta make sure nothin' else happen. Skinny guy talk to him an de guy push him. Skinny guy catch him inna jaw hard wid a elbow an de guy's out like a light. I nevah saw nuthin like it."

"Do you know Fred's last name and the skinny guy's name, Antoine?"

"Fred jus' be's Fred. I never heard anybody call skinny guy name. He ain't big though, like Fred. Maybe tall as me, maybe jus' as skinny 'cep' I fatten up a bit, now. Skinny guy, one mean dude, bro."

"You ever see much of Mother Nature?"

"Nah. She stay in her office. Sometimes Big Fred or skinny guy bring her a drink, mebbe sumthin' to eat. I never hear her talk to peoples. She allus watchin' her teevee, Gots mebbe five, six teevees in da office. All on a wall."

" Okay, thanks Antoine. That's all. You've been very helpful."

"I was? Whad I say?"

"What you told us was good. If you can think of anything else you think might be helpful to us, let me or Mr. O'Halloran know, Okay Antoine?"

"Okay." He got up, soda in hand, and calmly walked out of the room, the station, and headed for his shed without waiting for O'Halloran. He hadn't been gone two minutes when Crouse said, "Damn."

"What?" said O'Halloran, figuring something was radically wrong.

"I forgot to ask him if the skinny guy was white or black. It could have been Antoine himself, the way he described the skinny guy."

That night Antoine was quiet, almost sullen, as O'Halloran served up a country fried steak and green beans. What he was about to say to Antoine had been the only thing he could think about all that day. "Antoine, how long do you think we can keep this up, you staying here and me feeding you like this? I know you help out some, but I'm not a rich man and I can't afford this kind of arrangement."

"Okay, Missa O. I'll try to go back to Mother Nature's. My room dere was better den da shed, anyway. But not as safe."

"What do you mean, not as safe?"

"Oh, I dunno. Sometime dere be's trouble at Mother's. Here, nobody bother me in da shed. But guess in de winter, it get mighty cold in dere, huh?"

It seemed to Hamish to be a rhetorical question to which no answer was expected. He just grunted and kept on chewing a piece of gristle that had snuck into the country fried steak. Not an uncommon thing, he thought as he pulled a sinewy string out of his teeth.

That night, Antoine left. O'Halloran did not know when, he didn't say goodbye, he simply wasn't in the shed when Hamish checked next morning.

Chapter 10

A few minutes before 4:00 in the afternoon, North reported for duty, his uniform all freshly pressed, his black patent leather shoes dust free and gleaming. He always liked to look good in case he was up for a promotion. In larger police departments there would be a roll call but after all, this was just Pine Ridge.

The duty sergeant looked him over. Instead of the accolades North expected for his exemplary uniform, the sergeant merely said, "Lieutenant wants to see ya, North."

The Lieutenant! For a fleeting moment North was exhilarated, thinking he might get that promotion to detective, but it just as quickly evaporated when the cold fact that he had not done anything noteworthy recently slapped him in the face like a wet towel. His short lived feeling of glee fled, and his head lowered as he plodded to the Lieutenant's office.

Without waiting for him to finish his salute, the Lieutenant said, "Where is that incident report on that hospital case, Patrolman?"

Taken aback North stammered a bit, but finally was able to blurt out, "It's still under investigation, sir. The individual involved was still unconscious when I tried to speak to him. I'll go back today to try to finish up."

"See that you do. I want that report ASAP. Dismissed."

Frustrated by the Lieutenant's persnickety, terse demeanor, and his already low opinion of the chicken-shit Lieutenant, North moved out of the office as fast as he could before he let his temper get the best of him.

He got to the hospital fast but not fast enough. Tubbs was gone. Released. Sobered up. All better now, so the hospital ushered him right out the door. You think it might have had something to do with the fact that Tubbs was totally uninsured?

Anyway, finding out this crushing bit of information, North ran out of the front door of the hospital toward the parking lot as fast as he could in the fleeting hope that he might still be able to catch up with the drunk. He looked in every direction, but there was no trace of him. North realized he wouldn't have any idea what Lemmie looked like if the hospital orderlies had given him a bath and cleaned him up. He suspected they would have done that very thing, maybe even provided a disinfectant shower, something he knew they did every so often, especially when someone came in with lice or bed bugs or even fleas. Of course, North had come across Lemmie quite a number of times while on patrol, but realized he didn't know what the man actually looked like. Lemmie was just one of those people you glanced at but didn't see.

An hour later, the report, such as it was, lay on the Lieutenant's desk, along with all the other paperwork he generated. North had gone back out on his assigned patrol, walking the downtown Pine Ridge beat, hoping nothing would be happening, as usual. Nothing was happening as usual, that is, until he heard his name called from the shadows in an alley. Ossifer North," the voice raspy from drink, called out. "I needa talk wiv ya."

North was a little frightened. He couldn't make out who was calling. It was dark in the alley and he thought it might be a set up. He always carried the flashlight which could double as a billy club. He shined it into the darkness. "Damn, man. Turn that thing off. Iss blindin' me." The man shielded his eyes from the bright light with his arm. He stumbled forward as North turned off the flashlight.

North recognized him. "Oh, it's you, Lemmie. I've been looking for you. I need to finish my report about what happened last night."

"Huh? Oh, the hospital. I musta passed out. I was drunk, thass all."

Well, that had been obvious, even to Way North. But now he was stumped, for he didn't know what to put in his report, other than that simple truth. He thought of the Lieutenant's paperwork demands, and no longer cared what he thought. But he did care about Lemmie Tubbs for some reason, so he decided to check in with the hospital at the end of his shift, to get some particulars. That is, if the medical records people would give them up.

He was about to continue on his rounds when Tubbs grabbed him by the sleeve.

"What?" said North. Tubbs was stumbling, holding on to his sleeve to keep from falling, a powerful, fulsome odor emanating from him. It was in his breath, his clothes, his awful B.O.

"Ossifer, I wanned a tell ya som'thin'."

The patrolman's first thought was a fear that Tubbs was about to deliver his lunch on North's freshly cleaned and pressed sleeve. Instead, Tubbs turned and expectorated a gob of some gross substance into the street. Curiously, North marveled at the trajectory and distance, and then shuddered as he tried to guess the contents. But Lemmie was not to be dissuaded.

"Uh, Misser Ossifer. I wanned a tell ya I saw you in d'alley d'uddder night."

"Huh? What alley?"

"You knows, da one widda dead guy in it" He stumbled forward again, grabbing on to North's sleeve for support.

"I searched that alley, Lemmie, and I didn't see you or anyone else in it."

"Dass cause ya dint look very good. I was layin' on a pile o' trash wid a garbage bag over ma haid. Da van pulled in back'ards, an' dumped da body out. One o' de guys inna van got out an' da van quick like took off." Den youse showed up. I got down inna trash cuz I dint want no trouble."

"What color was the van, Lemmie?"

"Mebbe it was white."

"What did the man who got out look like?"

"Lemme think on it a minum. Hmm. Skinny black dude. I din't get a good look at his face." The mental exertion was too much for the drunk. He swayed dangerously and grabbed on to North's coat again, as he almost fell on his face. "Uh, Ossifer, I don't feel so good." He threw up and it was all North could do to get out of the path of the vomitus.

"Here, Lemmie," the officer said, as he led him a few feet to the protection of the nearest building. "You want me to have them take you to the hospital?"

It was too late. Lemmie had passed out, a trickle of greenish puke on the side of his chin. North was presented with a dilemma. If he called the EMTs he would have to write out another incident report, and the Lieutenant would be all over him for not preventing the second "incident." If he didn't, Lemmie might choke on his own vomit. So he called the EMT and went back on his foot patrol. He was two blocks away, checking doorknobs on businesses when the ambulance pulled up, found Lemmie, and dumped him in the bus like a sack of potatoes.

This time, North wrote it up as an interview with a witness in a suspected homicide. He did it up right, even noting that the witness had been consuming some sort of intoxicating beverage. Nevertheless, the Lieutenant searched for anything he could find to criticize, but finally, he grudgingly approved the report and sent it on to the department's only Detective.

The next day Crouse was flipping through the paperwork on his desk when he came across North's report. "Huh? What's this?" he said to himself, but loud enough so that the unit secretary glanced up at him. He immediately called Farrell. "Cuz, listen to this. Way North found us a witness. It seems that Lemmie Tubbs, the town drunk, was hiding in the alley when a white van dumped the body and our boy got out. Or at least a skinny black guy, according to Tubbs."

"Okay, that's good, right?"

"No. Tubbs is always drunk as a skunk. He couldn't find his ass with a paddle. His testimony is out, because there is not a single juror in this jurisdiction who would believe a word he said, but at least we know we're going in the right direction. Now we need to find that van and go over it with a fine toothed comb."

"Okay. I've got a full plate right now, and paperwork deadlines. Why don't you run out to Mother's and look around in the open area. Let me know if you find anything. If you do, then we can get a warrant. But don't go into that van if you find it, just get the make, model and license plate number. I'll do the DMV search."

"Come on Cuz, I'm not a rookie. I'll let you know what I find."

An hour later, Crouse was at Mother Nature's, circling the parking lot but there was no white van. He then drove around the area, searching for the white van. Not only did he see a white van, he must have counted twenty. Everybody in Pine Ridge seemed to be driving a white van. He had no idea where to turn in his search for *the* elusive white van.

Chapter 11

The next morning, as was his usual custom, almost an obsession, O'Halloran arrived at the Courthouse Coffee at exactly 7:30. No sooner had Doris plopped a mug of steaming coffee in front of him, amazingly not spilling a drop although the liquid sloshed a good two inches higher than the rim, when Officer Crouse slid in the booth across from him. Before either of them had a chance to say anything, they were joined by the esteemed Mr. Sparrow and Assistant District Attorney, Billy Brown, the venerable District Court Prosecutor. Crouse had a questioning look on his face as the two slid into the booth. Sitting next to O'Halloran, Mr. Sparrow held up his hand to indicate he was in charge. "Good morning, Officer. This is a little ritual we three have. Getting together for our morning coffee and a little camaraderie before braving the unknown perils of the practice of law in the Pine Ridge Court House. I hope you don't mind."

Crouse shrugged. "Okay, I guess I'll have some coffee too." He motioned to Doris to bring him a cup. "What I wanted to tell you, O'Halloran, is that we got another bit of information from a witness. He was a little drunk, but he saw a white work van pull out of the dirt road near the lot where we found the last victim. By the way, his name is Craig Craddock and he is a hardware salesman."

O'Halloran hadn't quite gotten his brain organized that morning. "Who, the dead guy or the witness?"

Ignoring his daftness, Crouse responded, "We need to speak to your boy again. Can you bring him in this morning?"

O'Halloran was a little bit agitated. "He's not my boy, Detective. Anyway he's gone. Must have left last night. I'm glad. Do you know how much that guy can eat? I can't afford to feed somebody with that kind of appetite."

Crouse snickered, "I thought you lawyers was rich."

O'Halloran was dead serious. "Look, Officer, I barely get by on my court appointed fees. If I wanted to get rich, I would've been a doctor, or maybe a banker. Or a Congressman. They're all rich, at least when they leave Congress. Why do you want to talk to Antoine again? Couldn't you get anything out of Mother Nature?"

Crouse faced Brown and then Mr. Sparrow. "Look you guys, forget you heard that. In fact, keep everything you hear today under your hat. This is an investigation in progress. Look Hamish, Mother Nature won't come out, in fact nobody seems to have ever seen her outside of her place in quite a while. For all I know she is a stiff lyin' in a casket in the parlor, there, holdin' a white lily. We need the kid to give us an intro to big Fred and to find out if he knows anything about a white panel van in the vicinity."

Since he had said what he came for, Crouse got up to leave. There was a little Laurel and Hardy routine as they shuffled places to let him out. The detective put his finger to his lips as he left.

Brown was deep in thought, but he was doing it out loud. "A hardware salesman named Craig Craddock. Hmmm. Oh yeah, I remember, now. Not a regular. but I believe he was in Court once before. Soliciting prostitution. About five years ago he was caught behind a strip mall with a guy named Ebony. Ebony used to go around wearing a very short, cheerleader type skirt, white knee socks and a dark brown wig which reached down to his butt. He also put some padding in whatever blouse he wore, you know, to give the impression he was a female. Boy he was not pretty at all with that badly busted nose, but he did seem to score a lot. Must have had a hell of a line. The Officer got to him when he was on his knees but before he could actually do anything, so the charge was only attempt. You should have seen the expression on Craddock's face when the officer called Ebony by his real first name, Larry. Ebony was a regular, all right. Must have been busted at least a dozen times. The john fainted when the cop took Larry's wig off and he found out he was about to get a little from a guy. That wasn't the first episode like that for Ebony."

Neither Mr. Sparrow nor O'Halloran laughed or even showed any evidence of amusement. After a rather long pause, O'Halloran said, "So, do you think his killing had something to do with his, uh, predilection?"

"Why not? Seems like the same type of guy turned up in the alley with your boy, Antoine's hand in his pocket. Sure, it's only a little coincidence but still..." Brown looked at his watch. "Gotta go. I'm late for the docket call." With that, he was gone, leaving one of the two friends to pick up his breakfast tab, and an agitated O'Halloran, because once again, Antoine had been called "his boy."

Chapter 12

The excitement of the discovery of two bodies died down after a while, and a relative peace descended on to Pine Ridge, the quiet ennui which characterized the little village returning. Crouse and Farrell made their calls, knocked on doors, trolled for eyewitnesses, and thought long and hard. All they had was two similar dead bodies, one found in an alley in Pine Ridge and the other in a lot out in the county, and a possible white panel work truck in the vicinity of one of them. Although there was actually no evidence linking her, their inner sleuths kept returning to Mother Nature's. They asked around a lot, Crouse in Pine Ridge and Farrell in Greeneburg, and got nothing. They became regulars at Lefty's, asking their questions, for some reason feeling that there was something there that could lead them to the perpetrator of the two murders, assuming it was just one person. It had been a week since they met with O'Halloran at Lefty's. Antoine had simply disappeared, but he had not been eliminated as a suspect and his court date wasn't for another week. The cop cousins had made a bet with O'Halloran, a cup of coffee, on his not showing for court. Ever the optimist, O'Halloran was secretly putting aside a few bucks to pay for the coffee for the three of them. Since the time Antoine left, O'Halloran had not heard a word from him.

The cops were getting desperate in their investigation of the murders, and faced the fact that they would just have to go to Mother Nature's and try to speak with Big Fred. They had no real reason to suspect him of any involvement, no facts they could throw at him, nothing to make him think the cops had a single thing to use against him. Big Fred was just a bouncer/manager at Mother Nature's, and that was it. All they could do was hope he would cooperate so they could at least rule out Alberta Joralemon, yet some primeval urging pointed to Mother Nature as being deeply involved in the murders.

It was a Thursday afternoon when the two cop cousins pulled into the dusty gravel parking lot. Set back from the road a good forty yards, Mother Nature's was an old Victorian house of the Queen Anne Gothic style, gables and architectural turnings adorning almost everything that came to a point. In need of a fresh paint job, the varicolored building was a show case of Nineteenth Century lathe turned ornamentalism and scroll saw wood work. It even had a turret. Near the road was a huge garish sign advertising the place in a none too subtle way, with a big arrow and blinking colored lights. There were even some windmill palms imported from Florida or South Carolina to add to the tropical effect. It drove the planning board nuts. Clearly a violation of every town ordinance having to do with good taste, the sign seemed to move across the county line every time one of the inspectors came to inspect hoping to issue a citation. Some low level county official must have had his palm greased enough to make a phone call every time the inspector got in his truck.

The detectives in the gray ford Taurus advertising they were cops like a neon sign, parked in the lot front of the stairs to Mother Nature's establishment. Nothing was happening, no other cars in the lot, the birds were singing, not a person in sight. After about a half hour, a large white truck pulled out from behind the place. It was decorated with a huge delicious looking cheeseburger with the uninspiring commercial words, "Restaurant Food Services" emblazoned on it in big red letters. "Damn, maybe we shoulda been hangin' out in the back," said Crouse. "At least that means there's somebody inside. I wonder if it's Big Fred?"

It wasn't. A few minutes later, a 1995 Nissan Pathfinder, badly in need of a paint job and some rust control, pulled up, a little faster than may have been reasonable, sliding to a halt, kicking up gravel. The SUV had a big metal cow-catcher type of guard in the front. The Pathfinder pulled up right next to where the detectives were parked and Big Fred got out. They knew it was Fred, because he was big. Boy was he big. About 6'4" tall and a good 260. He had skinny little bird like legs but a massive chest, must have been 60 inches around. Big Fred looked like he could bench press a raging bull at a rodeo. It was the cowboy boots that gave that away.

Fred walked up to the car and said, "Help you boys?"

Farrell got out since that was the side Fred was on. He felt like a midget even though he was an average size guy at 5'11", 200. "Fred, we're detectives investigating the murder of two guys. We were hopin' maybe you could help us out. Answer a few questions."

Fred stroked his chin in the traditional pose of one thinking deeply. "Sure officers, I'll do what I can, but first, how did you know my name was Fred?"

Farrell knew what to say. "We have a source said we should talk to Big Fred at Mother Nature's."

"A source, eh? Must be that skinny kid who used to sweep up here. Haven't seen him in a while. Anyway, go ahead, ask. But let's make it quick if you can. I got to make sure everything's ready for tonight."

The detectives were glad Fred didn't immediately lawyer up, but then, why should he? He wasn't under arrest, he wasn't a suspect and had nothing to hide, right? The detectives asked him a few standard softball questions and then asked if he knew the two corpses. Showed him pictures.

Again, he stroked his chin. "Hmm, Seems familiar. Not like that though. I remember them as being alive. I think they may have been in Mother's a time or two. I don't remember anything particular, you know, out of the ordinary."

"Fred, this is a bit delicate. We heard tales, you know, that Mother Nature's is a (cough, cough) brothel."

"Yeah, I heard that story too. Figured that is why they wanted to hire somebody like me, years ago when I started. Sorry I can't help you there, officers. We do hire some local honeys to come in and, you know, act like part of the decorations, draw the crowds in, so to speak. They hustle drinks, maybe sit down and talk to the fellas, strictly legit stuff, but I don't know about any of them going off with any customers."

"What about Alberta Joralemon? Some rumors follow her too."

"You know about her, eh? That old lady just sits in her room, keeps an eye on the security cameras. Has a fainting couch in there, she lounges around in her bathrobe and flannel pajamas. If there's nothing else, I gotta go in now. You can reach me here." He handed them a business card which announced he was the manager of Mother Nature's. Without objection, he turned and went into the bar.

"That went well, but we didn't learn a damn thing, did we? We are so back to square one."

Farrell responded with a grunt followed by silence. He didn't say a thing, even as Crouse dropped him off at Lefty's and his Ford Taurus. Crouse hoped his cousin was just deep in thought, but he wasn't sure. He listened for a snore. Some people sleep with their eyes open, he heard.

Chapter 13

Court day for Antoine. Patrolman Way North was there to make the case and testify if need be. Crouse was there to collect on his bet with O'Halloran. The courtroom was packed but O'Halloran didn't see his client, so he wrote Brown a note. "This looks like an all day affair. I'll be back after lunch. I represent Antoine al Aqwon, remember?" O'Halloran gave Crouse a sly wink as he left the Courtroom.

As usual, the Courthouse Coffee had become the Legal Lunch, as it did every day when Gus flipped the signs. Brown and O'Halloran were seated in their regular booth, having the daily special which wasn't so much, special that is. Today it was mystery meat, instant mashed potatoes, which tasted like shredded newsprint although I must confess I have never dined on newsprint, and green beans, Southern style, that is, cooked in an oily liquid until all flavor and consistency had been leached out, leaving only the green color.

Brown started the conversation as he tried to down a mouthful of something uncertain. "Sorry, Ham. I'm going to have to call him out when we start up again after lunch. My protocol is always to issue the orders for arrest right after lunch, in case somebody had a flat tire or morning dentist appointment."

Ham merely nodded because at that very moment he was concerned about what had gotten caught in his teeth. Perhaps a piece of mystery gristle, an uncooked part of green bean, or, God forbid, a hair. He shuddered at the thought of the cook, Gus's brother, a stocky, hirsute Greek who always smelled of garlic, tobacco, and sweat.

So when they went back to court, Brown called out a few of the recalcitrant defendants who had missed the morning, had orders for their arrests issued, and then called the name Antoine al Aqwon. Without waiting, he said, "Call him out, Mr. Sheriff." The Sheriff started by mispronouncing the defendant's name, "Antonio Alec Kwan, Come into Court as you are bound to do or your forfeiture shall be recorded." He repeated it three times sorely wishing the Defendant's name was John Smith or something easy. Ham tried to correct the Sheriff's pronunciation, and the clerk interjected that there was no forfeiture since he had been released on his own recognizance, but then the Judge said, "Wait just a minute, you all. Who is that standing next to you, Mr. O'Halloran?"

O'Halloran swiveled almost as if he was doing a military right face. There was Antoine standing not a foot from him, a big grin on his face. His pants and shirt were the same god awful color as the courtroom carpet, and if his complexion hadn't been so dark he would have been virtually invisible.

Brown was always quick on his feet. "Judge Howell, that is Mr. al Aqwon. The state asks for a continuance. I told Mr. O'Halloran I would dismiss this case unless we determined that the Defendant here had something to do with the demise of poor Mr. Lethbridge. Unfortunately, we haven't traveled very far down that road yet, so we'd like a little more time, maybe a month."

O'Halloran scowled. Judge Howell scowled. Nobody else said anything, so the Judge decided. "Okay. Last continuance for the state. When is Detective Crouse's next court date, Mr. Speedy?"

O'Halloran wrote the new court date on the palm of his hand, not having any paper to write on, before leaving the courthouse with Antoine not a step behind him. "What dat mean Missa O'Harran? Splain it ta me, please

"We need to talk Antoine. You got a few minutes to join me for a cup of coffee?

"Sure do. We gwine to your place?"

"No. Let's go over to the Legal Lunch. You eat lunch yet?"

"Nah, I ain't hungry."

Since it was well past 2:30 in the afternoon, the Legal Lunch was just about empty, the lunch crowd having completely vacated the place, leaving Doris, Gus and his son to scurry about, cleaning up, placing chairs upside down on the tables, getting ready to go home. Ham slid in to his usual booth and signaled to Doris to bring two coffees. "So what have you been up to, Antoine?"

"Oh, a little dis an' dat. Been pickin' up a odd job here an' dere. Dat kine a stuff."

"Where have you been living, Antoine? I need to be able to get in touch with you as long as this case is pending."

Antoine looked down at his uninteresting coffee with disinterest. "Say, Missa O'Harran. Kin I gets a cheeseburger? I guess I be's a li'l hongry."

O'Halloran noticed the deflection but looked up and immediately caught Doris's eye since she was carefully watching them. They were the only customers in the place anyway.

He ordered a cheeseburger and fries loud enough so she didn't have to come all the way over to their booth. It only took a couple of minutes for the order to be brought to them, and Antoine dug right in like a starving mutt. Of course, he couldn't talk very well with his mouth full so O'Halloran just sat there and waited, watching him. When Antoine was finished, he wiped his mouth with his sleeve, leaving his napkin still rolled up around the table ware. He didn't look up.

"So I take it you are still living on the street, searching dead men's pockets for anything of value. Tell me what really happened at Mother Nature's."

"Ain't nothin' happen dere, Missa O'Harran. Iss Okay. I kin go back if'n I wants to. Iss jus', sumpin' about dat place. I dunno."

"Okay, Antoine. You can stay in the shed for a month. After the case is over, you will have to find some other accommodations." O'Halloran wondered why he said that. He knew deep down he was setting a bad precedent. How many of his other court appointed clients would end up like Antoine, cadging meals off him and living rent free in his shed, cozying up to his lawn tools and all? He started to worry about his lawnmower again, now that it had been retrieved from crazy Robert's.

Chapter 14

Patrolman Way North hated that nickname. People who called him that were invariably contemptuous of him and used the euphemism as others might say he was a couple of cards short of a deck or maybe out to lunch. Way North considered himself to be smart, at least as smart as most cops, just not as lucky. He hated this part of the job, this walking the downtown beat at night. The truth was he was a little afraid of the dark. Ever since he was a kid suspecting monsters under his bed, he half expected someone to burst forth out of an alley and shoot him.

Pine Ridge didn't have many alleys but it also didn't have many street lights either. It was pretty dark and this particular night was downright eerie. The humidity was so high moisture was condensing on anything made of glass or metal. The few streetlights gave a diffuse glow, and made North think of the horror movies about the Boston Strangler or Jack the Ripper. When he did, he became so scared he couldn't control the drop or two that escaped uncomfortably dampening his underwear. North was sure some of the other cops knew about this fear and it really concerned him. He was certain that was the reason the Lieutenant always assigned him to this crummy beat.

He was approaching the same alley where he had found that body, the one with the homeless guy rifling through his pants. A couple of drops seeped out; he couldn't help that. His fear level was approaching paralysis as he stopped just at the alley entrance and took a deep breath. North took out his flashlight and cautiously peeked around the corner. At first, he was stunned, then he let out a little girlish shriek, as quite a bit more than a few drops spewed forth. There in the alley was what looked like another body. No one else was there, no one was rifling through the pants, for two reasons. The first was there was no one else in the alley. The second was that the body didn't have any pants.

Patrolman North froze. He stood there, his mind and body in a state of suspended animation. Then, as he became aware of the hated, embarrassing dampness, his presence of mind returned and he called it in. He was petrified because he knew he had to explain to the dispatcher what the apparent cause of death was, if the body was in fact a corpse. As he was listening to the dispatcher's questions, he inched forward, waving his flashlight from the body to the nooks and crannies of the alley, subconsciously looking for monsters. "What? Could you repeat that last question?"

"What are the particulars, Officer? Age, sex, apparent cause of death, clothing, that sort of thing. You know the drill."

"Yeah, Okay. It looks like a male, no wait, a female, yeah a female. Man's haircut, brown hair, no pants, white buttoned down shirt, big bloodstain on the chest."

The dispatcher knew North, and couldn't resist. "What about the boobs, Officer, how big are the boobs?"

"What?" North caught on and knew he was being conned. "You know I can't touch her clothes to check out her boobs. This is a crime scene for cryin' out loud."

"Okay, but is she really dead? Did you check her pulse, give her mouth to mouth?" The dispatcher was holding his hand over his mouth to keep from bursting out laughing.

"Just cut the crap and send the coroner and the homicide detective out. I'll secure the area." Which, of course, meant that North would do nothing but stand at the opening of the alley with his gun drawn. He didn't really think there was anyone still there, at least anyone alive that is, but you never knew about monsters.

In ten minutes, Crouse arrived still wearing the tee shirt he usually wore to bed.

"You homicide?" asked North, when Crouse rapidly pulled up to where North was standing, screeching tires, the soccer mom SUV, still bouncing up and down as he hopped out.

"No I'm the desk sergeant, dipwad. You know I'm the only detective in this glorious burg. What do you know about the stiff?"

North admitted that he knew nothing, hadn't touched a thing because he didn't want to disturb the crime scene.

"North, did you check her pants for a wallet or ID?"

For a fleeting second, North had that sinking feeling that he had forgotten to do an essential part of his job. Then he realized he'd been had again. The corpse didn't have any pants and was naked from the waist down, and Crouse knew that from the dispatcher. Damn Crouse.

North had been mesmerized at first, but then decided that porn was much better. There was something really creepy about a dead woman's pussy. But he did have a fleeting concern that the dead body still might belong to a man who had suffered an, ahem, terrible amputation. He couldn't get past the really short hair on her head.

While North stood there, making sure there was no telltale signs of life, like the heaving of an inhaling chest, Crouse carefully searched the alley while waiting for the crime scene techs. Invariably, the CSI team had to get dressed and put on freshly pressed uniforms when coming out to a crime scene. Their boss, the County Coroner, insisted on a good impression in case the media showed up, and didn't care about the extra fifteen minutes or so it might take. Corpses and forensic evidence weren't going anywhere.

Talking to no one in particular, except for North who was still staring at the corpse with a mixture of revulsion and titillation, Crouse said, "Alley's clean. It was a shoot and dump. She was killed somewhere else and just left here. We probably won't find any evidence at all, here, except for her." He indicated the corpse with a wave of his hand with the flashlight in it. "Here help me put up this Police Line tape."

In just a few minutes, the ambulance with the same two EMTs that had showed up to pick up Mr. Lethbridge in the same alley just a week before, arrived on the scene. Crouse watched them with interest as they approached the body, and in a futile obeisance to protocol made sure she was dead by checking for vital signs even though they all knew it was a colossal waste of time. The fat guy with the short arms turned her over and then turned her over again. He was just about to confirm there was no ID when the taciturn driver shivered. "I know her. That's Sydney Cole. She just broke up with her lover. Never thought it would come to her getting murdered. I just can't see that little thing shooting her like this." Businesslike, the two EMTs slipped the corpse into a body bag and onto a stretcher. Crouse was amazed at the strength and agility of the short-armed guy, but was more interested in what the other EMT knew.

"Wait Doc! Before you whisk her off to the morgue, can you tell me what you know about, uh, Sydney, and her situation."

"Sure, Officer. She was a dyke. Broke up with her girlfriend, Darla, who went back with her gorilla of a husband. Sydney was head over heels in love with Darla."

The given name of the big girl Crouse referred to as Doc was Marsha. She knew just about everything there was to know about Sydney's love life, but not where she worked nor where she lived. She looked on her cell phone, because she thought she might have her number. She did. She dialed it. There was no answer, probably because the phone was still in Sydney's pants, wherever they were. Marsha did not know what kind of car Sydney drove, just the dirt about her love life because it was a rather titillating topic of conversation in her circle, if you know what I mean.

The ambulance was just about ready to depart for the morgue when the long time county coroner arrived, braking a little too hard, causing the rear end of his state issued Chevy to swerve. Doctor George Bean was a chain smoking forensic pathologist who had been the County Coroner since Crouse was a rookie cop. He stumbled a little as he got out of the car. Wearing an overcoat loosely thrown over a pajama top and jeans with the fly half open, he had obviously been drinking and was quite embarrassed to see a uniformed cop standing there by the yellow Police Line tape. He quickly checked the body bag, confirmed that Sydney Cole was in fact dead, and was about to get back in his car when Crouse pushed him aside and got in the driver's seat. "I'm driving. North, here's my keys," he called out, casually tossing his own car keys to the surprised officer. "Meet me at the morgue in Greeneburg, in my car."

A few seconds after he sped off, Crouse chastised the Coroner. "Jeez, Doc, What were you thinking coming out here smelling like a brewery? I'm going to stop for a gallon of coffee for you before we head to Greeneburg."

There was an all night Dunkin' Donuts just inside the Greeneburg city limits. Pine Ridge was too small to have its own morgue. Sometimes they stuck a stiff in the interrogation room at the police station if there was some hang-up before taking it to the Greeneburg Coroner's morgue. Crouse smiled when he thought of the time he interrogated a murder suspect with a dead guy standing in the corner in a state of serious rigor with his face just visible in the partially zipped body bag. It was seriously creepy since the corpse had one eye open and that eye seemed to be locked on the suspect. The guy kept staring at the stiff and became totally distracted as his alibi morphed into a cold confession. *Good times*, thought Crouse, reminiscing, a trace of a smile on his lips.

The Coroner had considerably sobered up after consuming that gallon of strong black coffee, and heading to the rest room to pee, twice. When they arrived at the morgue, the ambulance crew was sitting on the rear bumper, ready to leave, just waiting for him. Crouse looked up at the clock on the stark white wall of the morgue which was colder than an igloo in winter. It was 3:35 a.m. He noticed Bean was still a little wobbly so he offered some advice. "Say, Doc, why don't you get a little shut-eye before you do the autopsy. I know you have a little cot in the back room there you can flake out on. I'm not in any particular rush to know that she died from a through and through to the chest. I'll check in with you about ten tomorrow."

Crouse left the befuddled Coroner and hoped the still tipsy official would take his advice. He went outside the morgue to wait for North. About a half hour later the uniformed cop pulled up in Crouse's SUV.

"What took you so long, Way. You get lost?"

"No, I got stopped by a damn Greeneburg cop. He even gave me a speeding ticket and one for inspection. Did you know your inspection is over a year out of date?"

"No, I didn't, Wayland. Okay, thanks for the tip. Give me the keys. I'm starving. I got to get something to eat." Crouse got in his SUV and had just started to drive off, a suppressed grin desperately trying to break out on his face. He was counting. After seven, he heard it.

A shriek-like "Wait. Wait," coming from Patrolman Way North. "Wait, Officer, uh, Detective, wait. How am I going to get back to Pine Ridge?"

Crouse stopped and rolled the driver's side window down. "I'm not going to Pine Ridge, North. I'm going to the Dunkin' Donuts in Greeneburg." He rolled the window up and drove off a few dozen yards before stopping and reaching over to open the passenger side door.

Panting a little when he reached the SUV, North was irate, but didn't really know how to react. He got in the car and said nothing, even after they passed the donut shop. The only thing he said was, "Thanks," as Crouse stopped the van by the alley with the yellow tape. He was still mad though. He hated being played, especially by Crouse, who really knew how to get North's goat.

The next morning at ten a.m., Crouse called the morgue. An assistant answered. When Doc Bean finally picked up the phone, the first thing he said was, "Did you get any sleep last night, Detective?"

"Nah, I'll get some sleep next week. Why do you ask, Doc?"

"Because I tossed and turned all night last night. Got up to pee six times. A whole goddam gallon of coffee, Crouse, a whole gallon. I won't be able to sleep for days."

"You all right for the autopsy, Doc?"

"Yeah, I'll be all right for the first hour, until I have to go pee again. Why do you ask? You looking for something in particular, Detective?"

"As a matter of fact, I am. Could you check her feet, the bottom. I'm lookin' for signs of dirt, mud, maybe even sand."

"Sand? You think she went to the beach and was killed there and then dumped in a forlorn alley in Pine Ridge?"

"Not likely, Doc. Just let me know if you find anything out of the ordinary on her."

Crouse, who had called from home, finished his coffee and showered, dressed and was back at his office at the station in twenty minutes. He checked his messages and emails, of which there were a dozen advertisements from police armorers and equipment companies, which he quickly deleted without opening. The chief wasn't in yet, probably out campaigning to keep his job. The chief's lips were in a constant state of pucker in case a baby showed up. Or the Mayor, with his big juicy rear always ready for someone to kiss. Crouse sat for a minute, doing some serious thinking, and then called Detective Farrell over in Greeneburg. "Hey Farrell, you hear about the corpse that turned up here last night, same alley as the Lethbridge guy? This one was a she and was naked waist down. Shot in the chest, through and through. A dump, but I got no idea where she was killed." He didn't have to say this last corpse may be linked to the other cases. That was just taken as a given.

Farrell was quiet on his end, but Crouse could hear papers shuffling. "Yeah, here it is. Note from the coroner's office about her. Sydney Cole. I'll check into her next of kin. I take it you didn't notify any NOK last night, right?"

"Nah. I got her cell phone number but there was no cell phone, no info on her address or work place."

"Okay, give me the cell phone number. I'll see what I can find out."

After the call, Crouse got a fresh cup of uninspiring, insipid machine coffee and settled in at his desk. He read the minimalistic reports about the three corpses to see if anything jumped out at him, but of course, there was nothing, including any noteworthy clues. He put his feet up on his desk and leaned back in deep contemplation, his eyes lightly closed. The only constant was sex. The first two liked to frequent houses of ill repute, and the girl was a dyke who had a bad break up with her girlfriend. What would I do if I was her after such an event? He just wasn't able to put himself in her shoes, being a straight guy and all, so he thought he'd find out about that. What was that short-haired EMTs name, again?

He shuffled through the reports, including the EMT call reports, and although he remembered she was called Marsha, the reports indicated the first responders were M. Grainger and M. Mendenhall. Typical. So which one was Marsha? He would have to make a call. Just then his cell jangled. It was Farrell. "Wouldn't you know it, Crouse, our girl has no next of kin in this area that I can find. I'm going to her apartment, which is in our county but over your way. Want to meet me there?"

A half hour later the two arrived at the apartment parking lot at almost the same time. They got in touch with the super who came out of his basement dwelling with a key and a three-day-old growth of beard. All he needed was a sweat stained wife beater undershirt and a beer to make a strong case for the stereotypical building superintendent.

The apartment of Sydney Cole was different, to say the least. First, it was spotless. Not a thing out of place, everything neat, put away in its place. There was no garbage in the trash can under the sink and it smelled as if a whole can of Febreze had just been emptied into it, The sink was polished, the counter sparkling — it was as if it was just made ready for a Mom of the year commercial. Interestingly, though, there was faint sheen of dust on everything, which clearly indicated to the detectives that nobody had been there for at least a week. Crouse scratched his head. "D'ya think maybe she was staying somewhere else?"

"Duh," said Farrell. "Your command of the obvious is really impressive, Crouse. You could make a fortune as a TV detective."

Crouse thought of his treatment of Way North the night before. "What goes around..." he mumbled to himself.

There was also no mail, no magazines with address labels on, them, no grocery store receipts, no bills, not even an electric bill or a cell phone bill and they were positive she had one of those. That is, if Marsha Grainger, or was it Mendenhall, was to be believed.

After a fairly thorough search, leaving everything as close to the way they found it as possible, Farrell commented, "This whole home scene looks staged, like she never actually lived here."

"Duh," said Crouse, a faint grin on his face.

"What a waste of time," they commented simultaneously as they walked out of the apartment and tossed the key to the curious superintendent who had been waiting by the door while they searched.

"Are you sure you didn't need a warrant for that?" asked the super, who obviously watched too many Law and Order shows on TV.

After a few calls, Farrell determined that Marsha would be on duty in half an hour so they did what cops naturally do to kill a little time. Dunkin' Donuts was not crowded but neither were the donut trays, so they each chose one from the paltry display of remainders to go with the rather strong cup of coffee they had each ordered.

After killing the required time, they proceeded to Greeneburg County Memorial, the hospital where the first responders often hung out, smoking cigarettes, waiting to be dispatched on a call. The cop cousins were sitting on the dock by the ambulance bay when Marsha came strutting up. "Uh oh," she greeted them, "What'd I do now?"

Farrell said, "Hi, Marsha. What's your last name?"

"No foreplay, eh Detective Farrell? It's Grainger, why do you ask?"

"Just wanted to know who was who, you know, for our reports. We went to Sydney's place, or at least the address we got from the cell phone people. It's a plant, a set up. No-one actually lives there. What do you know about that?"

"Look, I am — was, not one of her close friends. She was one of us, if you know what I mean. I saw her at get-togethers a few times, but she was always with Darla so I didn't get to know her very well." Marsha was delighted when the military did away with the don't ask, don't tell policy, which quickly devolved to apply to all quasi-military organizations like the Emergency Medical Service, but it had never been a secret for her. She was six feet tall, a good 200 pounds and strong as an ox. And with her short hair with a hint of gray, you just could never tell.

"What can you tell us about this Darla? She may have some more intimate knowledge."

Marsha groaned at the poorly disguised pun. That was the usual reaction whenever one of Farrell's myriad puns became public. He loved it but nobody else did. "Darla is Darla Fleming. She lives in Pine Ridge right near the county line off the interstate. I don't know the exact address but she lives in a brick rancher in a cookie cutter development out in the rural part of Pine Ridge county. Be careful with Butch, though. He's quick on the draw and usually carries a holstered pistol, a .44 magnum that could knock down the side of a house." She gave him Butch Fleming's description, the color of the big

Dodge Ram 3500 truck he drove, and the directions to the house, as best as she could remember.

Butch wasn't home, for which the detectives said a little silent prayer of thanks. Darla, on the other hand, was. Farrell had no idea what to expect but was genuinely surprised when an extremely pretty, really petite, actually tiny, very curvaceous blonde, adorned in a frilly, colorful dress, answered the door. She showed genuine shock when she was informed that her good ex-friend, Sydney, had been murdered. She bit her lip and her eyes welled up, but she stayed composed. After confirming the former relationship described by EMT Marsha, Farrell continued, "Tell us where she lived, where she worked, what you know about her family, next of kin, who else might have had problems with her. Things like that."

Darla took a deep breath, let out a little sob, and began, her words interspersed with an occasional snort and wipe of tears and snot on her sleeve. "She lived in an apartment not far from here, off the interstate near the county line. Her family lived somewhere out west, but she had to run away because of their reaction when she came out. I think it was Wyoming or maybe Idaho. She didn't talk about them. She didn't have any brothers or sisters that I know of, and no children either." Darla started to cry and just then the detectives could hear the rumble of a large diesel pull up and a door slam. In a second, a big brutish looking man with a serious five o'clock shadow burst in. "What the hell are you guys doing here?" He had the look of a wildly jealous man who was capable of killing both of them with his bare hands.

Crouse surprised Farrell when he boldly stood up, took a step toward the huge man, and replied, "Why Butch, is that any way to treat your guests?" Butch was a good six inches taller and probably a hundred pounds heavier than Crouse, but the effrontery confused the big guy, who clearly didn't have much going for him in the IQ department. He didn't know how to respond so he did what Neanderthals do in such circumstances. "Huh?"

"We are police officers, Butch, I'm Detective Crouse from Pine Ridge, and this is Detective Farrell from Greeneburg. We are questioning your wife with regard to a murder investigation. Now, you can leave and go into another room and not bother us, or we can take Darla, here, down to the Greeneburg police station and question her there. Your call, big guy."

"Take me to the police station. Please, officer, take me downtown."

This surprised both officers but they complied with the little lady's request and left, leaving a red faced Butch breathing heavy, without the presence of mind to ask who had been killed.

They all drove off in Farrell's Taurus, and as soon as the door shut and the car started to move, Darla thanked them profusely. "You saved me. Butch is so jealous I don't know what he might do if he found out about what my relationship really was with Sydney."

Crouse piped up, "I don't understand, Darla. Why would Sydney's death bother him? We heard he was really jealous of her, but wouldn't he be somewhat happy if she was gone?"

She was silent for a few minutes and then said, "I guess so." Darla didn't say another word until she was safely ensconced in the interrogation room, with the door shut and a can of some diet drink in her hand.

When Farrell closed the door, Darla seemed to breathe a sigh of relief as if she was safe in there from the demons outside. She started without being asked, "You don't know what it's like living with him. I'm petrified all the time, never knowing what might set him off. Once he killed our kitten because it meowed at him. When he hits me, he knocks me half way across the room. I started going out with Sydney just to get away from him, and you know, it kind of escalated. It was okay, I guess. I don't think I'm really a Lesbian, but I guess I must be. It was kind of exciting being with her, and going to some of her friends' parties, but then I began to feel, you know, as if I was doing something wrong. Eventually, I just told her I couldn't see her any more. She didn't take that very well, but she seemed to understand. Sydney was such a nice person."

Farrell and Crouse just sat there in amazement as Darla talked to them as if she was baring her soul to a psychiatrist. It must have been the trust factor some people have for the law. But it wasn't getting them any closer to solving Sydney's murder, or really finding out anything about her.

"Darla, when did Butch find out about you and Sydney?"

"Oh, he knew we were friends when I first introduced him to her, about a year ago."

"How did he react?"

"He was fine. He never knew for sure that there was anything sexual in our relationship. He used to call her that big dyke but that's about all. He's not too good figuring things out."

"Do you know where Sydney worked? What she did for a living?"

The two detectives lightly questioned her for far longer than was necessary. There was just something about the petite, pretty woman that captivated them. All three were smiling when they drove her home.

Butch wasn't. He was as irritated as a wet cat. Storming and threatening, he paced around in a tight circle. Darla ran into the house, and when she'd closed the door with Butch standing guard outside on their stoop, Crouse stepped up to him, almost nose to nose. Butch was a good six inches taller than Crouse so it wasn't quite, but Butch had never had someone so calmly and fearlessly stand up to him.

"Do you know what this is about, Butch?"

"Huh?"

"Somebody killed Sydney Cole. Did you kill Sydney Cole?"

Somehow, Crouse had grown a couple of inches taller and Butch backed up a step. "Sydney? Why would I kill Sydney? I hated her."

Farrell grinned. Definitely not the sharpest tack in the box. Absolutely not. Crouse turned around, stifling a laugh. Farrell took up where Crouse had left off. "So, Mr. Fleming, You admit you have a motive to kill Sydney, eh? Where were you last night at 3:00 a.m.?"

The cops did not really think the big goon killed Sydney. Maybe if she was strangled or beaten to death, her neck snapped in half, but shooting her in the chest was a little more conventional and too refined for this galoot. They were going to have a little fun with him, but when he started to cry they became concerned. This was definitely not right, this great big guy actually crying like a baby. This situation was going to take a lot of sorting out, a lot of deep thought, maybe even a visit to the shrink for the two cops.

Work was a dead end. It turned out Sydney worked for an electrical supply house, and the guys at the store considered her one of the guys. That's because she beat a big tattooed braggart in an arm wrestling contest. Cleverly, she bent her wrist just enough so that her opponent bent his in the wrong direction and literally became enfeebled. He was surprised and embarrassed, but Sydney did not have to suffer the taunts anymore, so she didn't gloat. She wanted to, but wisely kept quiet. Girls working in an all guy environment like that, had to have some kind of shtick just to get along. Nobody was willing to arm wrestle her anymore, lest they had to admit to their sweeties that they were bested by this girl down at the shop.

There was that confounding dichotomy between the spotless, sterile home environment, if she did in fact live there, and this otherwise rough and tumble woman. It didn't fit, at least to the detectives, who were taught to always look for something that didn't fit. They agreed to sleep on it and get together the next day, except they couldn't remember where Crouse had last parked his Taurus.

Chapter 15

When O'Halloran turned off the shower, he heard his phone ringing. It was the land-line and not connected to an answering machine, so it just kept on ringing. Incessantly. Dripping wet, the perturbed lawyer wrapped a towel around his waist and finally walked over to his bedside and picked up the phone. "H'lo"

"O! This is Farrell. Do you know where your boy is?"

"I don't know, Detective. I just got out of the shower. It is, uh, what time is it?"

"It's ten after seven. Did Antoine stay at your place last night?'

"I guess so, why?"

"We had another county line homicide. This one was a little different. Gunshot to the chest, female, sort of, and naked from the waist down. We just want to rule out your boy."

Calling Antoine *"your boy"* irked O'Halloran no end, but what are you going to do? The fact was he was a lot younger than O'Halloran, and hung around the house like he belonged there, coming in and out as if he owned the place, although he did seem to like sleeping in the shed. God only knows why. O'Halloran thought of the big dog bed he was sure was infested with fleas. "Look, Detective, I'm standing here soaking wet, getting water all over the floor. I'm going to have to dry off, wipe up these puddles where I'm standing, and then get dressed. Then I can check in the shed. I will be at the Courthouse Coffee at 7:30. Why don't you meet me there?" He hung up.

After hurriedly getting dressed and drying up his bedroom floor, O'Halloran walked out to the shed. Antoine was curled up on the old, extra-large size dog bed in the middle of the floor. O'Halloran shuddered. Who knew how many hundreds of fleas, mites and other critters of the insect phyla were rapidly multiplying on that filthy old thing? "Antoine, wake up. Did you kill anyone last night?"

"Huh? What you mean Missa O'Harran?"

"Never mind. Did you go out last night?"

"Uh uh. I was sleepin' here all night. Slep' like a baby. It be right cozy in here."

"Okay, I'm going out for breakfast. See you later."

Although it was just the beginning of October, it was a little cooler than it had been, as Hamish walked the few blocks to his favorite haunt. He always enjoyed this walk. It was still too early for fall, the leaves still showing the last vestiges of summer green. Some of the houses had potted asters in full bloom displayed on their porches or front steps, happily presaging the coming autumn. He noticed pots overflowing with the purple, rust, yellow and deep red flowers. He smiled as he thought of the flowers and then became sad. There were no such adornments on his own bleak porch or steps.

His cronies were already comfortably established in the usual booth, stained coffee cups full of the steaming black brew in front of them. As usual, a cloud of blue smoke hung at eye level throughout the place. Hamish couldn't tell whether the grill was on fire or the cigarette smoke pall was unusually thick today. He coughed a little as he walked over to the booth and bumped into Doris on the way. "Sorry about the smoke, Ham. Gus Jr. set the grill on fire and the blower isn't working right. We got Sam, the AC guy, coming over to bring one of those industrial size blowers in to clear out the smoke. We'll be fine in fifteen minutes. You want your usual?"

What with the grill smoke, the cigarette haze, and the fog from being called by the detective while he was coming out of a steaming shower early in the morning, Ham's mind was just as unclear as his environment. The best he could do was nod an ineffectual assent.

He breathed a sigh of relief as he settled into the booth next to Billy Brown and across from the steady presence of Mr. Sparrow. He took in a deep breath and almost convulsed since he'd forgotten about the smoke. After a sip of the water Doris had thoughtfully placed in front of him, he began to get back to normal, at least for him.

"Did you hear there was another murder last night? Brown was excited as he reported the news. "Patrolman Way North found another corpse in the same alley. That's three in less than a month, two of them dumped in the same spot. I think that's a record for Pine Ridge. Looks like we are going to have to beef up the night patrol."

Mr. Sparrow continued, "They all seem to have been murdered in another location and brought to the place where they were found. I wonder why they do that?"

"So the place where they were killed isn't identified because that's probably where the killer came from, or at least has a connection to. The first thing Crouse will have to do is figure out where they were killed, but I don't think there is much evidence to go on, from what I hear." Brown was a fountain of knowledge.

O'Halloran's cell phone jangled. "Hamish O'Halloran," he answered, vaguely curious. If he had looked at his caller ID he would have realized it was Detective Crouse.

"Okay, Ham. Now that you have had some coffee maybe you are awake enough to tell me 'bout your boy."

"He is not my boy, Detective, and from what I can tell, he was in the shed all night. He sleeps on a dog bed full of fleas. He must have some kind of natural flea repellent."

"Good to know, Ham. Talk to you later." Ham did not know whether the detective was glad to know that Antoine slept in the shed or had a natural flea repellent.

Brown and Mr. Sparrow looked at him inquisitively. "That was Crouse. He's interested in where Antoine was last night, as if I'm his guardian. The victim, he told me, was a half-naked woman. Unlike the others."

"This is getting really creepy. Does anyone know what the stiffs have in common?"

The always proper Mr. Sparrow was a little put off by Brown's use of the pejorative euphemism for the victims of these heinous offenses, nevertheless the trio discussed the possibilities without having enough information to make any real sense of the situation.

O'Halloran only had one case in court that day — a teenager with a massive attitude, probably intentionally developed to offset her intellectual deficit. There were four codefendants, high school classmates all from the same hood, who felt they were always being dissed, which was probably true, and with good reason. The female foursome decided to show the world just what they were made of and went on a crime spree at the local mall, stealing all sorts of worthless items; some costume jewelry, some see-through blouses that didn't even come close to covering their navels, non-essential stuff like that. When the store detective at the fourth store they visited arrested them, they were all self-righteous and innocent and demanded their lawyers. The store detective called for some uniformed cops who took them down town and they were booked and appeared before a judicial official for bond to be set.

The veteran magistrate, Anderson, was tired and his feet hurt. Nevertheless, he made them post a $250 bond. Naturally, Sharkey, a bondsman with the improbable last name, was hanging around the magistrate's office, trolling for potential new clients. When he heard about four female teenagers with a relatively low bond for a shoplifting spree, he volunteered his services. He was able to collect the required ten per cent, $25, from each of them, and then read them the riot act, showing them the chrome plated .38 revolver he always carried, in case they had any ideas about not showing up for court. Despite his dead seriousness, the flippant attitude of the girls persisted. They weren't scared. After all, they were just teenagers, still juveniles, what could the judicial system do to them?

Judge Howell was in rare form that morning, and the courtroom was still snickering from his last witticism, but when Brown called the defendants to the bar and the four snot-nosed teenagers paraded up in outfits that would have done a Las Vegas stage act proud, the good judge frowned. "Mr. Brown, looks like I got a bit of a conflict here. Miz Esleeck's father and I, well we're old college buddies. Let me see if I can get another judge in here for this one."

With that, he was out of the courtroom, disappearing through the door behind the bench. Two minutes later the bailiff called out, "All rise," and who should come through the door but L. Rita Axelrod, the Ax herself.

The kids didn't know about L. Rita. They just saw a dark black woman with a halo of white hair. They smiled to themselves. They had it made with this sister.

Brown and the cops smiled too. They knew what was about to happen or at least had a pretty good idea. The three other court appointed lawyers started to sweat. O'Halloran was totally without emotion because he simply didn't care.

He usually felt secretly vindicated when L. Rita came down hard on one of his clients, who usually deserved whatever he got. One of the other court appointeds, a young lawyer from the Public Defender's office, decided to brave it because, well, she had to represent her client as best she could, right? The Ax noticed her nervousness. "What is it, Ms. Robershaw? You have something to say?"

"Uh, your Honor. I would like to move for a continuance."

"Not a chance, Ms. Robershaw, unless either you or your client have an imminent gall bladder attack. All right Mr. Brown, you may proceed."

He took their pleas. All of them pled guilty. That was expected from O'Halloran, of course, who seldom pled a client not guilty if he could help it. It was just easier that way, and to O'Halloran, easy was good. But the Public Defender's office liked to test the system and often tried to force the DA's office to give them better deals by taking a lot of dog cases to trial. Clogging up the docket with trials, even worthless ones, sometimes got the more pragmatic prosecutors to cave. But none of the Public Defenders had the guts to try the patience of Judge Axelrod, so guilty pleas all around.

She heard the brief summary of the evidence. There was a prolonged silence. Two of the girls had their hands on their hips, jauntily, daring the judge. Of course, she wasn't about to relent. To Judge Axelrod, these kids were dead meat. She was just thinking of what voracious dog she was going to sic on them.

Calmly, she invited them all to approach the bench. Four nervous lawyers and four arrogant girls stood before her. "Not you. You four lawyers return to the defense table." This was highly unusual, being required by the judge to abandon their clients, unprotected, vulnerable to the vicissitudes of the system, so to speak, but this was the Ax after all.

The lawyers quickly made their way back to their assigned places safely behind the defense table, leaving their young clients hanging in the wind, with a sense of relief that it wasn't them standing under the glower of the Ax. They sat down and watched as a bit of the swagger deserted the girls just as their lawyers had.

"All right, young ladies. Turn around right where you are, right now, and face the audience." The order was delivered in a tone that brooked no deviation, so they sheepishly complied, staring nervously at the sea of faces watching them intently. The Judge said, "Call your next case, Mr. Brown. These young ladies will have a first-hand view of District Court for the rest of the day, standing right here in front of the bench, while I ponder what to do with them. This might just be a good lesson in civics for this crowd. You lawyers check back in at three this afternoon for sentencing. You think Court will last that long, Mr. Brown?"

"I can make it happen, your Honor."

The girls smirked, their youthful arrogance still dripping from their faces, as they looked into the crowd of defendants who had made bond and were waiting for their cases to be called, their friends and relatives, and their victims. But after just a few cases, the arrogance disappeared, replaced with a bit of *'I dare you'* directed toward any member of the audience who might feel a little contempt or even sympathy toward the girls. But as the cases were tried around them, the unfamiliar emotion of embarrassment began to invade their supercilious minds. Soon the smirks were replaced by a fervent *'wish to get out of this sideshow'* in which they were the freaks. The defendants that followed were all much more respectful of the judge, and much more humble than they might have been, under ordinary circumstances.

One of the girls wiped away a tear, and the others looked at her, commiserating with her plight, but trying to be stoic. By the end of the afternoon, as their lawyers silently snuck back into court taking their traditional seats in the jury box to await the fate of their young clients, the faces of all the girls were tear streaked and smeared with makeup and mascara.

After all the other cases had been dealt with, Judge Axelrod then read them the riot act. She frightened the bejesus out of them. One by one she asked them for a response. When they were all through with the 'I'm sorries' and 'I won't ever do it again,' the judge yelled. "Not good enough, young ladies. That is just not good enough. Thieves, that's what you are, just common thieves. Are any of you of the Islamic Faith?" Without waiting for any response she went on. "If this was a Muslim society with Sharia law I would have the right hand of each of you cut off at the wrist with a huge gleaming, razor sharp sword, and then cauterize the stump with boiling oil. But when I'm through with you, you all will wish for that sentence. What is the maximum sentence for this kind of thievery, Mr. Speedy?"

The old clerk, who was the antithesis of his surname, seemed to have just woken up. "Huh?"

"The maximum sentence for this thieving spree, Mr. Clerk." She already knew what it was, of course, but this was for maximum effect.

"Oh, uh, two years for each offense, yer Honor."

"Okay, that's eight years in jail, two years for each offense if I run them consecutively. You got that, ladies? You will be twenty-five when you get out of jail if I give you the maximum, those cute little figures of yours all gone to fat and flab. I often do that to people who embarrass my race, did you know that?"

The girls were all sniveling. And it was not just an act either, they were really worried, frightened, maybe petrified is more like it. She was no longer just another sister. Judge Axelrod was Ma'am, your Honor, and they meant it. She and God must be closely related, and these teens now feared both equally, fervently praying to the Judge's new found relative.

"Mr. Clerk, we will continue the sentencing phase until this Friday afternoon. Each of you girls will come back at 4:00 p.m. this Friday. You will each present a full two-page essay you have written, typed, single spaced, about why every society in the world has a proscription against thievery. And each of them better not be the slightest bit alike. I want a note on the Principal's stationary stating that you have attended school every hour of every day, including Friday, signed by the Principal or the Vice Principal. And bring your parents, both of them, or I will lock you up until you do. Understand?"

She did a roll call and the girls understood. When one of the girls tried to weasel out of the parent requirement, Judge Axelrod merely put her hand up in the traditional "halt" sign recognized worldwide. "No excuses, ladies. You, your parents and your lawyers will be here at 4:00 on Friday and if your parents don't want to come for any reason, tell them I may just cut off your hand. All right, then. Adjourn Court Mr. Bailiff."

She got up and stomped out of the Courtroom, an angry scowl lingering on her dark visage.

O'Halloran was energized. He really liked and respected Judge L. Rita, but of course, he wouldn't tell her that. She would think he was sycophanting.

Chapter 16

Tuesday was the kind of day when everyone was busy. In Superior Court, the jury trials had started; either the parties were in the midst of jury selection or the DA was putting on the State's case. In District Court, the dockets were full, Brown was maneuvering, making plea deals, hearing offers or excuses from the attorneys, organizing the docket, doing three things at once. But Hamish only had one lousy case, and rather than wait in Court for his case to be called, he took his crossword puzzle and went back to the Courthouse Coffee. He settled in to his normal booth and was soon engrossed in the relatively easy Tuesday puzzle.

He heard a plop and looked up, just in time to see the coffee settle back down in his cup. Doris eased into the booth across from him with her own cup of joe. "Want some company, Ham? Tuesday's puzzles aren't much of a challenge."

It started out innocent enough, talking about the weather, some banal Courthouse gossip, but pretty soon they were solving the world's problems. Neither one of these poor souls realized the other was so intellectually curious, so up on current events, so perspicacious. The more they chatted the more besotted they became with each other.

The bell over the front door tinkled as an elderly couple neither had seen before entered the restaurant. They looked like farmers, right out of the classic Grant Wood painting. He was wearing a Massey Ferguson baseball cap, bib overalls and a red checked flannel shirt, while she was dressed in an ankle length gingham dress with small blue flowers, her gray hair tied up in a tight bun. Straight out of a scene from the

Appalachia of the 1930s, it appeared that anything modern had just passed them by, as if they were in a time warp. Ham and Doris watched in silence as the couple meandered toward a booth, looking around the virtually empty restaurant, expectantly, seemingly unsure of what to do. Just as Doris was about to get up to wait on the couple, it seemed as if she had a sudden inspiration. She turned to Hamish, "Say Ham, want to come over and join us for dinner on Sunday? I'm having pot roast. It'll just be you and me and my daughter, Rachel. She's fourteen going on twenty-one, but it'll be nice. I want you to meet her. You do like pot roast don't you? Say 2:00? See you then." Clearly both excited and embarrassed, Doris got up and virtually bounded off to serve the farmers, and it never occurred to her that the awe struck O'Halloran had not answered a single one of her questions. She just assumed he didn't have any other plans for Sunday. He never did.

Not only had he not had time to think about the invitation or even answer, he was stunned. Speechless. No woman had ever asked him out before. He would not have known what to say even if he did have his wits about him. And he didn't; they were still frozen at five minutes ago.

He thought about Doris off and on all that week. By Thursday afternoon, while he was puttering around his house, he began to realize he didn't know where Doris lived. He planned to ask her Friday for sure, just to make certain he didn't wander around Pine Ridge in a fog when 2:00 rolled around Sunday afternoon. But thinking of pot roast made him think about beef and then he thought about Lefty's juicy heart stopper, with all the fixin's and the tantalizing blend of sugar and salt. He wiped his chin when he realized he was drooling. Thinking about juiciness caused him to think about Honey, so he went to Lefty's to get his fill of both.

Lefty's was uncharacteristically dead. Maybe not so uncharacteristically, since it was Thursday and most of the bikers didn't get paid until Friday, and had already used up their quota of beer money. The place wasn't exactly deserted but the customers were certainly sparse. The gurgle of beer being drawn from the tap, or a glass being set down hard on the bar echoed throughout the establishment. He went to his usual place at the end of the bar in the darkest part and settled his rump on a stool.

In a few seconds, Honey moseyed over in a rather provocative manner, and said, "Hello, big boy. What'll it be?"

O'Halloran couldn't help staring at her. Her cleavage exuded a little more skin than he remembered, and he had to forcibly make his eyes look at her face. "Huh?"

"Up here, Ham. My eyes are up here." She pointed to her face.

He was mortified. It wasn't the reflection of the Sam Adams sign that had turned his face red. "I'm sorry, Honey. It's just that you are so... so disarming."

She laughed. "It's all right Ham. Women like me are used to that reaction. For some of us it is part of our ammunition, if you know what I mean." She patted him maternally on the arm, but he didn't connect, maternally that is.

"Let me guess. You want a heart stopper and a giant diet coke, right?"

"You know how much I would love a heart stopper, but I don't think I could eat a whole one."

"That's all right, Ham. I'll tell the cook just what to make. Trust me on this."

He did, and waited with a mixture of anticipation, hope, and ... trepidation.

While he waited, Ham thought of the possibilities; he imagined her bringing him the dreaded breaded fish sandwich, a salad with red onions, oil and vinegar. He shuddered. Maybe even liver and onions, like his mother used to serve him every Monday. She had a routine she refused to vary, Tuesday was boiled chicken — he could abide that, especially with a helping of boiled potatoes. Wednesday was always boiled beef and cabbage with more Irish potatoes — the Irish boiled everything and knew nothing of sauces. Thursday was mulligatawny stew — that's what she called it but he later learned it was just traditional Irish stew, carrots, parsnips and boiled potatoes, sometimes with peas, and swimming in a tasteless, colorless broth. She couldn't tell you what was in it if there was even anything worth talking about. Friday it was boiled fish, boiled potatoes and boiled green vegetables. He loved his mother but she must have grown up during the famine. She had about as much culinary imagination as a food kitchen in the Sudan. And so he anxiously waited for what Honey would bring him, his pessimism in high gear, a fine sheen of sweat forming on his brow.

Ten minutes later she returned with a plate, hidden under a shiny metal food cover. He had no idea Lefty's even had such food accoutrements, for the joint wasn't what you would refer to as a gourmet establishment. She carefully placed the plate in front of him, her hands on the cover handle protectively. Watching his eyes until it appeared he could not stand the suspense any longer, she carefully lifted the lid. Sitting on a bed of lettuce, surrounded by finely cut French fries, was a mini-heart stopper. About the size of a tennis ball, dripping with cheddar, ketchup, chili and grease, it actually seemed to beckon the hungry Hamish. He breathed a sigh of relief, and looked up into Honey's seductive dark eyes as if she was the savior herself.

Honey watched Ham as he entered a state of bliss, savoring the none too good for him heart stopper. She didn't think he would go into cardiac arrest just then, but it occurred to her that O'Halloran did not have the most healthful eating habits. On a sudden whim, perhaps an inspiration, she said, "Say Ham, why don't you come over Sunday? I'll fix you a real good meal — a real healthy meal too, and we can talk a bit. Really get to know each other. What do you say?"

He froze mid chew. Stunned again. The antithesis of a Casanova, he had just been asked out by the woman he really liked. He couldn't say, "No. Sorry, Honey, I have another engagement," could he? No he couldn't, so he gagged a bit, trying to swallow the food he had greedily stuffed in his mouth, took a sip of diet Coke and when he could finally talk, said, "That would be great Honey, what time?"

What a schlemiel, but the gods saved him. "How about 6:00, Ham? I don't work, Sundays, but I will have to stock up the larder, and prepare the meal." She made no mention of what she had in mind, and he didn't even care. Just being with Honey would have been enough for him.

So he had a date for Sunday. Two dates actually. But maybe, just maybe, he could pull it off.

As Sunday approached Ham became exponentially nervous. He tried, but he couldn't eat a thing Saturday and actually threw up, his nerves were so taut. He was like a nerdy teenager about to go out on a first date with the prom queen. Saturday evening, sitting in his semi-dark kitchen, he was finally able to get some toast down, soothed by some tea. He was in bed by nine, staring at the ceiling, idly wondering about an old water stain, and how it might have gotten there. The exercise was like counting sheep and soon he was asleep.

The sun was high when he woke from a deep slumber, not too different from being in a coma. It took him a good fifteen minutes and a hot shower in order for him to be clearheaded, or as close to being clearheaded as O'Halloran ever was. After he had performed his morning ablutions, he looked at the clock and was astounded to see that it was already noon.

After his involuntary fast induced by a case of the nerves the day before, he was famished. Without giving it much thought he quickly scrambled a plate of eggs and toasted a couple of English muffins. He leaned back on his kitchen chair, and took a sip of instant coffee, which brought him back to the world. "Oh no," he agonized. He had two dinners to go to that day and he was already stuffed.

Having gotten the directions from Doris on Friday and written them down it didn't take him long to get to her house. By five minutes of two he was in a rural area spotted with cows and rolled hay bales, approaching her home. It was a double wide set back off the road at least a football field, framed by a forest of tall loblolly pines. He wondered if she wouldn't be afraid living in such a remote area, but then, he'd never known Doris to be afraid of anything. He drove up the long, rutted dirt driveway, parked the non-descript gray Japanese model, took a deep breath and got out of the car. He plodded up the two steps to the homemade wooden detached landing and knocked. In just a few seconds, Doris, wearing an apron, opened the door. He stuttered, "H-h-h-here Doris, these are for you." He handed her a bouquet of flowers he had picked up at the Piggly Wiggly on the way.

Doris was all animation as she let him in, talking a mile a minute, busying herself with last minute cooking preparations, flitting around efficiently just as she always did at the Legal Lunch. She was a real flitter, that Doris, and Ham liked that about her. Dishes clattered as the table was set, savory kitchen aromas permeated the house and Doris talked non-stop. There was a sudden lull as she appeared in the living room of the doublewide wiping her hands on her apron. Hamish had been sitting on a well-worn sofa pretending to read an old dog-eared National Geographic while she went about her preparations. He looked up at her. "Ready to eat Ham?" she asked, immediately turning to the back of the residence. "Maybelle, dinner is ready. Come on now."

O'Halloran's jaw dropped. He had no idea there was anyone else in the doublewide but now that he thought about it remembered that Doris had said she had a teenage daughter. On cue, a sullen looking teenager appeared, her midriff bared, some inartful makeup slathered on her face. "Mr. O'Halloran, this is my daughter, Maybelle. Honey, say hello to my friend, Mr. Hamish O'Halloran, a lawyer in Pine Ridge."

The girl nodded the most perfunctory nod she could muster, barely moving her head, her eyes nowhere. Doris showed Ham where to sit and served the meal, a Norman Rockwell Sunday dinner: pot roast, green beans and mashed potatoes. Ham stared at the plate, forlornly. It looked great, gravy steaming from a pool in the middle of the mashed potatoes, but he just wasn't hungry.

The voluble Doris was making up for her sullen dinner companions. Maybelle grunted occasionally, picked at her mashed potatoes a little and explained she wasn't hungry. Hamish was forcing himself to eat and making reasonable headway. At his very best, he wasn't much of a conversationalist, and he wasn't at his very best today. If Doris noticed his reticence she didn't let on. She didn't entertain very often, in fact almost never, and she wasn't going to let this rare opportunity go to waste. Her voice got a little higher, sort of the way hysterical people act when someone steals their car. But the meal was quite good, and Ham ate most of what was on his plate.

After they had finished dinner, Doris made a quick couple of trips to the kitchen clearing the table, while Maybelle disappeared into the cavern which was her room. They retired to the living room and as Ham collapsed into the sofa, Doris asked, "Want some coffee and dessert, Ham?"

Coffee sounded great but there wasn't a bit of room to squeeze a smidgen of dessert into his overstuffed system. She had pre-made the coffee and was back in a flash, babbling on about this and that, Ham barely comprehending as his lids fought to close. In ten minutes they succeeded and he was fast asleep, snoring like a buzz saw. Doris watched him for a few minutes, then let out an audible sigh and went to make sure Maybelle wasn't texting some pimply faced troglodyte who was her current beau, instead of working on the Social Studies report that was due on Monday. Doris came back into the living room and sat in a chair across from the loudly snoring O'Halloran. She sighed again, watching him as he slept, tears welling in her eyes. She knew of course, she had always known. He was what he was and there was no way she was going to make a silk purse out of this sow's ear. Well, at least she had tried. Doris began to accept the fact that she was never ever going to find someone to settle down with, and she would grow old alone, despondent and forlorn. She knew she deserved better, but just accepted her lonely lot in life.

After an hour or so, Ham woke himself up with a sleep apnea type extra loud snort, sort of like a sow rooting in the mud in a sty. As he snapped into consciousness, his face turned red from embarrassment when he became aware that Doris was watching him, a sad and curious expression on her face. He sat up and apologized profusely. There was nothing he could do to make up for this gigantic faux pas and to make matters worse, he was supposed to be at Honey's in — he looked at his watch — an hour. He made hurried apologies to Doris and skedaddled.

His belly was so full he felt as if he was driving while impaired, and he was, to an extent, but not because of alcohol or some illegal substance. His blood sugar was probably off the charts. He caught himself weaving and once, he actually nodded off, running onto the gravel shoulder of the road which jarred him awake. He pulled over and seriously considered calling Honey and begging off.

But there was something about Honey which stirred his libido in a way he hadn't experienced for decades, actually since he was a pimply faced teenager. He just couldn't chicken out. He drove to the closest convenience store and got the key to an unpalatably filthy rest room. He tried gagging himself, pushing in his stomach, doing anything he could to toss his cookies, but nothing worked. He was permanently full. It would take three days of bathroom visits before he could breathe without having a stomach ache. After a while he conceded, freshened up as best he could, given the circumstances of a washroom that looked like an abattoir. After slapping a little cold water on his face, but even that, he noticed, was brown, full of what he hoped were just flakes of rust, he headed out hoping the fresh air might rejuvenate him. It didn't. He still felt like a slug.

He stopped at the Piggly Wiggly and bought another bouquet of posies. The same clerk who had rung him up earlier looked at him warily, like he was some sort of gigolo. Spurred on by some primeval urge, a feeling which totally clashed with his uber-satiated self, he made his way to Honey's, driving a good twenty miles an hour under the speed limit, buying time, he hoped.

Honey's apartment had a security system which required him to punch in her apartment number and announce who he was. After hearing a buzz and a click he pushed open the door and walked up to the second floor. He took a deep breath and knocked.

When she opened the door, he gasped. Here he was wearing his amorphous sport coat, a colorful Bugs Bunny tie, on a caramel yellow shirt. He looked, well, blah. She, on the other hand, looked absolutely stunning in a low cut black dress, adorned with a necklace of faux black pearls, nestled comfortably in her ample cleavage.

She picked up on the gasp, smiled, and invited him in, gratefully accepting the proffered posies. She had taken the liberty of pouring him a drink. The aperitif was accompanied by a dish of mixed nuts and one of coated mint candies. Nothing much but subtle. Just to be polite, Ham took a few mints and sipped on the aperitif. His stomach rebelled and it was all he could do to keep it under control. After some small talk for a while, during which Honey noticed Ham's discomfort, he excused himself and found the bathroom. He tried everything he could think of to make some room in his saturated, stuffed stomach, but nothing worked.

Dinner was beautiful to the eyes, olfactory senses, and probably to the palate. At least it would have been to everyone else in the world, but not Ham. Honey had baked a terrific lasagna, using all sorts of specially selected herbs and spices, accompanied by a gourmet Caesar salad. She had uncorked a ten year old bottle of Chianti, and the tantalizing aroma just begged to accompany the lasagna.

He took a bite of lasagna — he felt he had to, but he just couldn't swallow. He coughed and expectorated the food into the linen napkin. Still coughing he ran off to the bathroom, leaving a stunned Honey just sitting there at the table.

Five minutes later a very sheepish O'Halloran returned to the table. He made a complete confession to Honey, in between the 'I'm sorries,' which were profuse. "I guess I should go, Honey. I am so, so sorry."

Whatever reaction he expected from Honey, he didn't get. "Shut up and sit down, Ham. Here, take a sip of this Jägermeister. It will help settle your stomach." While O'Halloran demurely sipped the drink, Honey cleared the table and puttered around in the kitchen. She returned with a cup of coffee for herself and one for Ham, served in fancy china cups. She served his black, and made sure it was strong, almost espresso strong. Years as a bartender had inured Honey to all sorts of peculiar personal peccadilloes, and she had developed a knack for always doing the right thing in response. They talked, and somehow O'Halloran became something of a conversationalist. She had calmed his fears, managed to get him over his innate shyness, and made him feel worthy, despite his horrendous social faux pas. He was totally enamored, that is until he felt a burp coming on, hoping against hope that was all it was.

Chapter 17

After Court on Monday, O'Halloran's mind was racing during the short walk to his house, thinking about all sorts of disjointed things. This confusion was typical of the Attention Deficit Disorder syndrome he suffered. He often wondered how in the world he ever made it through law school. Somewhere along the way, he became aware that he was being followed, but didn't look back since he anticipated it was his shadow, Antoine. It was. When he got to his home, instead of going into the house, he sat down on the front steps and turned to Antoine, who just then sat down next to him.

"Say Antoine, how did you come to be in that alley in the first place? You know, the one where you got caught with your hand in the dead man's pants."

Antoine hemmed and hawed, forgot, and didn't know. "Hmmm," said O'Halloran. "That is just not a good enough answer, Antoine. Remember, I'm your lawyer. I'm not going to tell anyone, but I do need to know the truth so I can deal with it when it comes out. It always does, you know."

"Huh?"

"The truth. It always comes out."

"Oh, yeah." He yawned, a big air sucking yawn. O'Halloran didn't know if it was a really tired yawn or a really stressed out yawn. He knew that people often involuntarily yawn when they are under a lot of serious imminent stress, like when they are about to jump out of an airplane, go into battle, or when their mom catches them with their hand in the cookie jar. Antoine yawned again. "I got to lay down, Missa O'Harran. I'm tarred."

"*And feathered,*" O'Halloran thought, as some serious suspicion began to taint the protestations of innocence of his own client in O'Halloran's mind.

Antoine, the shadow, snuck off to his dog bed in the shed to let nature deal with his tiredness, and Hamish went into the house intending to think about the murders and the possible connection to Mother Nature's. Orange Pekoe always seemed to hit the spot in situations like these. He was soon sitting, sipping, thinking, then, after a bit, snoring. Falling fast asleep while still sitting upright in the chair, his head fell hard on the table, hitting the saucer, spilling the hot tea onto the side of his head. Jolted awake, he shot up dizzily, the hot liquid in his ear. The vertigo caused him to fall out of his chair, landing unceremoniously on the floor causing a bruise on his rump.

"Ow!" He turned away from the bruised cheek and slowly stood, still wavering and unsteady, his head reeling. He picked up the chair and gingerly sat back down, his senses slowly returning to normal, at least what might be considered normal for him. The image of the slain girl in the alley, as described by Detective Crouse, burned in his mind, and it wasn't a comfortable feeling. He thought about what he knew about her. Not much, but he could just picture the dead woman lying half-naked in the alley. It wasn't like he had a prurient streak, far from it, but why was she half-naked? He would have to get Detective Farrell's take on that, what it signified, what it might indicate. That is, if the Detective would even deign to talk to him about it. Most law enforcement types instinctively distrusted defense lawyers, even those of his less than stellar ilk.

As he puttered around his kitchen, O'Halloran realized he was hungry, having skipped lunch again. He patted his belly, thinking he was putting on a little weight which reminded him of that magnificent feast he used to eat at Lefty's. There was something addictive about that heart stopper. Maybe it was the combination of sugar and salt in the chili and ketchup. Like a salivating automaton, without even thinking about it, he got in his car and headed for the county line.

It was almost dark when he arrived. The parking lot was full of gaudy, tricked out Harleys and plain Jane Ford Tauruses, making his boring little Japanese model look like it was a lost ragamuffin. He joined a trio of the biggest, meanest looking, tattooed bikers he had ever seen as they entered the dingy establishment. O'Halloran's eyes blindly searched the interior, desperately trying to adjust his sight to the darkness. He honed in on the fluorescent Sam Adams sign toward the back, and found a seat at the bar between a bearded behemoth with a bandanna and what was all too obviously a cop in plain-clothes. Honey came up to him and said predictably, "What'll you have handsome?"

There it was again, that 'handsome' ploy. Boy she knew how to push his button. He was amazed she still even seemed to like him, especially after that disastrous weekend. "The heart stopper, and..." He looked around at what the other men at the bar were drinking. "A draft, Heineken's, if you have it on tap." Keeping up with his macho neighbors at the bar, that was Ham O'Halloran.

"Sure thing, big boy. Coming right up."

He looked to his right and nodded to a vaguely familiar face, probably a plain clothes cop he had seen in court somewhere but whose name he couldn't remember. He looked over at the biker next to him on his left and in return received a glare as if he was a child molester. He felt a damp drip or two trickle down his leg, and vainly hoped it meant he had just spilled some of his beer. He gave an involuntary shudder, especially since he realized there was no beer in front of him yet. O'Halloran looked straight ahead, staring at the array of bottles lined up in front of a mirror, as if that would somehow save him. In the mirror, the biker was still glaring back at him. Honey rescued O'Halloran by plopping a tall glass with the correct one inch of foam resting atop the golden brew.

In just a few seconds, he forgot about the biker and salivated as he thought of the mouth-watering, tasty heart stopper. He took a sip of beer, sloshing the brew in his mouth to fully savor the taste, when a flash of blinding light erupted along with an unbelievably loud noise, which hurt his ears something terrible. Involuntarily, the beer in his mouth exploded forward in a fine mist. Everyone in the bar, whose pupils were already dilated because of the dim illumination, was instantly blinded by the intensity of the light, and seriously deafened by the earsplitting sound. Then there was another similar explosion and the men seated at the bar instinctively jumped off their stools in a panic. Disoriented and staggering, the crowd of customers began to run into each other, falling to the floor, tripping over bodies and bar stools, as they attempted to rush toward the door.

"Damn flashbang," shouted the plain-clothes cop, obviously familiar with the M-84 Stun Grenade, as he groped for the exit, unable to see, his ears ringing. The bar was a chaotic scene of cursing, swearing, moaning, and all sorts of associated noises, as the men bumped into walls, bar stools and each other. Brawny customers were falling on the floor, tripping over sprawled arms and legs, writhing in pain, holding their ears, even screaming. Imagine — grown he-men screaming.

O'Halloran was beset with the overpowering smell of acrid smoke. He coughed violently and repeatedly, a paroxysm of hacking imitated by so many of the others in the bar. He rubbed his tear filled eyes, and in a few minutes regained a modicum of sight. He could make out some of the chaos and the human carnage of writhing bodies, amidst the ghoulish sounds and cacophony of coughing emanating from the customers. Massive flames began to consume several parts of the bar, the flashbang grenade having caused most of the patrons' alcoholic beverages to be knocked over, the alcohol in them ignited, the fire quickly spreading.

Uncharacteristically, O'Halloran became overwhelmingly concerned for Honey's safety, but he couldn't see where she was. She'd been behind the bar, leaning over near him at the time of the explosion, so he lurched toward the bar bending as far over it he could, futilely searching for her. The fire emitted a flickering light but the smoke cancelled it out, eliminating any visibility. He crawled over the bar, getting soaked in spilled drinks as he did, and began to search on the floor with his hands. Somebody had gotten a hold of a fire extinguisher and was shooting acrid foam all over the place, totally without effect. O'Halloran stood up and got a face full of foam, and then tripped over something as he took a step forward. He fell face down, landing on a comfortably soft body, and heard a sound, "Oomph." It was Honey. For a few seconds, O'Halloran lay on top of the unconscious barkeep, savoring her scent, and enjoying a rare lascivious thought as he lay on her voluptivity, but then quickly regained his morality.

"Honey, Honey!" he shouted. "Honey, wake up." He picked up a half full bottle of beer lying on its side on the floor and sloshed some of it in her face. She sputtered and came to, sort of, as he tenderly held her in a sitting position, imploring her to get up, and hurry out of the burning bar.

There were a dozen burly bikers and cops pushing each other as they all tried to make it to the single door, the entrance to the bar, simultaneously. A couple of fat guys got hopelessly wedged together in the doorway causing a huge hullabaloo as the others stacked up behind them. All the patrons kept on pushing, shouting, and, of course, swearing the most inventive and noxious oaths. Finally, the door jamb splintered into a thousand pieces, and the whole kit and caboodle went tumbling into the fresh night air, cascading bodies piling on top of each other. In a few seconds, the place had emptied out, most of the patrons having regained some semblance of sight but still suffering a significantly dizzying and disabled sense of hearing, most with a vicious ringing negating any rational thought.

The parking lot was a mélange of moaning men. The bar was burning and outside a couple of cops, probably still on duty, had commandeered their cruisers and squealed their wheels trying to get out of the parking lot, but in keeping with the chaos, the cars collided heavily with each other. Both vehicles were disabled in the middle of the entrance, and nobody could get out of the lot. Or in. Fire trucks racing to the scene were forced to wait on the periphery as the Fire Captain organized a bunch of the more muscular, ambulatory patrons to push the wrecked cars aside so the fire trucks could get to work and put out the fire.

O'Halloran, with his arm still firmly around the shoulders of the shaking Honey, watched the pandemonium as they sat on the hood of his car.

Chapter 18

The next morning at precisely 7:30, Ham walked into the Courthouse Coffee. He seemed totally his normal self, oblivious to the world around him, not the slightest bit affected by the wild events of the previous evening. That meant he was still befuddled, befuddlement being his usual state anyway.

Brown was in the booth eating what looked like a heavily cholesterol laden breakfast of bacon and sausage patties, a couple of shmushed eggs, black with pepper, and of course, grits, a pool of bright yellow melted butter floating in the middle. "Heard you had a bit of an interesting evening, O. How's Honey?"

How in the world did Brown know every single thing that went on in the little village of Pine Ridge? He probably even knew what kind and color underwear O'Halloran wore. He was afraid to ask, though. Brown might actually know.

"She's fine, but she had a rough time. Got knocked out by the flashbang and inhaled a little smoke. Lucky I got to her, I guess, before the flames did. How'd you know about all that, Brown?"

Just then, somebody slid into the booth next to O'Halloran. "You all right. O? That was something out at Lefty's. The place is a wreck. I don't know whether he's going to teardown what's left and rebuild or just retire. I heard he might sell the property and move down to the Keys. Nobody got killed though. Lucky there. A lot of ER visits for the temporary blindness and deafness, a few burns, and one or two lacerations and broken bones."

O'Halloran turned to face Detective Crouse. "Do you know what happened, Detective? Who was behind it?"

"No. Usually the Fire Marshall investigates fires, but since Corporal Compton knew it was a flashbang, both from his military and police experience, we cops are going to do the investigation. He will probably lose a stripe though since his excuse about interviewing a perp at the time of the explosion didn't hold up. You know him, don't, you O? He's a Greeneburg gumshoe. Works with Farrell sometimes."

"Yeah, he was sitting next to me. Why would somebody do something like that, Crouse? Do you have any idea?"

"We're working on it. But nobody has claimed responsibility, like the terrorists usually like to do. We'll look into motive. Might be a business war between rival bar owners. Mother Nature's competes with Lefty's, I suppose, but Lefty wasn't any help there. Most of the evidence, if there was any, was burned up in the fire. Naturally, nobody saw anything, just the explosions." He paused, then almost as an afterthought asked, "How's Honey?"

"Look, you guys, lay off about Honey, Okay? Nothing happened. She was just shook up real bad, so I took her home with me. I slept on the couch. She just needed a little security and reassurance. So lay off. She's a very nice lady." O'Halloran was in a snit when it came to Honey.

"Where is she now, O?" Brown just couldn't let it rest. He was actually giggling. O'Halloran was not only a confirmed bachelor, rumor had it he was asexual, so a little blue gossip involving him was just too rich to be ignored.

O'Halloran, on the other hand, did not see any humor in the situation. "I don't know, Okay? She was sleeping when I left. She will probably call a cab and go home when she wakes up."

He was actually sulking, but Crouse thought it was time to deflect the attention. "Have her give me a call, would ya? I'd like to talk to her about anybody she might know who would have a possible motive to ruin Lefty's place. Maybe it was a vegan or Greenpeace guy, or maybe someone who was homophobic. You never know." He seemed lost in a private reverie for a moment. "But that heart stopper really was a great burger. I sure am going to miss that."

Shortly after Crouse left, they all broke for Court. It was a fairly light day, Court calendar-wise, the full moon not being out for a few more days. O'Halloran's only case involved an incredibly stupid seventeen-year-old who tried to pass off a Xeroxed copy of a twenty dollar bill. He had colored in the reverse with a green magic marker but the real giveaway was the paper. It was actually a piece of flimsy white cardboard, the kind used for index cards. When he handed the ersatz twenty to her expecting some real change for the candy bar he was trying to buy, the clerk had merely said, "Wait here," while she went in the back and called the police. The goofy kid was still waiting by the counter when a uniformed walked in. Even the Secret Service just laughed when they learned about the case and passed it back to the locals to proceed on a State counterfeiting and fraud charge. This was not the kind of case any decent Federal Court Judge would deign to allow in Federal Court. Plus in Federal Court the kid was a juvenile, and the Feds wouldn't touch it. There was nothing O'Halloran could do other than waive the probable cause hearing and hope he could work out some kind of a deal in Superior Court so the kid wouldn't get maxed out, although that might not be a bad thing come to think about it. If he met somebody else with a similar set of defective genes while he was still of age to father a child, putting more of such ilk into society would be an affront to the State.

He got home just before noon and was surprised to find Honey still there. She'd made herself at home and neatened the place up a bit; washed the dishes in the sink, and even made the bed, something O'Halloran hadn't done in weeks. She had prepared two egg salad sandwiches, with a sprig of fresh parsley she must have found in the yard, and a pickle, waiting for him. She had even brewed some delicious sweet iced tea, garnished with a couple of mint leaves. O'Halloran idly wondered where she had gotten all the herbs. He wondered what other herbs grew in his yard that he didn't know about. He was reminded of those neighbor kids, two fourteen-year-olds who seemed to have a great interest in a highly vegetated corner of his yard.

O'Halloran was filled with a new kind of dread. He liked the idea of somebody really nice, like Honey, doing something just for him, but for some reason was frightened out of his wits. He stuttered, "Why, why, thank you, Honey." He looked up at her and was startled to notice two things; one, she looked very nice, cleaned up, and without make-up. Two, she looked very nice, and... sexy.

She sat down across from him and watched as he ate, his nervousness palpable. "Do you like them?"

He did. At first he wasn't sure which 'them' she was referring to, but wisely guessed she was talking about the eggs. He could taste a touch of some spice, maybe oregano, or thyme, and maybe some nutmeg in the egg salad. He couldn't tell, but it sure beat the blandness of the food he was used to. He didn't even have to use salt or pepper on anything she prepared. He looked up at her and their eyes met. He immediately looked back down at the sandwich, blushing. Boy, he liked her looks, True she was no beauty of the sort you see in magazines like Vogue or Cosmo. But her features were even, her stoutness complemented by her curves, her black hair neat and shimmering. He was captivated and he hated it. Honey would ruin the comfort and security of his boring routine. First Antoine, now Honey. Damn. What was a guy to do?

After he had finished eating, they just sat and talked. About the fire that night, about being single, about the murders. She was a great conversationalist, something that O'Halloran was not very good at, but she carried him along without overpowering him. She was easy to talk to. When the conversation finally dwindled, Honey stood. "Well, my dear, it's time for me to go. You wouldn't mind giving me a ride home, would you, Ham?"

He didn't mind. The ride was mostly quiet because his thoughts were racing, not in any particular direction, more like racing amok. Honey lived in an apartment complex on the Pine Ridge side of Greeneburg County. It was a nice enough place, he thought. When he pulled into a parking place in front of her apartment, she leaned over and kissed his cheek. "You are truly a gentleman, Mr. Hamish O'Halloran, a rarity in these times. Thank you very much." He watched her with an unfamiliar sensation of longing as she ran sprightly up the few stairs to her apartment, turned and waved, and then she was gone.

O'Halloran just sat there for a good five minutes before he gathered up the courage to leave. This roller coaster ride he was on was a new emotion for him, and it confused him no end. He almost got lost on the relatively straightforward drive home. What an exciting twenty-four hours!

Chapter 19

On the way home, his mind totally dominated by thoughts of Honey, Ham almost ran off the road. Then he remembered Crouse's request. As soon as he got home he called her. Ham was the worst at small talk, so he got right to the point. "Uh, Honey, Detective Crouse asked me to have you call him. Here's his number. Uh…. Bye."

As soon as he hung up he stomped his foot and cursed himself. What a schlemiel! He couldn't even have a decent conversation with a girl he really liked. No wonder he was a bachelor. He desperately needed some fresh air to calm down so he went out in the yard to feed the dogs and pet them, especially Caesar, who simply loved it when O'Halloran scratched him behind the ears. There was something about the dogs, a way of communicating without words that enabled him to solve some of his more esoteric problems. They seemed to understand his darker moods, and their reactions often complemented them, brought him back to reality. He started to think about everything that had been happening lately. Ordinarily, Pine Ridge was about as blah as you could get. Nothing ever happened in Pine Ridge, the saying went. *Great place to live and raise a family, but I wouldn't want to visit there.*

After the mutts had their fill of O'Halloran's attention, they pranced off to search for something else of interest. His eyes idly followed them as they tore through the yard after each other. Noticing that the shed door was open, he went over and looked in but Antoine had gone which reminded him of Mother Nature's. What was it like? Could it have been somebody from Mother Nature's that torched Lefty's? He wondered what the food was like there. And since Honey had gotten his juices flowing he wondered about the girls. Would Honey be hurt if he went over and checked them out? Of course, but still….

He went.

He hadn't been out in years, and now he was going to visit his second joint in a week, and this one may be a … house of ill repute. What was he doing? He was about to turn around when the county line came in sight and he saw Mother's, a big old, brightly painted Victorian era house in the carpenter gothic style with all sorts of tracery and turned wooden ornamentation. Standing prominently in front of the building near the road, was a gaudy neon sign advertising the place, complete with a palm tree and parrot, blinking lights on the sign's border, and all. It was definitely cheesy, South of the Border-esque, you might say. There were more than a few cars in the parking lot which surprised him since it wasn't even dark yet. Almost, but not quite.

Just then, a deer darted across the road causing him to jam on the brakes in order to miss her. An omen, he thought? He pulled into the parking lot still thinking about the deer, and what it could mean. O'Halloran was quite superstitious about things like that.

There was a short line waiting to get in, so it really must be quite a joint. When he approached Big Fred standing guard at the door, he was intimidated by the sheer bulk of the man's upper torso. Big Fred said, "Cover charge, twenty bucks unless you're a member, then it's only ten."

Twenty bucks! O'Halloran would never pay money just to get into a place where he would end up paying more money. He turned around to leave but Big Fred put his big hand none to gently on O'Halloran's shoulder. "Say, aren't you the lawyer representing Antoine?"

Embarrassed at being recognized outside the courtroom, he merely nodded.

"That's Okay. Forget about the cover charge. Have a good time," and Big Fred stepped aside, gesturing for O'Halloran to enter. As he passed by, Big Fred whispered, "Psst. Your fly is open." O'Halloran shuddered, giving his fly a quick zip, as he felt like he was entering the gate to hell. A sheen of sweat formed on his face as he recalled the line from Dante's *Inferno* "*Abandon hope, all ye who enter here.*"

So abandoning hope, he felt compelled to enter, although an inner voice warned him not to. That voice had been quiet for a long time, ever since he was a pimply faced teenager when he went into a Puerto Rican pool hall with blinking *cerveza fria* signs in Newark, New Jersey when he was in the service. He got beat up and rolled that night after ignoring that voice.

The place was not nearly as dark as he expected. Lively music of an ersatz Caribbean beat was playing and scantily clad girls were hustling all over the place. He sat down at an out of the way table and was immediately beset by a couple of beauties who looked like they were fourteen, but must have been at least old enough to get working papers. One of the girls quickly left and the other took his drink order, a plain Coke. It was the cheapest thing on the menu, everything else in double figures. The waitress, exuding sexuality as if it was sweat, was eye popping gorgeous, and made Honey look like a middle aged bartender at a biker bar. Still, thinking of Honey made him feel guilty.

The décor was dime store faux tropical. He didn't see any banaquits or any other live birds except for the two tethered parrots. There were pictures of snakes and monkeys, some plastic parrots that didn't look a bit genuine, a stuffed leopard in a fake tropical tree, but nothing else real, not even a close approximation. But green was the predominant hue, a few fake palms back lit with a green light, and even some of the customers seemed to have verdant visages.

Hamish looked around taking in everything he saw. There were a couple of bikers he recognized from Lefty's the night before, but he didn't see any cops or guys who he could immediately tell were gay. Mostly middle aged men, maybe middle managers or traveling salesmen, all getting off at having a teeny bopper come on to them even if it was so obviously a ploy. The girls were laughing without a hint of sincerity, and the guys were such pathetic phonies, lapping it up.

Trudi, that was the name the obviously underage waitress gave. She had a squeaky voice reminiscent of a teacher drawing her fingernails across a blackboard, which made him shudder. It wasn't too long before she came back and leaned provocatively over the table, displaying her wares perilously close to his face. She carefully put the Coke in front of him on a cardboard coaster with a dramatic portrayal of Mother Nature's on it. She made sure to wiggle in an exaggerated manner, and linger a little longer to let him have a good look at her package, enhanced and pushed up as it was. Hamish didn't recognize the voice within him that whispered approval, so he ignored it. Trudi scooped up the tenner and disappeared. The drink was $7.50 but O'Halloran was sure that he would never see a shekel of change. His inner cheapness rued the rip off, and vowed that would be the last cent he spent there.

Trudi brought a menu but no change, quickly dropped it, and turned away in search of more lucrative prey. Hamish was astonished at the prices as he pored over the menu. No wonder Lefty's was creaming this joint, business-wise. When he saw the price for a plain burger, fifteen dollars, O'Halloran lost his appetite. He looked around trying to spot Mother Nature, but didn't see a female over twenty-five. He did spot a dark window in the second story with a good view of the goings on, but couldn't tell whether the glass was tinted or nobody was home.

The bartenders were identical twins, both just barely twenty-one, if that, but beautiful and buxom with swept up dos, like the waitress on a 1940s Coca-Cola ad. He could see a tip jar on the bar overflowing with bills, and not just ones either. He watched as a girl with a nametag advertising her as Betsy walked by, her chest preceding her by a good few seconds. She settled in on a red bearded biker, wearing blue denim bib overalls, and after just a minute or two chatting each other up, the two left together, escaping through a curtained side door. Craning his neck, O'Halloran concluded there wasn't a cop in the house, which made him wonder.

A sound like a loud, hoarse whisper drew his attention. A big bird he recognized as an African Gray parrot fluttered but since it was tethered to a tall stand in a corner, it couldn't go anywhere. Another, similar bird answered from another corner. There was a smattering of applause which confused him since he didn't know what there was to clap about. Then he realized the smattering of applause was because the bird's behavior announced that Betsy and the biker had bonded and linked up. The word 'clap' lingered in the air like an evil irony.

The Coke was flat and tepid and after a few sips, he really did abandon all hope. As he was thinking about leaving, a huge hand laid heavily on his shoulder. Big Fred leaned over and stage whispered in his ear. "I'm sorry, sir. You will have to leave, now." He pulled O'Halloran up on his feet as if he was a rag doll.

"What did I do? Why do I have to leave?" O'Halloran was really upset, even though he had been about to leave anyway. Big Fred was quite professional, but persistent, and perp walked O'Halloran right out of Mother Nature's. A number of customers eyed him warily wondering what kind of dire deed he had done. With more than a little irony, they looked at him as if he was some kind of weirdo or pervert.

As soon as he was rather unceremoniously shoved through the door, he turned and demanded an explanation. Big Fred merely pointed to O'Halloran's crotch and said, "We run a decent establishment here, Mr. O'Halloran. We can't have any of that kind of exhibitionism going on, here." He turned and slammed the door.

O'Halloran looked at where Big Fred had pointed. His fly was still partially open and he realized he had failed to fully take heed of Big Fred's advice as he was going into the place. But worse, a four inch tail of his orange shirt was sticking out of his fly, waving in the breeze. Oh, the shame of it all!

But he basically got what he'd gone there for. He understood the layout at Mother Nature's, and what kind of an establishment it was. The cheesy atmosphere and the blatant sexual solicitousness of the young serving staff catered to the shallow, sexually deprived and even depraved. Any lingering questions could be answered later by Crouse or Farrell, except he had learned nothing about Alberta Joralemon, and he had not seen hide nor hair of the Skinny Dude.

After the humiliation and anger had worn off a little, O'Halloran, perhaps spiked by the prurience of the place, found he could not stop thinking about Honey all the way home. But he was still hungry for some decent food, so he stopped at a McDonald's for an all beef patty, special sauce, on a sesame seed bun and a 99 cent Diet Coke. Shows you what O'Halloran's culinary standards were.

When he arrived home, the snub he received at Mother's was replaced by some rather steamy images of Honey etched in his mind. He wondered whether it was the shape of the McDonald's buns that reminded him of Lefty's former barkeep or maybe some new emotion that he completely did not understand. It was still relatively early, so he called her and made a date for the next night. He was surprised she was available, and seemed so…anxious. He had convinced himself Honey would be hesitant after the Sunday dinner fiasco. His embarrassment over his lack of *savoire-faire* was assuaged when he considered Honey might have been a little forgiving because of his heroism during the fire at Lefty's.

He didn't have long to be surprised, because she called back in two minutes. "Ham, I was just thinking. How would you like to come over to my place for dinner Sunday evening instead of going out tomorrow? I'm still a little shaken up by that fire at Lefty's, and I also have to start looking for a job. Do you know anybody who might want to hire somebody like me with no clerical skills?"

O'Halloran thought about it a minute. Going out to a movie, or even a restaurant was something he considered to be quite awkward. He was pretty much a stay at home type guy. On the other hand, going to Honey's apartment for a dinner sounded pretty nice. He could relax in that environment, take it slow, no pressure. Honey was the kind of person who could make you feel comfortable without expecting anything in return.

Chapter 20

"What the hell were you trying to do at Mother Nature's, O?" Farrell was angry, but Crouse, squeezed in next to him in the booth in the Court House Coffee the next morning, seemed unconcerned. Big Fred thinks that somehow you are associated with our investigation. He knows we're interested and is keeping a choir boy like profile. He even had the damn nerve to call us to complain about you. Said you were an exhibitionist." Mr. Sparrow was seated next to O'Halloran and seemed worried for his friend, as O'Halloran merely blushed, not responding.

"Why can't you be like other lawyers and stay the hell out of police business?"

O'Halloran had no idea what to say and realized that anything he did say would seem really lame, so he just shrugged. He didn't even try to ward off the exhibitionist charge. He thought about it, but telling them his fly had been open with his shirt tail hanging out, an orange one at that, didn't seem like it would help the situation.

Brown came in and stood there a minute, looking at the full booth. He pulled up a loose chair from one of the nearby tables and sat. "Good morning, gentlemen. Seems a little thick in here today."

The cloud of blue cigarette smoke still hung at eye level, but they all knew what he meant. Nobody tried to explain so he kept quiet for a while to see if anyone was going to let him in on what the fuss was about.

Finally, O'Halloran asked, "Have you gotten to talk to Mother Nature, yet, Detective?"

"No," Crouse answered for Farrell who was not about to clue O'Halloran in to anything. "We really don't have much to go on yet on any of the killings. All the crime scenes had been sanitized, or were clean because it was a shoot and dump. Nothing other than a white van seems connected to any of the murders. Butch Fleming is a simpleton but a killing with a single shot to the chest is just not his style, in my opinion. If he had killed Sydney, he would have roughed her up. Vented his rage and maybe strangled her or broke her neck or beat her to death with his bare hands. The guy is a gorilla, but dumb as a box of rocks."

"Why don't you just go find a reporter and tell him everything we don't got, Dimbulb."

"Look Farrell, these guys know to keep mum and maybe with these people looking, people that know the system, guys we can trust, we can find something. As it is, we got squat. No forensics, no eye witness, nothing."

"Who is Butch Fleming?" O'Halloran asked.

"A person of interest is all. We'll clue you in when and if you have a need to know."

"Okay, if that's the way you want it. But there is still my client. That's something although I don't know what it is. And when I went to Mother Nature's, I did see a white van there."

This was followed by a chorus of hmmmms.

"Where is he, O, your boy?" Farrell's ire had dissipated.

"I don't really know. He just took off the other day and I haven't seen him since. He wasn't at Mother Nature's, which was one of the reasons I went there. To look if he might have gone back there. You know they got a lot of teeny boppers serving drinks there. The one that served me looked like she was still in middle school. They have to be under age. Did you check into that?"

"What for? We are homicide, not vice. Let the P and P boys check that out."

"P and P?"

"Porn and Pot squad. Vice and narcotics."

Sullenness returned, covering the group at the table like a wet blanket, but Brown was not about to let that happen. "I still have to dismiss the case against Antoine if you don't have anything connecting him to that alley murder by the next court date. You do realize that don't you?"

They realized it all right, and visualized their only suspect with even a hint of knowledge about what actually happened to Leonard Lethbridge disappearing into the morass of homeless creatures who sporadically congregated around the Christian Mission on 17th Street in East Greeneburg.

Farrell got up. "Let's go do something, Crouse, anything. I want to have a look at a county map. You got one in your office? Maybe we can see this thing from a different angle." He turned to the prosecutor. "We'll let you know the minute we have anything substantial to hold Antoine on. If we don't get back to you by the Court date, I guess you will just have to let him walk."

Crouse's office was a closet. The desk was wedged in so tight that you just about had to slide over it to get to the office chair, a cheap fifty dollar World-Mart model. There was a metal folding chair in front of it which Farrell parked his ample behind on. "The map, cousin."

"On the door behind you."

Farrell turned around and looked at the map of Pine Ridge County. It took up most of the door and included just a little bit of neighboring Greeneburg County, enough to see where part of Mother Nature's was situated. Crouse had penciled in the location of the usual suspects — perennial thugs, registered sex offenders, known johns, and areas frequented by prostitutes. He had already marked Lefty's and Mother Nature's with map pins as well as the location where the bodies had been found.

"Impressive, Crouse. Here's the thing. We got two bodies in the alley in Pine Ridge, but no connection. We got two dead whoremongers found in different places. No obvious connection there except for their sexual proclivities. We got two guys shot in the head, a semi-girl with no pants shot in the chest. All were picked clean with not a bit of forensic evidence or identifying documents. All shot with a .44 caliber Magnum, close range, two in the back of the head, execution style, one in the chest. We got nothing as far as suspects on the two guys, and a gorilla as a maybe, probably not, suspect on the girl. Motive — none on the guys, a possible jealousy motive on the girl. We got a white van, maybe, in the vicinity. What else we got?"

"We got a flashbang at Lefty's. Maybe connected."

"Maybe not. What's the motive there? Can we make any connection from any motive we can think of?"

"Let me think about that." A couple of minutes later, after he had gone to the break room and retrieved some tasteless, boiling hot machine coffee, a cup for each, Crouse came back, hopped over the desk, plopped in his chair, and continued. "With Lefty's out of the way, Mother Nature's can pick up some business. Lefty's had been jammed the last couple of times I was in there; Mother Nature's, not so much."

"The two in the alley; other than being shot with a .44, do you think there is any connection between them?"

"Other than probably the same shooter, no. I am always suspicious of convenient coincidences so I think we're looking at one perp. We'll have to wait for corroboration from ballistics but we may have to wait until next year at the rate they work. The motive, though.... The motive is a mystery right now, but we'll find it."

Farrell disappeared into one of his moods. Crouse was sort of used to this behavior from his cousin, like the lights were on but nobody home. He waited for him to come to.

After about five minutes, during which Crouse wasn't even sure Farrell was breathing, he came around. "There must be a connection, Crouse. The motive is usually money, with sex and power a distant second and third place. Sometimes it's revenge that's the motive, but that is unlikely since we can't find any connection between the vics, yet. There was no evidence because the shooter was a pro, he probably had help to clean up the dump scenes. I like the white panel van being involved. But if Antoine was involved, why was he left behind in the alley? It doesn't seem like he had any real function in the alley if he was connected to the van. It was already sanitized. We took a look at Sydney's place, talked to her co-workers, her lover and her lover's husband, but haven't followed up on the two johns. Let's see what their grieving widows have to say."

The widow Lethbridge lived in a small but nice brick ranch, well maintained, the type that were built by the thousands in North Carolina in the sixties. Crouse had called and set up an appointment and told her to make sure Armand, the pool guy, was there, too.

Leora Lethbridge was not an unattractive woman, just into her forties, with blond hair showing a bit of gray at the roots, and an extra pound or two hugging her hips. After they introduced themselves, she took them into the kitchen and offered coffee. A very nervous Armand was sitting there, fidgeting as if he had the DTs. Interestingly, at least to Farrell, Leora seemed right at home.

She was cooperative, in fact downright voluble. In five minutes, they knew all about Leonard's philandering, a sordid tale of the storied traveling salesman. He had come down with a couple of STDs, left evidence all around, from red hairs on his suit coat, to a pack of Trojan prophylactics in his suitcase, and the proverbial lipstick on his collar. But they also learned that Leonard was one of these guys who just didn't care. He was a mediocre salesman of storage racks and bins after having been fired for non-performance from some pretty decent sales jobs. He didn't care if Leora knew about his adventures, or had adventures of her own. When he was home, he sat around in his underwear, watching the sport du jour on his big screen TV, chugging a beer, and making all sorts of demands on his wife. "Get me a beer, Leora; get me some potato chips, get me this, get me that." He was the lord of the manor and she had been his slave. Leora kept the house, mowed the lawn, checked the oil in her car, and worked part time as a school bus driver. She was used to Leonard, and didn't have the confidence to leave him and find another guy to marry. She didn't want to deal with kids and the other issues divorced guys in her age range came with, so she just put up with the toad. At least until she met Armand, the pool guy.

The detectives switched their attention to the pool guy. Immediately, they picked up on the fact that Armand's accent didn't fit with his name. "So, Armand. What's your real name, and don't give me this BS about being French. You're from the Bronx, aren't you?"

He stood up as if to leave, but Crouse was behind him and pushed him back into the chair, not so gently. "So what's the con, Armand, you planning to marry this nice little widow for her money, is that it?"

Armand feigned indignance. "You got something on me, lemme know what you got. I ain't talkin' without a lawyer."

"Now you got our attention, Armand. What's your real name, no aliases, and tell us where you live?"

Leora's jaw dropped. It wasn't an act, she was really surprised as the cops jacked Armand to his feet and searched him. Farrell found his camo canvas wallet and flipped through it. "Nestor Pina y Lopez, huh? Your driver's license says you live in New York City. What're you doing down here, Paco, trolling? Cuff him Crouse. He's got a couple of joints in here, for starters."

Out in the driveway, while a still seething Armand watched, complaining about the lack of warrant, they searched his car, a 1995 Sterling, under the search incident to an arrest rationale. "Jeez, Crouse, I haven't seen any of these since they were mandatory rides for crack dealers. It even has chrome plated profiles." The search yielded a crack pipe, some coke residue, and surprisingly, a computer, but no .44 or any other weapon.

Farrell walked back up to the widow. She was standing on the stoop, her hands on her hips. "That is one stupid Paco, Leora. He knew he was going to talk to detectives and he comes in here with dope and paraphernalia. What were you thinking?"

"Take a good look at me, Officer. I'm over the hill, my hair is totally gray under this dye job, and I am at least fifteen pounds overweight. My husband is always running around with whores, I drive a goddam school bus full of loud, snot nosed brats, I keep a supply of penicillin, amoxicillin and all sorts of other cillins, like normal people keep aspirins. Until this guy showed up, I hadn't had a decent lay in years. Leonard hasn't touched me since that last STD which took the most powerful antibiotic there is to cure, and on IV at that.

What a pathetic existence. Sure I figured Armand wasn't exactly what he said he was, but what the hell." She was quiet for a few minutes. Farrell didn't say a word. Crouse was still wrestling with Nestor, securing him into the back seat of the cruiser.

After a few minutes, Leora broke the silence. "Do you really think he had anything to do with Leonard being shot?"

"Not right now, Leora. I think he might be too dumb to pull off a hit like that, but you never can tell. It's still early in the investigation. But he did focus on you, you were obviously vulnerable, and Leonard is dead. And he did lawyer up." He paused, then added, "And to tell you the truth, Leora, I really don't like such coincidences."

Leora didn't respond and the two of them just stood there, she with her arms now crossed under her breasts, accentuating them; Farrell looking up at her from the sidewalk. Both were evaluating the other thinking the same thing, *If circumstances were different…. Well why not?*

But Farrell broke the spell as if he had doused the two of them with a pail of water. "Don't get too complacent, Leora. The spouse is always the principal suspect in these type of cases, right up until the very end."

Finished with the Lethbridge domestic drama for the time being, they went back to the Pine Ridge police station. Farrell took off for Greeneburg, while Crouse booked Nestor and thought about the report he had to write up. He slid over the desk, settled into his cheap chair, and began to write the report, when a knock on his door immediately followed the entrance of Lieutenant Bollard.

"How you coming on those alley murders, Crouse?"

He was surprised. He didn't like the Lieutenant and knew the Lieutenant felt the same way about him. Distrust, relying on completely different policing methods, political correctness, etc., but Crouse knew the lieutenant was smart, and more important, he was somehow related to the chief, maybe through the Chief's termagant wife.

"We don't have much evidence, have a couple of possible suspects, but no motive linking all of them. We are pretty sure the same weapon was used in all three killings."

"Three? Wasn't the one found in the field actually in Greeneburg County?"

"Close, but actually inside the Pine Ridge county line. Virtually same MO and same type of vic. We are working with Greeneburg because we have an idea that it was a shoot and dump and the shooting took place over there."

"Look, we have a lot of crimes to close. I'll give you another day or two. If you can't get anything concrete, we'll mark it cold and you can concentrate on something you can come up with an arrest on pretty quickly."

"Numbers, eh? We got to come up with arrests, and the hell with a serial murderer running loose in the County, is that it?"

"Be careful, Detective. You don't want to be considered insubordinate, especially by me. Let me know where you are on this by 5:00 tomorrow." He turned and slammed the door just for emphasis. Crouse started thinking about running for sheriff.

Chapter 21

The pall of blue smoke still lingered at eye level, as if it was a permanent decoration, irritating the eyes of any standing patrons, but the conversation at The Legal Lunch was much livelier than usual. The full moon had been extra bright for a couple of days and crime was way up. What with the three murders and the fire at Lefty's there was a lot of gossip fodder and just about everybody had their own opinion as to the identity of the perpetrators, from deranged psychopaths roaming the streets and alleys of Pine Ridge like Jack the Ripper or the Boston Strangler, to aliens from planet X.

Lieutenant Bollard strolled into the Lunch and looked around. The commotion and conversation fell eerily silent as if someone had suddenly turned off the tap. His presence at the Lunch was a rarity and he was as popular as a rabid skunk at a church picnic. It soon became apparent he didn't see what he was looking for, probably a wayward Way North or his only Detective who should have been out hustling up clues to the alley murders. He turned and left but it took a few minutes for the conversations to restart and even then the patrons were all a lot more subdued. Soon the Court crowd drifted back to the courthouse, leaving the only noise the clatter of Doris and Gus Jr. busing the tables and stacking the chairs.

Oblivious as usual, O'Halloran was hiding behind the crossword puzzle in the daily newspaper and didn't notice he was the last patron in the establishment. The door opened, jangling the little bell over it, announcing a potential customer. A small, nervous little man, thin as a reed, horned rim spectacles which seemed way too big for his face, came in. Spotting O'Halloran, he cautiously approached the booth.

"Ahem," he coughed into his hand, "Excuse, me. Mr. O'Halloran, can I talk to you a minute?"

The reclusive lawyer, surprised to be rousted from his reverie, looked up at the little man and nodded, pointing to the seat in the booth across from him.

The man continued, the nervousness causing his voice to waver. "I have seen you in my place a few times, and Honey says I can trust you. I, uh, think I need a lawyer."

O'Halloran scoped him out. "I know you. You're Lefty, the guy who owns that biker bar that got firebombed, right?"

"Yes," he said, extending his hand. "My name is Lev Lefkowsky, but everybody calls me Lefty." He paused a bit but then had to add a clarification as if it mattered. "Actually, I am right handed."

Doris came by and interrupted them. "I'm sorry, sir, but the kitchen is closed. I can get you something to drink, though, if you'd like to sit here a while and talk while we clean up."

"A cup of coffee would be fine," he said.

Lefty seemed as nervous as a whore in church, constantly fidgeting, looking around as if someone was after him, so O'Halloran tried to break the ice. "What's up, Mr. Lefty? Why do think you need a lawyer?"

"You know about the fire, right? You were there, Honey told me. You actually saved her life." Lefty sounded like a machine gun on full automatic. He was talking faster than he was thinking so he stopped a minute. "Well, the insurance company claims they won't pay, because they are still investigating the fire. They say maybe I did it to collect the insurance money. Another lawyer I talked to said it might take years to get resolved, and he wanted half the proceeds to take the case, along with a five thousand retainer up front, just to cover expenses. What a Jew!"

"Uh, Mr. Lefty, what's that hanging from your neck?"

"Oh this? A star of David, why do you ask?"

"That means you are Jewish right? And you just made a disparaging comment about a lawyer who was a Jew. I don't get it."

"Oh, sorry. I just got mad because he was trying to gouge me. Look, don't tell me you never heard of the stereotype. I need you to represent me to do two things. First, get the insurance company to pay this legitimate claim. Second, find out who did this to my business and why. Can you do this? How much will it cost?"

"First things first, Mr. Lefty. And let's slow down a bit. I can't even think as fast as you talk. We have a very good detective who will be looking into the cause of the firebombing. Let law enforcement do their job in investigating the case and getting enough evidence to charge the perpetrator. Granted, that may take a little time."

"Time? Time is what I ain't got, Mr. O'Halloran. That's my business what was destroyed, my livelihood. My business, you understand? The money I make there, I pay my staff, my mortgage, my expenses. Without that I am in such financial trouble you can't imagine. Not only me, everybody who works there. And I had a lot of good people working there."

"Okay. But I am sure you know insurance companies make money by not paying claims. They delay them, discount them, go to court over them, find every little thing they can in order to avoid paying the claims that their actuaries have already set aside money for. And fire claims are the worst because in most cases the evidence to support the claim has burned up in the fire, so the owner of a fire claim can't prove the amount he actually lost. You do understand that, right?

Plus there are some business owners who actually do torch their own businesses in order to get the insurance money, so naturally insurance companies think every business fire was set by the owner. But I was there when the fire happened, so I am sure that wasn't the case with you. Do you have any idea who might have thrown that flashbang into the bar?"

"Oy veh! Of course not. Sure, I know I got a good business, but who do I compete with, McDonald's? There isn't another bar like that anywhere near my place."

They were quiet while Lefty tried to catch his breath and compose himself, while O'Halloran was thinking, sort of. Lefty grabbed a paper napkin and wiped the sweat off his brow.

He picked up his coffee and drank the whole cup as if it was water and he had just come out of the desert. O'Halloran looked at the little guy and kind of felt sorry for him, even though he served the most unhealthy food on the planet. But it sure was the tastiest unhealthy food. "Talk to me a minute, Mr. Lefty. Tell me about your business, how it got started, about your unusual clientele, if you know of anybody at all who has a grudge against you, that sort of thing."

Lefty took a deep breath and told him. He spoke so fast he sounded like one of those TV announcers spouting mile a minute disclaimers in the latest gotta have drug commercial. He didn't intend for it to become a biker bar, at first, but after a few came in and seemed to like it, he called a policeman he knew in Greeneburg and asked him to stop by, just to maintain the decorum, you know. He did and pretty soon the bikers and cops came by in droves. The two groups respected each other, seemed to have something in common, maybe it was the macho thing, who knew, and then some of his gay friends started coming in and soon they found they got along with the bikers and cops, too. It was like cats and dogs who lived in the same house. It seems their natural animosity wasn't so natural after all. The diversity actually appealed to them. Lefty admitted he was always on pins and needles, expecting a major donnybrook, but it never came. Even when the black guy from Mother Nature's came in, all he did was scope the place out, talk to a few of Lefty's patrons, but that was all. Nobody ever complained to Lefty about anything. It was what it was and that was it. Lefty told his story without taking a breath, it seemed, and he said it all in a minute. O'Halloran was still trying to remember what he said, long after Lefty had finished. Then he thought of the tasty heart stopper and Honey, and that clinched it for him.

"Okay, Lefty. Here's what I can do. I will take on the case against the insurance company. My fee is $100.00 per hour. I have to charge by the hour because who knows how long a case against the insurance company will take? Like I said, they can get pretty inventive in causing all sorts of delays. I will need a retainer of $1,000.00 which will cover the first ten hours of my time. You will also be required to pay any fees and costs, such as for expert testimony, our own private investigators if I think we need them, court reporters, deposition fees, court costs, anything reasonably necessary to advance the case. I will tell you about any fees as they come up. I will talk to any law enforcement people who have any connection to the case, investigators, the fire marshal, anybody with any knowledge. I will let them do their job and will keep them informed of any evidence I uncover. If you want to settle it for less than what you consider to be your total loss because of whatever reason, legal fees, expedience, whatever, that will be up to you because it is your case. I need for you to cooperate with me in whatever reasonable requests I have, such as keeping me informed of ways of getting in touch with you. Do you agree?"

"So how much is this going to cost me total?"

"Is it going to rain on your birthday in two years? How do I know? If the insurance company agrees to pay you after one phone call, you get most of your retainer back. If they want to make a federal case out of it, and drag it out for ten years.... How can I possibly know that?"

He stopped as a weird thought invaded his normal, uncomplicated mind. *Was he even up to this kind of tough case, or should he back off?*

"One thing you can bank on with me, Mr. Lefty. Unlike some other lawyers, you know, the stereotypical shysters, I am not going to do all sorts of legal shenanigans just to jack up the amount of time I spend on your case. That's the deal with insurance company lawyers, though. Their lawyers may charge a lower hourly rate but they make up for it by all sorts of stalling tactics and finding thirty hours' worth of charges in a twenty-four hour day, They do it sometimes when they think a fairly expensive claim can make a Plaintiff give up and go away. You have already had some dealing with the insurance company, so you know what I mean. Of course, you can always get a lawyer with more clout; some silk stocking type from one of the high rises in Greeneburg. In fact, you ought to call one just to compare."

That was O'Halloran's way of getting out of this case. He could just see what a pain this case could be, but he sure would like to see Lefty get some justice. Let the insurance company work on getting retribution from the perpetrator of the flashbang arson, and pay what he considered to be a legitimate claim.

Lefty thought about it and once again looked over O'Halloran and his uninspiring surroundings.

"Could you go maybe $80.00 an hour?"

Chapter 22

O' Halloran was whistling zip-a-dee-doo-dah as he walked home after court the next day. He had represented three pathetic defendants in crummy court appointed cases, pled them all guilty, and figured he would make about $225- $250 in court appointed fees from the State of North Carolina, that is, if the State was flush. Not bad for him. It ought to just about cover his electric bill for the month. That and the discounted grand sitting in his trust account from Lefty, just waiting for action on the insurance case, would pay for his expenses for the month, but he had to do something on the case before he could touch any part of the nine hundred. That meant he had to keep records of the time he spent on the case. *Bleah.* Record keeping was just about O'Halloran's least favorite activity.

He was actually surprised Lefty had chosen him. The little guy had made a few phone calls and decided what the heck, a lawyer is a lawyer right? He wasn't going to get involved with a fee generating firm charging $250.00 or $300.00 an hour. He knew how they worked, padding bills, generating frivolous fee eating depositions and motions. Plus they wanted a $10,000.00 non-refundable retainer. The decision to go with O'Halloran was easy, especially since he agreed to come down to $90.00 an hour. Such a deal…or was it?

As O'Halloran neared his house, he noticed someone sitting on one of the old wooden slat backed rockers on his porch, the one with the least amount of mildew on it. He was going to have to get some bleach and wash off all that mildew or the chairs would soon turn black. When he got closer, he saw the visitor was a very attractive, very, very petite woman.

She actually had to jump off the chair when she stood up to greet him as he got to the steps. He had to look twice to make sure the person was actually a woman and not a little girl. "Mr. O'Halloran? I'm Darla Fleming. I need a lawyer. Can we talk?"

O'Halloran wondered what had happened to all the other lawyers in Pine Ridge. All of a sudden he was the most popular guy in town. He had gone for months without a retained client and now he was about to have two; Lefty and this tiny pretty lady. Pretty? She was gorgeous.

He made some iced tea as Darla sat at the kitchen table. She climbed up on one of the slat backed wooden kitchen chairs with her feet actually resting on the top cross rung. The rough surface of the old table was scarred with scratches, burn marks, and water stains from sweating glasses left on the table. She watched him, a curious expression on her face as if she were evaluating his tea making ability, her eyes traveling up and down his amorphous form, unobtrusively. Then he handed her a glass and sat across from her at the table for two. He didn't say anything, just looked at her with unabashed curiosity and admiration.

"Before we start, you may want to tie your shoes, uh, and tuck in your shirttails." She turned a nice shade of fuchsia for her effrontery.

O'Halloran blushed a little but not too much for this wasn't the first time one of his prospective clients had corrected his usual state of unkemptness. He once even had a nice looking, older woman come up close, face to face. He thought she was going to kiss him, but instead, she redid his tie, patting him motherly-like on the chest when she was done, saying, "There."

After quickly attending to his sartorial deficiencies, O'Halloran looked at the woman again and he could tell she was getting a little nervous. He was, too, because women always made him nervous, especially one as good looking as this petite lady. "I need a lawyer," she began, "and this nice looking, very neat older gentleman I met at the courthouse suggested I talk to you. He said he was a lawyer but did not take on domestic violence cases. Do you know him?"

"Oh yes, he's my friend, sort of. Mr. Sparrow."

"Well anyway, the reason I'm here… Is this your office or your house?"

"Both, actually. I didn't think I needed an office since I'm alone and live so close to the courthouse."

"Oh. Anyway, my husband beat me up again, and something just has to be done to make him stop." O'Halloran studied the bruise on her cheekbone under her eye and a red mark on her left temple. She paused for a few seconds until she was sure O'Halloran had processed her injuries. Processing her physique, now, was another thing. Everybody did that. "He smacks me around a lot. He is huge, 6'6", and I am barely five feet, as you can see."

She was lying. Four-eight was more like it and that might be seriously pushing it. He could just picture the two of them together. Talk about an odd couple.

"I have this friend, had actually, and she and I, well, we became intimate. After she was murdered a little while ago, I told my husband and he went postal and beat me up."

"Whoa," said O'Halloran. "Murdered? What do you mean murdered?"

"She was that tall girl who was found in the alley in Pine Ridge, shot in the chest." Darla said this simply with no emotion, as if it was just an ordinary, every-day occurrence for your lover to be shot in the chest and dumped half naked in a dark alley.

O'Halloran was stunned and had nothing to say in response for a good minute, which seemed a lot longer as he studied the doll-like woman.

He was thinking about what she said and then, his mind re-diverted. "What do you mean, 'Went postal?'" O'Halloran was not current on the latest hip slang.

"Lost it. Just went wild, yelling at the top of his lungs and breaking things. Then he hit me hard with his fist right here," she said pointing to the bruise. "He knocked me clear across the kitchen into the refrigerator. See? Feel the lump on my head. That is probably the tenth time."

O'Halloran was scared to death to touch this fragile wisp of a woman, so naturally he took a step back and ignored her request to feel her lump. Maybe it was because he thought she might break if he did, but more probably because the little voice in the back of his head was buzzing like mad with the danger warning. He had long ago decided that the buzzing was a survival instinct, an atavistic alert which he had better believe in and listen to.

"Did you take out a warrant? Go to the domestic violence people at the courthouse? What did you do after he hit you?"

"Sure, I always do that, but that domestic violence thing is totally bogus. Most of the time he says he never will do that again, we go to counseling, he apologizes, tells me he loves me, and the warrant gets dropped. It's really a bunch of bull, especially if a guy knows the system and how to beat it."

"If he has beat you up ten times, why didn't you leave him before now?"

She just shrugged. "Loyalty, I guess." Darla paused to let that sink in, and then added, "Plus he's terrific in the sack."

After his face went through a series of prismatic changes from violet to pink, and his sensation satiated mind returned to thinking in legalese mode, O'Halloran still could not understand the trade-off of great sex for being mauled by a grizzly, but what did he know? Great sex, any sex for that matter, was just not in O'Halloran's repertoire.

O'Halloran assumed the classic *"Thinker"* pose, and was quiet for a minute or so, frowning. He didn't believe that loyalty stuff for a minute. There had to be more, maybe it was an incipient sense of loyalty, perhaps she depended too much on his income, or maybe it was one of those weird psychological dependencies he knew virtually nothing about. He wondered what Butch did for a living, and whether he would have to fork over part of his retainer to pay for a psychological expert.

She was quick, was Darla, and despite whatever intellectual shortcomings she might have, she knew and understood people, even the oddballs like O'Halloran. Since she figured O'Halloran wasn't totally buying her story, she added, "And I think he might have wanted to get revenge and maybe do more than just knock me around, if you know what I mean."

There must be a lot more to this mess than she is letting on, and he really didn't know what she meant. But he just nodded, got up, and rummaged through his desk and returned with a couple of sheets of paper, a typewritten form, slightly wrinkled. "Here, please fill out this form and write down your version of the incident."

He waited, wordlessly, still as a church mouse, as she struggled with the written assignment. He began to understand why she stayed with her thug of a husband. A clerical job would be agonizing for her and anything else would probably be a part time McJob that wouldn't bring enough to pay the light bill. When she was done with the paperwork, she handed it back to him, seeming uncertain. He looked it over carefully, initially surprised by the fact the penmanship was that of a third grader, replete with decorative curlicues and exaggerated serifs, until something caught his eye.

"You are not working now, I take it. For previous employment, you put down "hostess." Where was that?"

"A place by the county line called Mother Nature's. It's just a high priced bar and restaurant."

"Hostess?"

She didn't answer, while he was clearly lost in thought.

"Did your husband also work there, as a, uh, sort of, uh, bouncer?"

"Yeah. How did you know that? But he got fired when he bounced a guy too hard. Broke his jaw and his arm."

"Did they give you a special name at Mother Nature's, one that you went by while you were there, or maybe was on your name tag?"

"You seem to know a lot about that place. Yeah, they called me Tiny-Mite. It was just a name because, you know, I'm not very tall."

"Do you know when it was that your husband broke the guy's jaw?"

"No! Why are you asking me all these questions? What does that have to do with representing me in a divorce case?"

"Well, there are a lot of things I need to know, in case I might have a conflict, or in case your husband may have some kind of a surprise defense I need to know about. I also need to know what your position is on alimony and equitable property distribution. I take it there are no children involved, right?"

She settled down and Ham thought about why she might have suddenly gotten a little testy. Was it because she had something to hide about her employment at Mother's? Sure she did. All the girls there did. But there was something else, which right now, he couldn't figure out.

After a while, the deal was sealed. O'Halloran was salivating over his retainer in five brand new one hundred dollar bills, and Darla was told to pack at the first opportunity and move out. There was always the women's shelter, he had told her, and it might be a considerable time before a hearing could be held in order to be awarded temporary possession of the home place, maybe even a couple of weeks, but at least it would be safe from the likes of Butch Fleming. After escorting his tiny client to the door, he went back in the house and started writing out the complaint in longhand on a yellow lined pad, legal size, pausing to think gratefully on his new found popularity and the swelling of his oft empty coffers.

Chapter 23

Crouse showed up that evening. "Any sign of your boy, O?"

"Don't you have a life, Detective, or do you work all the time?"

"24/7, that's me. One hard working cop. That's why they pay me the big bucks. Antoine, you seen him? "

"No."

"Let's talk a minute. You got any tea?"

Hamish was surprised at this sudden gushy, friendliness, but invited him in. After Crouse had settled into his chair, the same one the tiny Darla Fleming had occupied just a few hours earlier, sipping a surprisingly good cup of special tea, he said, " Okay, Ham, this is what it's all about. You not only have more information about this mess than any other civilian, I think you may have some ideas we haven't thought of, even if you haven't thought of them yourself yet."

O'Halloran was confused. He looked up at Crouse as if he was an alien, and then got the picture. "Oh, that bad, huh. Is it your Lieutenant hassling you?"

"You got it. This baby becomes a cold case if I don't have something by tomorrow. What gets me is that there is still a murderer on the loose, and all the Lieutenant seems to care about is numbers. I don't know if it is one, two or three perps that are involved in these murders, but I feel like I got to do something. Any ideas? Lawyers always come up with something. Some of the stuff I hear in court. You guys go to a special school to teach you how to make these things up?"

"Are you kidding? Let me think about this a minute, detective."

They sipped their tea in silence. Occasionally Crouse looked up at O'Halloran to see if he was still awake. At one point Crouse actually thought he smelled wood burning.

Finally, Hamish came to a decision. "I have a new client, Detective. It's a domestic violence matter. Her husband used to work as a bouncer at Mother Nature's. He got fired for hurting a customer. He has a really bad temper. And he is very jealous." O'Halloran was very careful to only talk about the husband.

"What! Are you trying to set me up? Trying to get me to do the dirty work so you can win a divorce case?"

"Fair enough. I just thought you might want to know. His name is Butch Fleming."

That got Crouse's attention. O'Halloran slid the handwritten complaint in front of him. After all, it would be a public record the next day when he filed it, so he wouldn't really be revealing any client confidences.

"You have pretty nice handwriting for a lawyer, O. Do you actually file stuff like this, in this form on yellow lined paper?"

He didn't answer for a few minutes. Then as Crouse looked at him expectantly he said, "What do you think, Fleming killed the girl North found in the alley?"

"Beginning to look more and more like it, but I'll tell you, O, I know Fleming. This character is too dumb to pull off a hit without leaving a bunch of clues so obvious, it would be like an advertising billboard. That is, unless he had help. So, where's your boy? Didn't he used to work at Mother's?"

O Halloran reached for his cup of tea and a sudden spasm, not an uncommon occurrence for the uncoordinated lawyer, caused him to knock over the cup, spilling a major splash of the hot tea on the complaint. He quickly blotted up the tea with a napkin but the complaint was all splotchy, part of it unreadable.

"Looks like a do-over, O. Do you remember what you wrote?"

O'Halloran was frowning as he pored over what remained of the complaint. He blotted up a little more liquid which was on the table and obliterated the document in one more place.

"Tell you what, O. Listen to me. Take that nice retainer you just got and go down to World Mart and buy a computer. Or better yet, they are having a seized property sale this week at the Sheriff's office. They usually have some computers there and I bet you could pick one up real cheap. Might have to hire a techie to erase all the porn and get you started. Hey, do you think your new client might be involved in some way?"

O'Halloran was taken aback, struck by the accusation. *Where did that come from?* Then he remembered that Crouse already knew about Darla and Butch Fleming, at least to some extent. But he knew he had to be very careful in what he told the detective. He couldn't divulge any client confidences. Worried about his law license.

"Look Detective, you know it would be a breach of my responsibility to protect the confidentiality of my client to tell you something like that, even if I didn't believe everything she told me."

Crouse looked at O'Halloran for a minute and then nodded. He understood.

After his visit with O'Halloran, Crouse decided to check on the lawyer's new, potentially volatile domestic violence case because of the oh-so-tenuous connection to Mother Nature's place. On his way to the Fleming house, Crouse thought of how he was going to handle the situation. It was late and he knew Butch had a vicious temper and could easily out muscle him, so he called his cousin, let him in on the plan. He knew it

167

was dumb but didn't think it was as stupid as Farrell made out on the phone. He had a bit of an edge on when he pulled into the Fleming driveway. The big Dodge Ram was sitting there, all shiny and bright. Ready to roll — and intimidate.

Butch answered the door. "What do you want? I ain't talking to no cop about that dyke's killing, so you can just get lost. I already talked to my lawyer."

Crouse quietly said, "Step outside, Mr. Fleming. I don't want to mess up your house."

To Butch that was a major challenge. He pushed past Crouse into the yard and had his dukes up when Crouse followed him.

"What, you want to fight me, is that it?"

Butch was already getting himself psychologically prepared for a real brawl. There was a little voice that warned him that Crouse was a cop and it was not going to end well, but Butch's alligator brain had already kicked in, so rational thought had disintegrated like a wisp of smoke. This was primeval Butch. He took a swing, a big roundhouse right telegraphed a mile away. It would have knocked down a building if he had connected.

Crouse ducked just enough to make sure Butch's huge balled fist sailed over his head, the breeze from the swing cool on his crewcut. The detective responded with a spinning karate chop in the neck with the side of his open hand, stiffened, which was like being hit by a board. Butch was irate but he could barely breathe. He was bent over, gasping for breath as he tried to introduce some level of oxygen into his system, but his neck swelled and his larynx began to close.

"Look, doofus, I ever hear of you so much as raising your voice to any woman again, I will finish the job, and I guarantee you, your breath will never be coming back to you." Just as a point of emphasis, Crouse hit him a short sharp blow with an extended knuckle, right in the solar plexus, as Butch tried to stand erect. As Butch fought to take a breath through his severely constricted diaphragm, Crouse pushed him over like he was a pin in a bowling alley.

"Where did you learn to fight like that? In sissy school?" He watched Butch writhe on the ground for a few seconds until his attention was distracted by a movement at the window of the house. Crouse noticed a little girl, or maybe a very small woman peeking out from behind a curtain. He turned and left, with Butch still fighting for a little oxygen.

As Crouse was about to get in his car, Farrell pulled into the driveway fast, skidding to a stop. Butch, on his hands and knees, was still in agony, trying desperately to force some air into his paralyzed lungs, past the closed up epiglottis and contracted diaphragm. He was turning red, panicking from the lack of air, and thought he was going to die.

Farrell jumped out of the car and approached the big man whose contorted face had turned dark fuchsia. He looked over his shoulder and asked, "You kill him, cousin? Is he going to die?"

"No, but it will take him a few minutes to begin normal breathing again and he will be hurting for a week. Every time he swallows it will remind him what will happen if he even thinks about knocking little Darla around."

Farrell asked what he meant and Crouse told him all about it, everything he had learned from O'Halloran, and a good bit more that was just surmised. Farrell went up to the agonized man, who was struggling to get to his feet. "You want me to call an ambulance for you, Butch? If I do, I have to write up the whole incident. You might even get charged with attempted assault on an officer."

Butch was red faced but had recovered enough to be able to get just a little air into his lungs. He shook his head no, and tried to talk, but that was too much of a hassle, according to the pain in his neck, so he just nodded no again, turned around and staggered into the house. He stumbled past Darla who was holding the door open. She smiled and demurely waved to the officers as she slowly shut the door.

Farrell thought about that. Something was odd. During the entire ride back to Greeneburg, he was thinking about just what little Darla's role in this whole scenario was.

Chapter 24

They were in domestic relations court. The Judge, as always, was Sam Hill, who seemed to have a permanent appointment to this depressing venue. He had no use for people who committed domestic violence, and this included women who pushed their men to the limit. But Sam sure did like a good looker, and his eyes made sure Darla knew that as she stood next to her lawyer. What a contrast! The beautiful miniscule Barbie doll like woman, not a strand of hair out of place compared to her super sloppy lawyer who looked like a troglodyte that crawled out from under a rock. As super confident as Darla normally was, she stood shaking next to O'Halloran, maybe a little fearful of the obvious interest shown by the Judge, an interest that was no doubt prurient according to his leer, maybe fearful of what Butch was going to do to her later, when he had recovered and could breathe normally again and get his hands on her. She was certain that would happen. Hamish seemed to have puffed up a bit, being brave, now, showing off for his cute client. Of course, a couple of armed bailiffs hanging around in their intimidating brown uniforms, straining to hold in bodies enlarged by hours of heavy lifting, tasers and spray cans of mace hanging from their belts, may have helped his bravado no little bit. Judge Hill kept looking over at the petite beauty, drooling with lecherdemain.

Butch didn't have a lawyer but seemed to know the drill. He was polite, contrite, promised never to do it again, but since this was only a preliminary bond hearing, his words didn't have much force. The judge released him on a $10,000 unsecured bond, on condition he move out of the marital home, have no contact at all with Darla, and turn in all the weapons he owned during the pendency of the case. And of course, there were those conditions that were all the rage these days, submit to random drug and alcohol tests, and the dreaded C word — counseling. Butch had been there before but just didn't understand all the hoopla about counseling.

Later that morning, a sheriff's deputy went with Butch to his home while he gathered up his stuff, handed over a sleek, well cared for Winchester 30-30 rifle to the deputy, making sure to get a receipt, and proceeded to his big Dodge Ram truck to drive off to the home of his aged mother. Darla was standing on the stoop and yelled after the deputy, "He has a .44 caliber Magnum in the glove compartment of his truck."

The deputy heard Butch mutter, "Bitch," but he handed over the gun without a problem, a nice, blued, snub nose. Butch sped off, planning to spend the next couple of months with his mother. Such crass irony. He hated his eternally carping and complaining mother.

Over the next few days, Darla began to pester O'Halloran. She wanted to know what would happen to Butch, could she call the whole thing off and go back with him, did he think Butch killed Sydney, stuff like that. As was often the case with O'Halloran, he just didn't know. If he tried to speculate what would happen based on his previous experience, which predictably was quite limited in domestic cases, he invariably got it wrong. It seems women domestic violence victims always tried to get hooked up with a tough woman lawyer or one of the good looking younger men just out of law school. He thought about that and concluded that he did not engender a great deal of confidence for his clients in these kinds of cases. It wasn't just his slovenly appearance, or his lack of Brooks Brothers tailored competence. He just came across as generally unconcerned, out of touch, even apathetic, maybe even incompetent. Ouch. It hurt him to think about that. Maybe if he had a new computer he could project a more capable image. If he could only learn how to use the new-fangled technology. Just thinking about that confounded him and addled his brain.

After initially being annoyed by the beautiful, tiny woman, O'Halloran started to think. Thinking was not normally his forte. He usually let thoughts drip off his brain like water off a duck's back, but some of these thoughts were beginning to sink in, and the shallow thoughts were gaining some serious perspective. He was beginning to ask himself questions. And then he started asking her.

"Darla, who do you think actually killed Sydney?" The doll like woman was quiet for a few minutes, lost in apparent thought. To O'Halloran, she was feigning actual thought and was trying to figure out the best angle in answering the question.

After an inordinate amount of time, she responded, "Why, I guess Butch must have done it. He did have a motive, didn't he? He hated Sydney. He said so himself."

"How do you think he did it?"

"Why, he must have shot her with that big ol' .44 caliber Magnum he always has with him. Don't the police have it now?"

"Yes indeed." *They sure do. And you made sure of it with that domestic violence complaint.* But he didn't say it. She was, after all, his client, and his suspicion wasn't evidence. Yet. He would tell Crouse in the morning so the detective could pull a ballistics check on the .44. He was certain Butch's gun was the murder weapon, but he wasn't so sure the galoot was the actual killer. No he wasn't. He looked at his pretty client again, this time with a somewhat jaundiced eye.

"Darla, if Butch killed Sydney, why do you think he left her half nude after he killed her? Does that make any sense to you? Isn't taking her pants off some sort of statement? What do you think happened to her pants?"

It seemed apparent to O'Halloran she hadn't thought of having to give an explanation for that. That left another unanswered question, especially if she was the one who was really behind Sydney's killing. O'Halloran stroked his chin in deep thought, and realized after a few minutes, that Darla had avoided answering the question, and he was getting a headache. He was aware that he was developing some sort of strong emotion with respect to Darla, but wasn't sure if it was a perverted attraction or deep seated loathing. He was well aware that his seriously mixed emotions about his beautiful little client was not a good thing, at least insofar as objective zealous representation was concerned.

Chapter 25

At nine the next morning, the two detectives were standing in front of the recently widowed Mrs. Craddock's house. She had opened the door, and was standing in the doorway without the slightest hint of any emotion. Dressed in a gingham housecoat, the kind that went out of fashion at the beginning of the last century, she quietly ushered them into a 1950s plain living room. They sat on a brown and pale yellow plaid sofa, with partially wooden arms, a faint unpleasant odor of disuse and cigarette smoke causing their noses to involuntarily crinkle. An oval wooden coffee table, stained and scratched, sat on an oval rag rug, a holdover from, the Depression Era. The room smelled slightly of mildew and cigarettes, a glass ashtray with what looked like a racy Las Vegas decal on it already full on the coffee table.

For a minute the detectives just stared at Cressa Craddock without saying a word. A cigarette dangled tantalizingly from her lower lip with no hint of what caused it to be suspended there. Her hair was festooned with pink plastic curlers. Dowdy, that was what she was. She was mashed potatoes plain, but then she wasn't wearing any makeup. Still.

After introductions all around, they finally got to explaining why they were there. Cressa Craddock just shrugged. Speaking in a monotone, she explained that she lost all libido after the birth of her child. Never found it. After that, Craig just became weird. He gawked at all sorts of porn sites on his computer. When she caught him at it, he asked, "What do you care for?" She really had no response, so she just let him be. He paid the bills, gave her a little allowance to supplement her meager income as a bookkeeper at a condo complex. The two of them lived completely separate lives, Cressa Craddock playing bingo at Saint Bede's Catholic Church twice a week, and Craig out gallivanting, trolling for poon, buying a night of sex if he couldn't otherwise score, which was most of the time. Cressa told the officers that Craig was a salesman, but she didn't know what he sold or where he did it. Their worthless, deadbeat son was in jail after becoming a meth head. Her life was the pits, she knew it, and couldn't think deep enough to figure out how to escape her miserable existence. And as long as she had a television to watch all night long, she just wasn't much motivated. She liked *Hoarders* and *Storage Wars*, television shows like that.

The deceased Craig Craddock had a small insurance policy, enough to bury him and pay off the paltry mortgage on the old, dilapidated ranch style house. Cressa thought about moving back to Cleveland to take care of her ninety-year-old mother, but she really didn't want to do that. Cleveland! Was the Cuyahoga River still burning? The widow Craddock was rooted in her past like a plant. She couldn't make any decision that took her outside her long established routine and that included leaving Craig, the scoundrel philanderer.

The detectives got nothing, but learned from the income tax return they found among the papers she willingly provided, that he worked for a food distributor, and made a very good commission, which he must have spent most of on the honeys. They found charges for all sorts of night spots, usually in the hundred to two hundred dollar range, and some for the services of a urologist and prescriptions from a pharmacy for amoxycillin. But what most caught their interest was a number of charges at Mother Nature's, six months ago or more, but nothing since.

So they confirmed what they suspected the stiffs had in common. All led loveless lives, forlorn in a pathetic sort of way, but nothing else that would indicate any motive for a common killer. And yet, there was that flimsy Mother Nature's connection.

Chapter 26

Taking the tip from the detective, O'Halloran learned of a sheriff's sale two days hence at 10:00 a.m. He planned to take Crouse's advice and bid on a computer since he was flush for the first time in quite a while. It had taken him hours of agonizing trying to justify the leap into the new age of technology. They had a printed list of items for sale which he got from the Sheriff's office. He was amazed at all the interesting confiscated or forgotten stuff that was for sale, much of it seized from perps who would have no use for it for a very long time, and could already be considered abandoned; at least practically, if not legally. A lot of it had been judicially declared to be ill gotten and ordered sold, the proceeds scheduled to be going to the school fund.

He looked longingly at a single line, a "1968 Camaro Convertible. Theft recovery, unclaimed." He remembered that kind of car from when he was a kid. Sigh. He idolized the '68, the epitome of cool. He could just picture himself parading around town in a spiffy '68 Camaro convertible. At that image, though, he remembered the rather seedy, unattractive one he saw in the mirror every morning. His mind's picture of a handsome young man with a stylish pompadour sporting about in a new convertible, like his ego, evaporated. He had always wanted such a ride but just didn't have the chutzpah to actually try to purchase the hottest car of the time. Plus, he knew that not only could he not afford it, his slovenly appearance would be a total insult to the beautiful style of the old car. At breakfast the next morning, he broached the subject of the computer with Mr. Sparrow, but just couldn't bring himself to mention the Camaro.

"Wonderful, Hamish, welcome to the 20ᵗʰ Century," the venerable old attorney said. It was the 21ˢᵗ but who's counting?

He had never been to a Sheriff's auction and hadn't a clue of what to expect. But at 9:45 Thursday morning he was standing among a growing crowd of prospective buyers in the Sheriff's vehicle confiscation lot, which was surrounded by an eight foot tall cyclone fence, topped with a roll of razor wire. O'Halloran looked over the motley group, seeing everything from tattooed bikers with beards, to corporate executives looking to score a cheap deal, and even a few soccer moms thrown in. He didn't know it but these queens of the eBay made a fortune buying merchandise cheap at auctions like this and selling them online for healthy profits.

At precisely 10:00 a.m., a tall rangy deputy appeared and quickly got the crowd's attention. "Before we begin I have an announcement. The blued .44 Magnum snub nosed pistol advertised in this auction has been "withdrawn." A chorus of boos and other assorted sounds of disapproval erupted and the deputy held up his hand. "I'm sorry but there is a murder investigation and it seems like that particular gun maybe was used in that shooting. It may come back on the auction block after the trial. Sorry." There was a big commotion and at least half the crowd left. O'Halloran was surprised when a goodly number of soccer moms joined the crowd leaving the lot. He had no idea that plain old housewives had any interest in blued, snub nosed .44 caliber Magnum pistols.

The first items were bicycles. There were about a dozen of them, all sorts and sizes. Most had been found abandoned at the rec center, and had probably been stolen by some juvenile druggie and just left there, unclaimed, the owners oblivious to their whereabouts. The deputy seemed bored as he quickly disposed of them for around $20 apiece to a wizened old black guy. O'Halloran looked closely to make sure it wasn't the lawn mower thief, but it was somebody else. When he caught O'Halloran staring at him, the old man lowered his head and said, "I got a used bicycle shop over toward Greeneburg." O'Halloran wondered why the man felt he had to explain.

There were some other odds and ends, including an old TV, an Osterizer, and a bunch of broken things. O'Halloran could not understand how they ended up in the Sheriff's possession. When there were no bids, the deputy started bundling the items and sold a boxful to an old man for a dollar. The crowd started chanting, *cars, cars,* so the deputy responded by saying, "I usually get to them last, but I'll throw in a teaser or two."

Followed by the crowd, all of whom were eager for a bargain, he walked over to a shiny black Cadillac Eldorado, with chrome profiles and an exaggerated chrome hood ornament of a graceful naked lady, art deco style. The crowd voiced some *oohs* and *aahs* and O'Halloran salivated. It certainly wasn't his style of ride but it sure did catch his eye. The bidding started at a grand and was quickly up to ten. After a flurry there were two final bidders, both straight out of Hollywood casting. One was a wise guy with slicked back greasy hair, dressed all in black, a silk shirt with a skinny white tie and a pair of oversized, white rimmed sunglasses, almost the type Elton John might wear. O'Halloran wondered where this guy had come from. He certainly wasn't a Pine Ridger, probably not even a Southerner, not looking like that, he wasn't.

The other bidder was a tall, skinny black guy, with a faint resemblance to Snoop Dogg. Sporting a purple satin shirt, open almost down to the waist, a pair of pink unisex pants, and purple winklepicker boots, with a prominent gold buckle with at least a pound of bling, and aviator glasses, O'Halloran pegged him as a certified drug pusher. He decided to stay far away from the bidding on this beauty. These two characters were determined to outbid each other, but the cost of the old Cadillac was clearly getting to be much more than it was worth. Finally, when the bidding got up to $16,500, the wise guy gave up and it was sold to the pimp, or maybe he really was a drug pusher, whichever.

A couple of Sterlings went fast to some rather shady characters, also dressed up in the costumes of your traditional drug dealers, and their names and addresses were quickly recorded by the DEA plant in the crowd, along with a rather secret cell phone photograph of each buyer. Later, they would check with the lady deputy who was collecting the cash for the names and addresses, most assuredly phony. Then the deputy auctioneer went back to the electronic stuff. O'Halloran was encouraged when the first two computers went for about $100 each. Then the deputy held up a simple black Acer model and started the bidding at $25 bucks. O'Halloran held up his hand and the deputy recognized his bid. As he tried to encourage more bids, another deputy behind him held a fine, almost brand new Dell in his hand, a seventeen inch monitor, and was looking at it almost lustily, carefully wiping a little dust off it with a clean handkerchief. The crowd's attention was on that Dell and nobody else bid on the Acer, so the deputy announced, "Sold to the gentleman with the pony tail for $25.00." The bidding on the Dell was fast and furious as Hamish walked over to the table and handed $25.00 cash to the woman deputy collecting the dough and handing out bills of sale.

When O'Halloran returned to the bidding area the deputy had gotten through most of the electronics and was drawing the crowd's attention back to the assortment of seized vehicles for sale. Several pretty banged up models went cheap, for about the value of the used tires. There were three convertibles. The first two were newer models, pretty nice cars, probably seized from drug dealers or tax cheats. One had a bullet hole in the driver's side door, and if you looked closely you might find a little blood on the seat the detailers missed. There were several active bidders on these snazzy models. By the time the deputy came to the Camaro, there were just two interested buyers left, O'Halloran and a fat guy, a really fat guy. There was no way this character could even fit in behind the oversized steering wheel of that era, the size of a garbage can lid. O'Halloran gaped at the Camaro, even drooled a little. Okay, it was a little rough. It had a few dings and the top had a little rip in it. It certainly was dirty, but the black paint job looked pretty good under the thick coat of road dust. At least O'Halloran imagined it did. The interior was a light gray leather, which seemed to be in pretty good condition, and O'Halloran was hooked. He was going to bid until tomorrow if he had to.

The fat guy pulled out his wallet and fanned a wad of c-notes that made the wallet look just as obese as he was, and O'Halloran's miserly heart sank. The chubby guy opened the bidding at $100 and Hamish quickly countered with 2. Then the fat guy started to raise his hand, hesitated, and grabbed his throat instead, falling forward right on his face. There was a big hubbub as medics rushed to the stricken man, turned him over and started administering CPR, eschewing the mouth to mouth routine in case he egested whatever undigested intake that was the cause of his collapse. He was quickly transported away by ambulance. It took three medics and a couple of civilians to lift the guy onto the gurney, while O'Halloran just stood there, frozen in a state of astonishment.

When the commotion had subsided, the deputy resumed the auction, but there were no other bids on the Camaro. O'Halloran had gotten the car of his dreams for $200, but as he went to pay, self-deprecating doubts filled his mind. The car must be jinxed, he thought. He became convinced there had to be a major problem with it, like for instance, maybe it was a flood car and all the wiring was shorted, or it didn't even have an engine under the hood.

But just to make sure, he checked. After lifting the hood, O'Halloran was ecstatic. Not only was there an engine but the air filter on top of the carburetor was chromed. Joy! That meant the former owner had been an aficionado and probably maintained the car very well. In addition to the not so fancy Acer computer, he now had a new old Camaro. He had not spent so much money at one time in quite a while, and he had not gotten such fantastic deals, ever. But his euphoria subsided a bit as he realized he would now have to learn how to use the computer and clean all the unwanted stuff off it. He was stunned to learn later on that a professional tech service was going to charge him $200 to clean all the unwanted smut and other illicit favorite sites and set it up with a basic Windows program. The Camaro started up, right away, but was running rough, smoke coming out of the exhaust. He knew a decent tune up was going to cost him what he paid for the car. At least. He began to question his own judgment, that fear of venturing into anything new coming back to haunt him, as well as the fear of violating the security of his innate inner miser.

Chapter 27

Finished with a boring day in District Court, O'Halloran thought about going to the Legal Lunch, or the Court House Coffee since it was still early. Instead, he walked home to play with his computer, and maybe gain a modicum of competence. He turned it on. Nothing happened. He sighed. This was his life, O'Halloran thought, nothing ever worked the way it was supposed to. He was about to walk back to the restaurant, but it was starting to drizzle and the clouds overhead warned him he was going to get soaked very soon. So he got in his brand new old Camaro and drove, finding a serendipitous parking place right in front of the place. He scurried in, avoiding the rain and protecting the refurbished ACER as if it was a newborn, and set up his computer in his usual booth. It was not quite time for the name change and the place was empty as a synagogue in the Vatican City.

Doris came over with a cup of coffee, set it in front of him, and slid into the booth. "What you got, Ham, a new computer?" She was as surprised as anyone, for she was well versed on the old lawyer's propensity to write out all his legal pleadings, correspondence and stuff, on a yellow legal pad.

"Yeah, but I can't get this thing to work."

"Let me see it," surprising Ham as she reached for the laptop, "I know a thing or two about these things."

"You do?" Ham was really surprised for he just could not imagine Doris having anything to do with the new electronic age other than an old television set, with rabbit ears, even.

"Where'd you learn about computers, Doris?"

"I've got a fourteen-year-old daughter, Ham. If I didn't keep up with these electronic gadgets, who knows what would be goin' on. She'd probably be sexting and into all sorts of stuff I wouldn't approve of. You got to stay one step ahead of these teenagers these days, Ham. They're smart and sassy. Now let me see. Hmmm."

She quickly had it up and running, rapidly explaining everything to him as her hands flew over the keyboard. "You need a password, Ham. This thing wants one with at least eight characters including one number. What'll it be?"

"Huh?" Ham was clueless.

"Password, Ham, something only you know so everybody else can't get in here and find out all your secret stuff, especially about clients. One that has a number in it. You type it in here, and you are the only one with access to what's on your computer."

Ham thought for a minute, looking out the window at his Camaro, thinking about his father for some reason, and the old man's 1926 Essex which he had idolized. His Dad even had a raccoon skin coat which was all the rage back then. "Uh, how about 23 skidoo?"

"Ooh, good one. No one will ever think of that as a password. We can't have a space so we'll just run the letters and numbers together, no capitals." Her hands were a blur as she set it up. "Okay, what do you want to do, write a letter, pleading, do legal research, what?"

"Legal research? You can do legal research on that thing?"

"Sure. You are a member of the State Bar Association, aren't you?"

"Yeah, but only because I have to and they have a magazine."

"Actually you don't have to be a member to practice law, but since you are a member, what's your number?"

O'Halloran was thinking about the cash he had to put down each year for the Bar Association dues, that he didn't have to pay if he actually wasn't required to be a member. He was ticked at first, but then he started to get interested in what Doris was saying and began to listen to her intently.

In a few minutes, O'Halloran was logged in, had an account number that made no sense but he had written down the jumble of letters and numbers that was the password so he wouldn't forget it, and was soon doing legal research. Amazing. Actually he was amazed at Doris, He looked at her with a new found sense of respect as she lit up a Marlboro and blew out a cloud of blue smoke, which wafted up and settled at eye level merging with the permanent cloud.

They talked for a few minutes and he messed around with the keyboard a bit, hunting and pecking, like he had never seen a typewriter set up. He had, but it had been thirty years or more.

Some customers came in and Doris jumped up, leaving the burning cigarette in an ashtray, a wisp of blue smoke wafting up to merge with the thin cloud. "Gotta go," she said, and was gone.

O'Halloran looked after her, watching her move with the same sense of that foreign feeling he always had when he watched her like this. It both troubled and pleased him. Then he went back to his computer, thinking of things he wanted to research.

He started thinking about Darla, Butch and then the killings. He thought of the detectives and their interest in Antoine. Wondering where Antoine was hanging out these days, himself, he typed in Antoine al Aqwon, half expecting nothing to appear. But it did, an arrest sheet for Antoine al Aqwon, aka James Matheson, for Simple Assault. The case was dated several years ago and was from Greeneburg.

This made absolutely no sense to O'Halloran. He typed in James Matheson and made three spelling errors before he got it right. Matheson, James, Member of the Greeneburg Better Business Bureau, Chamber of Commerce, Lions Club, etc. An upstanding citizen. This confused O'Halloran more than the computer itself did. This just could not be the Antoine who lived off and on in his shed behind his house like a homeless person. James Matheson! He would have to ask Antoine about that. Maybe he should let Detective Crouse or Farrell know about his serendipitous discovery.

Just then, Mr. Sparrow came in and slid into the booth across from him. "What do you have there, my friend, a computer?"

But the smile on Ham's face dissolved in an instant as the screen went blank, and the quiet hum of the electronic device stopped, followed by silence.

He looked up at Mr. Sparrow with the goofiest expression on his face. "My computer just died. I was looking up someone and it just went blank." He was truly devastated.

Mr. Sparrow was sympathetic, knowing his friend's befuddlement with new gadgets of any kind. "The battery probably just needs to be recharged. Do you have a cable we can plug in to a USB port and power source? I am certain Gus doesn't have Wi-Fi here."

To O'Halloran, Mr. Sparrow was speaking a foreign language. He didn't respond, just kept that goofy blank expression on his face. Mr. Sparrow understood his predicament. "Ham, using this computer requires under-standing of a host of new terms and ideas for you. My suggestion is that you take a course at Pine Ridge Community College to properly learn how to operate a computer and learn the jargon."

He showed O'Halloran the USB port, explained about connecting the computer to an external power source, simple stuff that was like learning calculus in Braille to O'Halloran.

But Mr. Sparrow mercifully directed him to Conley's Computer Company on the outskirts of town for his crash course in cybernetics.

Chapter 28

They met after Court the next day, Crouse a little perturbed since he had just been assigned a burglary case that he wanted to start working. "What, O? What's so important that you couldn't tell me over the phone?"

O'Halloran told him about his computer, about Antoine al Aqwon aka James Matheson. Crouse slapped his forehead with the palm of his hand, the traditional, *I am so dumb*, gesture.

"I never thought to look up Antoine on the PIN database. This is a good score, but you know what? You can't represent him anymore. You are now a witness, sort of, in the murder cases and you have a conflict. That bother you?"

Ham thought for a minute. "No, not really. I kept getting the feeling he was playing me. I don't know what he was after but he stuck around for a reason. Who would want to sleep in an old garden shed on a dog bed full of fleas anyway? I wonder if that was an act he was putting on," especially if he really was this James Matheson guy.

Crouse talked to him like he wasn't there, bouncing ideas off him, not expecting a response. Ham wasn't thinking fast enough to respond anyway. His mind was still on Antoine, his alias, and why a man like him would stay in the shed with that musty smell and all those fleas, hanging around, volunteering to do chores like a menial servant. Finally Crouse, said, "I am going to call him in, find out what this James Matheson business is all about, and dig as deep as I can to try to put all these oddball pieces of this puzzle together. Thanks, O. Be in touch"

He got up threw a couple of bucks on the table, and left. O'Halloran was still thinking about Antoine sleeping on a flea infested dog bed, his brain addled and stuck in idle.

It didn't take Crouse long to find Antoine. A phone call to his cousin, an afternoon trip to Mother Nature's, and Antoine was in his patrol car.

"What's dis 'bout, off'cer? I din't do nothin' Why's I gotsta go wid you to da station?"

"Something came up, Antoine. We need to ask you some questions."

"So Ize unner arrest, huh? Wha' fo'? You gonna read me ma rights?"

When they got to the Pine Ridge police station, Crouse escorted Antoine to an interrogation room, put a can of Coke in front of him and walked out, closing the door perhaps a little too hard. It was quite a bit more than a few minutes later, when he and Farrell came back in.

"Antoine, you know Detective Farrell, here, from Greeneburg. We have a few questions to ask of you. First off, is your real name James Matheson?"

Antoine appeared stunned. He looked from one officer to the other. After a long pause, he said, "You did not read me my rights, Detective Crouse. Unfortunately, I will not be able to answer any more questions until I have had the advice of my attorney. If I am not being charged with any specific crime, I take it I am free to leave, right?"

Now it was the officers who were stunned each looking at the other, then at Antoine, then back again. Finally, Farrell, asked, "Do you want me to call Mr. O'Halloran for you?"

"No, I think I will retain someone from Greeneburg. Since I don't believe I am under arrest for any specific criminal offense, I suppose I am free to leave. I would like a ride back to Mother Nature's if you don't mind. Detective Farrell. I assume you will be traveling back that way in a few minutes, aren't you?"

The change in Antoine's diction was mind boggling. They were not just dealing with some dumb or deranged street person. This was a shrewd, intelligent man, according to the dramatic transformation in his speech, and his acute understanding of the situation.

Farrell, the more experienced of the two, got up. "Be glad to, James. I'll be back in a minute. Just one or two administrative things to take care of. I'll be right back."

The two officers left the room and as soon as they had shut the door, Farrell said, "Cuz, run a quick check on NCIC for James Matheson, see if there are any warrants out for him under the name James Matheson, black male, age about thirty-five. Also check whatever you can on any computer data base. See if there is anything we can pick him up on by the time I get to the county line. Make it fast."

Farrell returned to get Antoine and the two left the building, Antoine still sipping the Coke. "James," Detective said, "Department policy. I have to search you again before you get in an official vehicle. Spread your legs, hands on the vehicle, take a step back." He patted Antoine down, thoroughly, very thoroughly. He felt the man cringe as he ran his hand up the inside of his leg. He found something he didn't wish he had, but said nothing.

"This is mortifying, Detective. I demand to know what's going on."

As they drove back to the County line, Farrell told him. "Antoine or James, whatever your name really is, we like you for the recent murders, but we haven't got solid evidence on you. Yet. Just so you know. Right now we are looking into motive, and I got an idea that when we find it, you will not be able to wiggle out of this one."

Neither man said a word for the rest of the ride. As they approached the County line, Farrell's cell rang and he immediately pulled over, explaining to his passenger, "Can't use the phone and drive at the same time. Department policy."

Antoine doubted it but said nothing. He was only about a quarter mile from Mother Nature's and could easily take off and hoof the last few yards. But when he noticed there were no door handles in the back of the patrol car, he decided to sit where he was, and wait to see what was going on. Farrell spoke into the phone. "Nothing except that, eh?" he listened for a few minutes more, started the cruiser and drove the four hundred yards to the restaurant. "See you Antoine, or James, or whatever."

As soon as Antoine was out of the car, Farrell did a u-turn and headed back to Pine Ridge.

Chapter 29

O'Halloran looked at the bill in astonishment. $241.38 for a tune-up! He had made arrangements for Mr. Sparrow to drop him off at Marty's Motor Mart, the only garage in Pine Ridge that was still reputed to be anything more than a shade tree mechanic's repair shop. Still, there was an old oak tree out behind Marty's garage that had a rusty block and tackle set-up hung from a limb the size of a man's torso. He could just picture Marty thirty years ago using the block and tackle to pull out a straight six out of a '55 Chevy to replace it with a powerful V-8.

He eased into the front seat of the Camaro after paying Marty with $200 in cash and a check for $41.38. Marty had itemized everything from five quarts of oil, a filter, wheel balance and the proper air pressure, to new sparkplugs, replacing a battery cable and tie rod. The Camaro started right up and purred like a kitten. Hamish was elated as he drove home, the top down, the scented Pine Ridge air cooling the very top of his forehead. Picturing the Joe Cool of his youth in his mind's eye, he pulled in front of his house. As he was about to turn off the engine he noticed what looked like a foot operated button on the floor. He thought it must be the high beam for the head lights and pushed down with his left foot just it check it out. AAAAROOOGAH. The loudness of the musical claxon of the novelty horn almost blew him out of his seat. At the very moment the horn blared, the neighborhood brat, little Billy Maloney, was driving by on his refurbished Schwinn Challenger bicycle. The horn blasting right next to his ear caused him to become discombobulated, and veer off, crashing into a fully loaded garbage can across the street. Fast food wrappers, uneaten food scrapings and all sorts of odoriforous kitchen detritus cascaded into the street. As Billy pulled himself out of the trash can, he exclaimed, "That was so cool, Mr. O'Halloran. Where can my Dad get a car horn like that?"

O'Halloran was more concerned with the boy, especially since the red stuff dripping from his temple was either ketchup or blood. There was a lot more stuff dripping from his head and a cheesy paper from Hardees was sticking to the side of his neck. O'Halloran deftly removed it, determined that the red stuff was definitely just ketchup. "You are Billy Maloney, aren't you? The kid that lives around the block from me," O'Halloran asked. He'd seen the boy around the neighborhood but wasn't sure who he was.

"Yup, that's me, Billy Maloney, but everybody calls me Bony on account of I'm so skinny."

"How old are you, Bony?" O'Halloran felt funny calling the kid Bony.

"Eleven years old, but people think I'm older because I'm tall for eleven. Not the tallest kid in my class but close. Big Barbie is bigger than me by a couple of inches."

After determining there was nothing broken and that the kid suffered more from a serious case of garbage immersion than anything else, O'Halloran said, "What do you say we pick up all this trash?"

As he was unenthusiastically retrieving selected items from the garbage can, which had spewed into the street, Billy asked again, "What about the horn, Mr. O'Halloran? My father really needs one of those."

O'Halloran responded, "I don't know Billy. It came with the car. Your Dad probably needs to stick with his standard factory horn. You need to go home and wash this stuff off." He turned his head, grimacing when he got a good whiff of

Billy's hair and realized it might not have been just the garbage.

As he was picking up some pieces of flotsam blowing around on the street, O'Halloran noticed the front wheel of Billy's bike was askew. The wheel was at a forty-five degree angle to the handlebars. He hoped the wheel wasn't bent. Using a little leverage, he was able to get the wheel roughly perpendicular to the bars. "I think you can ride it Billy, but ask your father to fix it right and tighten up the handlebars."

Billy wobbled off and Hamish hoped the boy was all right, and then started thinking about the claxon.

Chapter 30

After O'Halloran had spent an hour at the one room, jam packed Conley's Computer Company outlet near downtown Pine Ridge, he was smiling. Conley had removed what turned out to be a plethora of porn, set him up with a few basic programs like the latest Windows and an anti-virus program just as Doris had instructed him. The rain had stopped and the oblique afternoon sun shined brilliantly, casting the little village in a glorious glow. Colors were sharp and the shadows and rain slicked streets exaggerated the feeling of contentment he felt. In a few minutes, he pulled up in front of his old clapboard house on Main Street, carefully parking on the street a few inches from the curb. The rain had washed the Camaro and it sparkled proudly. Life was good.

That is, until he got inside. He put the bag of the various items he'd bought on the kitchen table and as he was looking at one of the manuals, the telephone rang. It was Darla, and he sensed what seemed to be panic in her voice. She had to talk to him right away.

Darla! What a pain. Although he enjoyed looking at her in a perverted sort of way, the perfect little beauty, not fully formed, more like a miniature painting, she brought him nothing but discomfiture. The emotions she evoked were a combination of attraction, revulsion, distrust, unsettlement, even loathing. But it was like a diabetic's addiction to sweets, he just couldn't say no, so in half an hour, she was sitting at his kitchen table.

"Would you like some tea, Darla?"

"Oh, that would be lovely. Thank you so much, Hamish."

He shuddered at the informal use of his first name. He wanted to be called 'Mister' by her. Keep some sort of barrier between them. He knew she was purposely becoming familiar, but he didn't know what her purpose was. He knew it was not a sexual come-on for she hadn't expressed any romantic interest in him before. How could she, as decrepit and unattractive as the mirror reminded him he was every morning? It had to be something sly, even nefarious, for he really did not trust her. What was she after?

He served some Darjeeling oolong, no cream or sugar. Staring into the cup of dark golden brew, a sense of mystery emanating from the liquid, his confused mind was racing. He didn't understand what possessed him to serve her this fine, expensive tea, but some inner force compelled him, as if he wanted to impress her, and this was the only manner in which he could.

She looked at the thick honey colored liquid and carefully sipped. "Oh, this is delightful. You must be a tea connoisseur, Ham."

There it was again, even more familiarity. He blushed involuntarily.

"Why did you come here, Darla? What was so important that you had to talk to me in person and not on the phone?"

He'd retrieved her file from an ancient wooden file cabinet he bought at a yard sale years ago. The manila file only had a few yellow lined sheets of handwritten notes, and a copy of the newly typed complaint with the time stamp from the Clerk's office. Studying it carefully as if there was some hidden code in his notes which would unlock his malaise, he realized she wasn't answering him, but staring almost seductively at him. He checked his fly to make sure it was zipped up. Sometimes, when he forgot, people would stare at him like that. Clearing his throat, he said again, "Darla, why did you come here?"

She had that look, like there was something she really wanted, lusted after, even. He was reminded of the look of euphoria on the faces of heroin addicts after they had just shot up, experiencing the last pure bit of pleasure before the inevitable painful crash. There was absolutely no doubt that Darla was blessed with an over-abundance of raw sex appeal. Or cursed. It was the one tool whose use she'd mastered.

She took a deep breath, accentuating her curves, as if she was exuding a last gust of overpowering sexuality. "Oh, I, uh, just wanted to see you." She pretended to blush, not quite pulling it off, but it still had the desired effect on O'Halloran. "I think Butch wants to get back together with me. He called me a little while ago."

"What did he have to say?" O'Halloran was thinking about having Butch picked up for violating the domestic violence restraining order, his protective instincts toward his little client strangely in high gear.

"Oh, he was nice. Said he missed me. That he hated living with his mother. Wanted me to drop the charges."

"And how did you respond to that?"

"I don't know. I have mixed feelings. I guess part of me still loves him, but I do hate getting knocked around by him or even being in the same room with him when he gets mad. And it seems that lately every little thing seems to set him off."

"Like what?"

"Like when I talk about going back to Mother's, or about Fred."

"Fred?" She really piqued his interest now, and he forgot about any nascent lust that might have been building up.

"Fred, you know, my brother Fred. He's the bouncer over at Mother's."

O'Halloran was stunned. First, how could one set of parents produce two such dissimilar offspring? Fred was huge, Darla was a midget compared to him. Compared to anybody for that matter. Fred looked like he could throw an anvil a mile, while Darla couldn't even move one an inch. "What did you say about your brother that set Butch off?"

"Just that I miss him. We were close as kids, very close, and I haven't seen him since I left Mother's."

"Then why did you leave?"

"It was getting pretty tense there. You know, the guys always hitting on me and Butch wouldn't let me do lap dances, but I did anyway. For the money, you know. Some of the men really dig the little ones like me, and they get real generous. But one day Butch came in and he and Fred had it out. The cops came and broke it up. They took Butch away. He's had it in for Fred ever since. Butch is the type who always has to have somebody else to blame for his problems."

O'Halloran was quiet as this revelation sank in. There was something fishy about this tale Darla was spinning, despite the obvious truths. He was getting the feeling he was being set up, but he couldn't see what the reason was, or where this was all going. O'Halloran was beginning to have a suspicion that perhaps even Butch was being set up. He was deep in thought when Darla interrupted him. "Mr. O'Halloran, are you all right?"

He breathed a sigh of relief. It was back to the formal Mister, and he plummeted down from his reverie. "Okay, Darla. I will need a little information. What is Butch's mother's name and where does she live; what is Fred's last name and where can I get in touch with him without going to Mother Nature's? I kinda was barred from there."

"Oh, Mr. O'Halloran. I can fix that. I'll just call Fred. You wouldn't want me to fix you up with a lap dance would you?"

This blush was for real, a deep claret, causing the little woman to form a disingenuous smile, but Darla gave him the information he asked for. "Darling? Fred's last name is Darling? Your maiden name was Darla Darling?"

"Yeah, cute isn't it. Sometimes I wish I had kept my maiden name. It would have really helped business at Mother's."

She got up to leave, but sidled over to where he was sitting and kissed him on the cheek. Or maybe it was the forehead. Anyway, it seemed like she was actually bouncing as she skipped down the porch stairs to her car parked next to his fine shiny Camaro.

Still feeling the heat from the deep blush he had experienced long after she was gone, O'Halloran remained frozen in his chair at the kitchen table, thinking hard and occasionally taking a sip of the fine, but now tepid, Darjeeling oolong. The tea seemed to stimulate his brain, but in a good, clearheaded way. Not like the time he took a Darvocet after having his wisdom teeth extracted. He was so out of it then, he had actually walked into a wall.

His thoughts ranged from the lingering magic of the pervasive aura of sexiness of the petite beauty, to what the hell was going on? This whole thing seemed designed to steer him away from something, not toward it. He hadn't had a reason to think this hard for at least a generation. His Attention Deficit Disorder, something he had worked hard to conceal all these years, had his thoughts bouncing all over the place like a superball in a concrete walled jail cell.

Still thinking about Darla, and soothed into a sentient sense of well-being, his reverie was suddenly shattered by an ear splitting *AAAROOOGAH*. Another blast of the claxon and O'Halloran was running out the door. There sat Billy in the driver's seat of the Camaro, as the evening light was fading, happily blasting the horn. *AAAROOOGAH*. O'Halloran tried to open the driver's side door but Billy was too quick, and pushed down the old car's door lock. O'Halloran ran around to the passenger side but Billy quickly slid over and locked that too. Neighbors were coming out onto their front porches to see what all the commotion was and to find out who and why their peaceful evenings were being disrupted. *AAAROOOGAH*. O'Halloran was frantic, pleading with Billy to get out of the car. But the little imp responded with another *AAAROOOGAH*.

"I'm going to call your parents."

"Go ahead," came the muted reply. *AAAROOOGAH*. Billy was cackling with glee.

O'Halloran ran into the house, and quickly called the Maloneys. In a few minutes a small posse of neighbors had gathered around the car, begging, cajoling, threatening the bratty boy, but his response was always the same. *AAAROOOGAH*. Mr. Maloney seemed awfully quiet and stayed sort of in the background. Hamish thought he smelled a strong odor of alcohol, but Mrs. Maloney was irate. "Get your butt out of that car right now or you'll be restricted to your room for the rest of your life, you little brat." *AAAROOOGAH*. His laugh was now downright devilish, devious.

In a last ditch effort, O'Halloran yelled through the closed driver's window. "I'm calling the cops now, Billy, if you don't get out of the car right now."

"Go ahead." *AAAROOOGAH*. All the neighbors were yelling at Billy. Mrs. Maloney, red faced and apoplectic, was screaming as Officer Wayland North strolled up.

"What's going on? Who is making all that noise?" *AAAROOOGAH.* "Get out of that car now," demanded Officer North, but Billy just shook his head and stepped on the horn button again.

Finally, Mr. Maloney, who had been watching the scene several feet away with his arms crossed, took a few steps forward and softly said, "Lift the hood, Mr. O'Halloran, and I'll disconnect the battery. I think the horn is battery operated." His speech was slurred. The Camaro was made in the days before the only way to pop the hood was from a latch on the inside, so O'Halloran got to it and lifted the hood. In a few minutes, Mr. Maloney returned with a wrench and removed one of the battery cables, and that was it. The neighbors looked at the kid who was desperately stomping the floor button to no avail, but after a few minutes they all went home, except for North and O'Halloran.

"You want me to arrest him, Mr. O'Halloran?"

Hamish thought a minute and said, "What for? I never heard of someone being charged with trespassing in a car. I guess maybe a disturbing the peace charge might stick, but he's just an eleven-year-old boy. What judge do you think is going to want to deal with that? Leave him be, Officer, I'm going to go back inside."

Peace returned to the little neighborhood, but every so often O'Halloran would check, peeping out of the living room curtain, and Billy was still in the car vainly stomping the floor board, a dejected expression on his rascally face. It was not until the serenity of evening settled in, calming the old lawyer's frazzled nerves, that O'Halloran realized he could have used his car key to open the door and forcibly evict the juvenile from his Camaro. Even after he turned off the light to go to sleep thoughts of his fading intellect plagued him.

The next morning when Hamish woke from an extraordinarily deep slumber, he was confused. His alarm had not gone off and when he looked at the clock he saw it was 9:00. This was much later than he had ever slept, for O'Halloran was devoted to his routine which meant that he had to be at the Courthouse Coffee at 7:30. He panicked as his addled mind reminded him he had to be in Federal Court in Greeneburg that morning. No time for breakfast or even coffee, he threw on some clothes and ran out to his car. He tried to start the engine. Nothing, not even the coughing sound of a bad starter. He got out, and popped the hood and remembered the chaos of the evening before. Billy was no longer in the car but the battery cables were there, unattached. He ran in the house, got a wrench and quickly had them on and tightened. As he stood up he banged his head on the hood, causing a little gash, and more than a little blood. Hamish swore a blue streak as he rubbed his sore scalp getting so much blood on his white handkerchief it looked like a cowboy's bandanna. Then he started up the Camaro and was off to Greeneburg in a flash.

He got there in record time, brazenly parked in the 7-Eleven lot and ran into Court, without a briefcase or even a file. Judge Mulvihill was sitting there, an aura of smoke emanating from her ears, incessantly tapping a pencil. Everyone stared at him, a sense of pity on their faces as he breathlessly ran into the Courtroom.

Sweating and shaking, O'Halloran thought Judge Mulvihill was about to deliver her famous sermon on professionalism, or worse, find him in contempt of court for being late and slapping a big fine on him, when she stopped short. O'Halloran looked much worse than his normal level of dishevelment. His clothes were dirty and streaked with grease, his head bleeding, the blood mixing with sweat as it poured off his brow.

"I don't even want to know, Mr. O'Halloran. Take five minutes, go to the restroom and get straightened up, wash up, and get right back in here. Fred, call a five minute recess." She directed the bailiff as she shook her head in disgust.

O'Halloran ran to the rest room, took off his shirt and started washing with a wet paper towel, the ultra-cheap kind bought by corrupt government purchasing agents in huge quantities which naturally disintegrated under the slightest pressure. He was finally able to stanch the blood on his forehead, wipe off all the sweat, and most of the grease stains on his hands and arms, get reasonably dry, but there was nothing he could do about the grease stains on his shirt. It just happened to be the only white shirt he owned, too.

He was back in Court in five minutes standing before the judicial terror, Federal Judge Bridget Mulvihill. He was still shaking, this time from abject fear. Judge Mulvihill, had that kind of reputation, you know.

"Now, Mr. O'Halloran, just what are you doing disrupting my Court today?"

He was stunned. He looked over toward the arrogant federal prosecutor, Beau James, who had suffered a series of embarrassments at the hand of O'Halloran in the not too distant past, and was not about to throw him a line to help him out of this one. James just glared at O'Halloran. Hamish flapped around a bit like a recently beached fish, but had no idea what he was doing there, either. "I don't have a case here, Judge?"

"No, Mr. O'Halloran, you don't. I suggest you call your secretary to find out where you are supposed to be. Oh, that's right you don't have a secretary, do you? You might want to get checked for senile dementia, or maybe even Alzheimer's.

Now get out of here so we can take the plea of that Defendant sitting behind you whose lawyer just got an urgent phone call from home. Oh, here he is now. Oh, and Mr. O'Halloran, I will need a written statement of explanation and an apology if you don't want a big fine for contempt by interrupting this proceeding. That's all."

O'Halloran couldn't get out of there fast enough, but did notice a big smirk on James' face.

Chapter 31

"So, what is this? I'm your new best friend, O? Don't you have anybody else to harass?"

O'Halloran feigned having his feelings hurt. Then he told the detective what Darla told him, at least what he thought was public knowledge, such as the relationship with Fred and their last name. He was careful not to tell Crouse about her job at Mother Nature's, especially the lap dances. He lost his train of thought just thinking about that.

"O, you here? Earth to O'Halloran."

"Oh, sorry. My mind was somewhere else."

"I can just imagine."

O'Halloran proceeded to relate what Darla said about the feud between Butch and her brother. That piqued Crouse's interest.

"I would love to see a battle between those two bruisers. It would be like an earthquake. Both of them act real tough, but I wonder... I know Butch is mostly mouth, but Fred, Fred seems a lot more intelligent, even though he looks like he could squeeze the air out of an elephant with a bear hug. Thanks, O. This is some info I'm going to look into. You know, follow up on, especially now that we know who Fred Darling is. I am also going to check the civil records on Mother Nature. I got a feeling about her."

"Have you ever actually talked to her, Detective?"

"No, she's never available. We even put an undercover in there but the place seems pretty well run and we didn't catch anything illegal going on. A lot of the girls looked underage, but the few we looked into checked out. Just barely. What about your boy? Seen him lately?"

After his initial exasperation at Antoine being once again referred to as *his boy* had passed, and he had collected himself, O'Halloran wondered about the whereabouts of his boy, as well.

But while O'Halloran was wondering about Antoine, Crouse was thinking of something else. "You know what doesn't make sense? Genetics, that's what. Darla can't be, what, four feet six? And Fred is maybe six-two, two-sixty? He looks like a barrel on stilts, and she looks like a miniature Barbie doll. If Mother is her mother, I wonder what Father Nature looks like, or maybe Father Darling."

Crouse chuckled a little, but that got O'Halloran to thinking, too. "Maybe you should detect a little about Father Darling, Detective."

Even though O'Halloran was a far cry from a clever detective, when Crouse left they were both thinking about the same thing. O'Halloran had already given Mother Nature's his best shot, feeble as it was, and came up empty, but maybe the next time he saw Darla he could find out about her father. He had an ominous feeling about that. He wondered whether Darla got the genes for her miniscule height from her father, or maybe some visitor in the night. Or maybe some random mutant gene. Then he wondered if delving into Darla's family history was just his own morbid curiosity or whether it actually might have something to do with her case.

O'Halloran had time to kill before his court case was going to be heard. At breakfast Brown had already told him not to come before the morning recess, so he wandered into the deepest recesses of the Clerk's office, into a room rarely ventured into by the uninitiated, that tiny cadre of lawyers, clerks and paralegals, who actually searched titles back as far as the BCE (Before Computers Era.) The room was redolent of must and disuse, a thin sheen of dust covering everything like new fallen snow. He stood before an intimidating array of very large old cloth bound books with red leather corners. These contained various indexes for all sorts of information before they were subject to computerization after 1983. They were just hanging around, gathering dust, these old carefully maintained records. It wouldn't be long before some energetic, enterprising young intern in the clerk's office got around to relegating them to the basement of some old, never used, storage building to where they consigned old archives, gathering dust and cobwebs in perpetuity, lingering undisturbed until some archival archeologist disinterred the disintegrating remnants.

He pulled out the tome he thought contained what he was looking for, and with great physical effort, plopped it on the high, slanted counter used for such investigations. It was awkward and must have weighed twenty pounds. As he hefted the huge tome up to a high, slanted table, like the old British "clarks" used, a shot of pain surged through his lower back and he was sure he slipped a disk.

Beginning with the vital statistics, he paged through the volume. He had two last names to look up, Joralemon and Darling. Under Joralemon, he found no record of Alberta's birth, but did see a marriage license that was issued on October 4, forty years ago. Alberta Joralemon and Marquis Darling were married three days later. There were no birth certificates under either Joralemon or Darling, which meant that Fred and Darla were born somewhere else, maybe in some other county, probably Greeneburg, but perhaps not even in North Carolina. Maybe Alberta and Marquis weren't even their parents. They could be adopted. That would make more sense than the same parents producing such vastly different offspring. He would have to check with the state

Bureau of Vital Statistics to confirm their parentage if they had been born in North Carolina.

Finding no death certificate for Alberta, he looked up the name Darling. Nothing, except the same marriage license. Oh, well, that was at least something. He looked up the tax records and wasn't surprised to find no real property under Joralemon but there was nothing under Darling either. Hmm. Then he remembered Butch's last name was Fleming so he checked under that name and found a house listed under Darla Fleming and Arnold Fleming. Arnold? That explains why he went by Butch. Despite Schwarzenegger's model, Arnold was just not a very macho name these days. The address of the house was the one Darla had given him so that didn't tell him anything. He was going to have to call Farrell and ask him to do a little deeper detecting. He shuddered. Hamish knew Farrell wouldn't take kindly to such a suggestion from him.

Looking up criminal records on both suspected parents, O'Halloran was surprised to find a number of entries. For Marquis there was a sheet as long as your proverbial arm, from possessing non-taxpaid liquor, the euphemism for moonshining, to fraud, but nothing violent. It appeared from his record that Marquis Darling was just a sleazy guy, who scammed his way through life. He wondered what kind of scam he used on Mother Nature to get her agree to marrying him and consent to having his child. If she did. A whole panoply of thoughts he wished he didn't have flooded his mind.

He went to pull one of the case files for one of the misdemeanor charges against Marquis Darling, but found they had all been tossed, nothing remaining but a microfilm. He sighed and went through the necessary antiquated procedure to bring these old documents on the screen. It took him twenty minutes, but he finally found out what was in the shuck, the manila envelope that contained the various forms required in each misdemeanor case. There was a warrant which had no personal information other than the name address and charge. But there was a also a bond sheet which showed such things as height and weight, tattoos and scars, identifying characteristics, stuff like that. O'Halloran was intrigued by the Cupid tattoo on the right arm of Marquis Darling, but thought it must be a clerical error when the bond sheet listed his height at only 4'. But when he saw that Marquis weighed only 87 pounds, he was beginning to understand, although it might still have been 6' and 187. A typographical error? He wasn't sure about that, but it was food for thought and he sure was thinking hard now.

What if Darla's father really was a midget only four foot tall? That would explain Darla's diminutive stature, of course, but Fred was anything but diminutive. Maybe Fred's father wasn't Marquis after all, but some Jody who just happened by when Alberta was horny. O'Halloran determined to locate Marquis, who must be closing in on 65 now, according to the paperwork. He wandered up to District Court to try to sort out this conundrum in his mind as he waited for his case to be called.

O'Halloran was sitting in a cushy comfortable seat in the District Court jury box, a thigh high wall separating the jurors from the courtroom action. He was thinking, but as usual his mind was wandering all over the place, so typical of one plagued by Attention Deficit Disorder. Of course, there was no such diagnosis when he was in school. As a school boy in the third grade, he was so rambunctious, so out of control, the teacher had tied him to his seat to try to get him to sit still. Eventually, he just learned to deal with his impulsive behavior without Ritalin which hadn't been invented yet, and most of the time he was able to control his mind when it went on a rampage.

He looked at an empty chair in front of him. What a waste of money! District Criminal Court never had juries, juries were strictly for the Superior Court, but then he figured maybe some old District Court lawyer with a little clout had persuaded the county attorney to put in these comfortable chairs just as a benefit for the lawyers, plush seating disguised as a jury box when they built the new courthouse thirty years ago. That was nice. Now he was thinking how warm the courtroom was. The warmth was comforting. He began to be overwhelmed by a need for sleep, and had just started nodding off when he heard his name called out loud. "Mr. O'Halloran, you with us here? You represent this defendant, Barney McGlurkin?"

It was Judge Howell and he did not look particularly pleased. "Huh? Oh yeah. I mean, yes, your Honor." He was awake now, rubbing the sleep out of his eyes. He stood up too quickly, suffered a wave of vertigo, and felt for a minute like he would fall flat on his face, but he shook it off before the catastrophe. It was close, though, and everybody had noticed what must have looked to them like an inebriated stagger.

He walked up to the Defense table, still a little unsteady on his feet from the sleep residual, and a number of spectators whispered to each other that the lawyer was surely drunk. There was a guy standing at the defense table who O'Halloran had never seen before, or at least didn't remember ever talking to him. The Defendant was waiting expectantly, a curious expression on his face, maybe showing a little contempt. Maybe a lot. The man was in his forties, clean shaven and neatly dressed but not overly so. He looked like he worked in an office, mid-level manager maybe. O'Halloran whispered, "Are you the Defendant? Did you do it?"

The guy just sighed, looked up at the ceiling with a disgusted look on his face. He was toast. This was the last time he would opt for a cheap, court appointed attorney. Brown arraigned the Defendant, "Mr. McGlurkin, you are charged with indecent exposure," throwing O'Halloran a bit of a line. "How do you plead, guilty or not guilty?" with just the slightest emphasis on the 'not.'

O'Halloran quickly stepped up. "Not Guilty, your Honor." The Judge and everybody else looked surprised. O'Halloran opting for a trial on a misdemeanor in District Court? O'Halloran was surprised too, but since he didn't know a thing about the case, he thought he might as well throw the dice and try to learn something. Plus, McGlurkin looked like the type who might send a complaint to the State Bar and O'Halloran didn't need that hassle right now.

Brown called his first witness, a ten-year-old girl with pig tails. She testified she saw the guy sitting on a park bench with a bag of something on his lap, she went close by and saw he had a peeled banana in the bag. She tentatively ID'd McGlurkin as that man. That was it. "Huh?" Brown, asked her again, "Are you sure it was just a banana? Was it yellow?"

The girl nodded shyly. Brown looked helplessly at the Judge, and shrugged. The Judge looked at O'Halloran, who looked at McGlurkin, who looked at the girl, who looked at the Judge, who just shook his head, then the girl looked at her mother, shyly. Her mother turned beet red. She was about to say something, perhaps to explain or even protest, but the judge shook his head, held up his hand, and said loudly, "Next case, Mr. Brown." The confused girl's mother was seething with righteous indignation as they stormed out of the courtroom, still convinced the banana eater was a pervert.

As the numerous pathetic cases on the District Court docket droned on, O'Halloran decided to go to the coffee room for a cup. His heavy lidded eyes signaling a desperate need for a jolt of caffeine. The room was empty, which was a relief for O'Halloran, who often eschewed conversation, especially when the sands of sleep still lingered in the corners of his eyes. He put a couple of quarters in the box, poured the last drop of a black, thick substance which passed for coffee, and might have been simmering there for a couple of days, for all he knew. He noticed with some distaste a bunch of grounds floating ominously on top of the oily surface. Shuddering, he knew that it would taste like burned mud, but he needed the zap from the caffeine. He plopped down in the faux leather sofa which had most of the stuffing squeezed out of it a long time ago. Taking a sip, he shivered at the awful taste, and then, spurred no doubt by the caffeine, had an epiphany.

He jumped up and ran down to the Clerk's office, thought a minute, and called the Greeneburg Clerk of Court's office from the phone on a Pine Ridge Deputy Clerk's desk. He talked to a very helpful clerk with a lisp, and asked her to look up Doe, Jane, and gave her a range of dates. After a little while she returned to the phone. There was only one entry that caught her eye. "Doe, Jane, aka Mother Nature." That was all the anonymous defendant would say to the cop who arrested her for procuring prostitution at a place called Pretty Polly's. O'Halloran got all the information from the arrest sheet.

But all that told him was that his suspicion was confirmed.

O'Halloran decided to skip the Legal Lunch since he had a large can of the Chef's tasty ravioli, loaded with MSG, waiting for him in his cupboard, plus he needed to think undisturbed by the cacophony of the local restaurant, and a cup of fine orange pekoe would be just the thing to get his thoughts in gear. Plus, he still had the taste of the awful, stale coffee in his mouth, as well as a few errant coffee grounds stuck in his teeth. A cup of excellent tea might be what he needed to erase the taste and rinse the remnants. He had not seen Antoine for a while, and while it was curiosity that got him to thinking about 'his boy,' he wondered if the seemingly simple soul could possibly have anything to do with the shootings. There was that tenuous connection to Mother Nature's, and the unexplained fact that he was found in the alley, rifling the already empty pockets of the pitiful Mr. Lethbridge, when he was discovered by Way North. Thinking about it, O'Halloran realized that Antoine had cleverly ducked the chance to explain when the question was put to him. Did he do that on purpose?

O'Halloran lifted a big soup spoon full of the yummy ersatz ravioli to his lips and was just about to enjoy it when he heard a single thump outside. "Damn, what was that?"

With catlike curiosity on hold while he sucked the stuff off his spoon, O'Halloran swallowed and got up, overwhelmed with a need to find out what was going on. It was unusual for such a sound to emanate from his yard. As he opened the screen door to his back porch he was relieved to notice the dogs seemed unperturbed, going about their canine concerns, Caesar asleep, the others doing their business. Literally.

The back yard was ominously silent. There was no evidence of the source of the noise in the yard, so he decided to check the shed. He swung the door open and there was Antoine resting on the big dog bed, his hands behind his head, but he jumped up when the afternoon light shined in on him. "Damn, what you doing man?" he said, squinting.

"Antoine, where have you been? What are you doing here? I thought you left?"

Antoine was quiet for a minute, not responding, an expression close to a grimace on his face. Then he got up, silently, with more than a bit of menace in his eyes. Which was increased exponentially when O'Halloran saw the gun in his hand. He started to stutter out some sort of objection, but Antoine just pointed the pistol at O'Halloran. "You know Hamish, you are starting to be a real pain in the ass. You couldn't let it go, you just had to stick your nose in my business, in the business of the club, in big Fred's business. You nosy twerp. I hadn't planned on doing this in this manner, but...."

He cocked the hammer on the pistol, a revolver, but since O didn't know squat about guns, he wondered what caliber it was, even under this dangerous circumstance. Attention Deficit Disorder is like that. But he did have a normal enough reaction to back away from the shed, as he said, "Your accent, Antoine, what happened to your accent? You don't sound like some clueless, homeless person."

"Ha! You completely fell for it, you simple dweeb. I have a degree from State in Criminal Justice, and I am definitely not homeless. Fred and I live in a rather large estate in a gated community over near Greeneburg." He took a step toward him and O'Halloran reacted by taking two steps backward, stepped on an untied shoelace and fell flat on his rump. Antoine followed up by sticking the gun in O'Halloran's right nostril, pushing the helpless lawyer prostrate on his back in the mud.

"Wait." O'Halloran was almost shrieking, fear causing a panicked tremolo in his falsetto voice. "Wait, you and Fred? I don't understand."

"We are married, you old coot. Fred and I got married in Maryland a couple of years ago, after his mother died."

"Wait, wait. Are you telling me Mother Nature is actually dead?"

"Sure. I think Fred, or probably Darla, might have poisoned her. Anyway, I took the body to my cousin Marvin's in Paducah. He has a funeral home there. What the Hell, I'll tell you and then I'll shoot you right up this wide nostril of yours. It will blow your homely head to smithereens. Marvin invented an embalming fluid that makes the corpse rock hard. That very life-like rigid corpse has been sitting up there in the window watching over her girls for four years now, while we rake in the profits. Don't even need to feed her, but I take her a plate every now and then. It verifies the spoof to the staff."

At the instant O'Halloran fell back on his rear, the dogs became suddenly vigilant, the two mutts acting like pointers, frozen in place, every sense focused on O'Halloran. Caesar, sensing that his beloved benefactor was in dire danger, stood up, in four point alert. Then he lunged forward, the thick chain that restrained him, which was thick enough to tow a semi, snapping like a pretzel. With just a couple of frenzied bounds, the dog raised up in full flight, his huge front paws landing squarely on Antoine's back, sending him flying. The impact caused Antoine to pull the gun back and over his head. Reflexively, he pulled the trigger. It went off, with a tremendous boom. The bullet whizzed skyward and hit a big old branch high up on an old oak overhead , square in the middle, causing the sodden and semi rotten log to crack in half with the result that the huge branch dropped right on top of the head of the hapless O'Halloran, knocking him out cold.

The crack of the pistol was a disturbing sound on the normally quiet residential street. Old Misserus Eula Clampitt, a reformed moonshiner, now a devout Baptist, who was herself known to fire her ancient .38 revolver at intruders when she had run a still in the mountains long ago, knew it was a large caliber pistol and called 911. As luck would have it, North was working foot patrol in the vicinity at the time, having traded with another officer so he could go out on a date with a local cutie that night, his first in four months. He was in the back yard within three minutes.

The hapless patrolman was stunned at what he saw, and in true North fashion, didn't know what to do. O'Halloran was sprawled on his back in the mud like a dead man, blood seeping from a wound on the top of his head, right in the middle of the highest part of his high forehead. Naturally, North thought he really was dead. A .44 Magnum snub nosed was sticking out of the mud a foot or two from Antoine's hand. The would-be murderer was lying virtually face down in the reddish slime, whimpering like a hurt child. Caesar was in complete control, his huge jaws encircling the exposed neck, a low, terrifying growl steadily emanating from the giant canine.

North knew he had to do something, especially if he ever wanted to make detective, but there was no way he was going to mess with that vicious wolf. So he called for the EMTs and tended to O'Halloran, who was breathing now, a shallow pathetic rale. Slowly, O'Halloran started to come around. He sat up, rubbing the bloody knot on his head, smearing blood and mud all over himself. As his mind began to focus, he assessed the situation. "Grab that gun, Officer," he said, pointing to the .44's barrel sticking up out of the mud. When North had retrieved the pistol, holding the barrel with his thumb and forefinger as if it was a stick of dynamite, O'Halloran called off the dog.

After releasing his vice-like grip on the neck of the fear-paralyzed Antoine, Caesar trotted over to O'Halloran, licking his blood streaked face, while the always uncertain North pointed the gun at Antoine. "What am I doing this for, Mr. O'Halloran?"

"Tell him what you told me, Antoine."

"Hah, fat chance I am going to say anything without my lawyer present. Officer, read me my rights."

North did, but when he came to what Antoine was charged with, he hesitated.

Just then, the ambulance pulled up to the front of the house, sirens a blaring, catching the attention of everyone in the neighborhood who happened to be home. Mrs. Clampitt was watching the whole shebang through a gap she had pulled in the venetian blinds on her kitchen door. This was better than any soap opera she ever saw. North started to go toward the house to let the emergency responders in, but O'Halloran shouted, "Wait, Officer, give me that gun while you get the EMTs."

North realized only then that Antoine would have taken off if given half a chance, so he gave the pistol to O'Halloran with much hesitation, since he thought O'Halloran might actually shoot the now cocky Antoine, and then ran off to direct the EMTs. Meanwhile Antoine was about to do just that, having started to quickly plan his escape, when O'Halloran said, "Sic 'em, Caesar." No kidding he said just that.

Caesar responded with relish and in a flash the mud streaked face of Antoine was looking up into the gaping jaws of the huge dog, the familiar awful growl starting up again; the vicious canines of the vicious canine just about to close in on Antoine's jugular. He could feel it. His life started to flash before his eyes, and he started whimpering again, a pathetic, fear filled sound. Caesar knew the fear and smiled. Dogs do smile, you know.

North, and the burly, short-armed EMT, accompanied by good ol' Marsha, trotted into the yard, but stopped short, twenty feet from the sobbing man.

"Tell 'em, Antoine, or there will be nothing anybody can do when I let that dog loose. He is very well trained and will tear your neck off, if I let him."

If Antoine had been thinking, he would have realized that Hamish didn't have the heart to do that, but right now, he just wasn't thinking clearly, and wasn't sure, and certainly didn't want to take the chance. Especially, with the huge wolfish dog's hot putrid breath engulfing his head, and razor sharp teeth pressing into his soft flesh, perilously close to sinking deep into his tender, quaking neck, and maybe puncturing a jugular.

Antoine spilled his guts, in between the slobbering, snot, and tears.

Then the light came on and North finally figured out what to do and cuffed him. Watching the two of them walk off, Antoine, with his face smeared with drying mud, looking like a vaudeville comedian in whiteface, O'Halloran wondered what would have possessed a man like that, intelligent and articulate, when he wasn't putting on the homeless act, to shoot three people in cold blood. Although the actual murders themselves were solved, there were a lot of questions still to be answered.

Chapter 32

As soon as North typed up his report, misspellings and all, Antoine was booked and immediately lawyered up. What, did you expect a full confession when the huge wolf was not growling and scratching his mud-streaked skin with his razor sharp teeth? North called Crouse and let him know what had transpired and Crouse just said, "Damn." There were a dozen reasons for that reaction.

The next morning at precisely 7:30, Crouse walked into the Courthouse Coffee, with a vengeance. Waving his arms in a futile attempt to dissipate the cloud of lingering blue smoke, he found O'Halloran ensconced in his favorite booth, a stained mug full of just poured steaming coffee in front of him. "You're early today, eh O? Did ya hear about your boy?"

O'Halloran just looked at him with that questioning look on his face. O'Halloran wasn't very good at dissembling. "I was there, Detective. Didn't Way North put that in his report?"

"Oh, yeah. So let me hear your version of what happened. I'm not sure North got it right."

O'Halloran took a sip of his coffee, and immediately spit it out. "Damn that's hot." He fished an ice cube out of his water glass and sucked on it for a few seconds, plopping the remainder into the coffee cup. "Well, you know he was going to kill me. Pointed the gun right between my eyes." He just couldn't bring himself to admit that Antoine had stuck the barrel well up his nostril, and omitted the part about peeing his pants. A man has to have some dignity, you know. "Then I don't remember anything. I guess I got knocked out. When I came to, my head hurt and was bloody, see?" He pointed to the knot on his head and the large scab which had formed over the wound. There was a skinny bandage almost covering it. "North was there, and Caesar had Antoine face down in the mud, his jaws wide open around his neck. He was snarling and growling like I never heard him before."

"Yeah, I got that. And then your boy confessed did he?"

"Right. Antoine told us everything. I couldn't believe that guy could murder those three people in cold blood. I thought I knew him."

"It was a voluntary statement, right? There wasn't any duress. No little bit of coercion, like holding a gun on him or having your wolf at his throat?"

O'Halloran was silent, staring into his coffee cup, waiting for the magic ball to pop up with the answer. Since there was no magic ball, just a wisp of steam, he understood that the confession could not be used against Antoine in Court. At least they knew what happened and now just had to figure out why. "The confession is out, is that what you are saying, Detective?"

"You're the lawyer, genius. What do you think?" Disgust was just dripping from the detective.

O'Halloran let out a sigh. "What was I to do, Detective? Just let him grab the gun and then I would be just another stiff whose death you would have to investigate?"

"No, from what I got from Way North, you did what you had to do. You might have saved us all a lot of Court room hassle if you had just drilled him, claiming self-defense, or let the wolf finish him off. But then we wouldn't know about big Fred and Mother Nature."

Doris, the all-seeing server, having just plopped an unbidden cup in front of the detective, was off in a flash, not really wanting to have any knowledge of this ultra-serious conversation. Crouse got up and took a sip of the hot coffee in front of him, but not before taking a hint from O'Halloran and dropping an ice cube in it. "We got the shooter, O, and maybe we can hold him for a bit while Brown tries to figure out what he can realistically charge him with, and actually prove. Maybe I can get a warrant, search his house and the bar, but in the meantime, the reason for these deaths is still on the loose. I would watch my back if I were you, O."

Crouse abruptly left, the bill for his coffee unpaid. O'Halloran had a raft of conflicting thoughts coursing through his brain. Even though he was no longer Antoine's attorney, technically, he felt a lingering professional obligation, despite the fact that he would in all likelihood have been another of Antoine's victims were it not for his loyal shepherd. He realized there was so much about Antoine he neither knew nor understood, including the reason for his duplicity with O'Halloran. The attorney was not known for his perspicacity and even he knew he could be naïve sometimes, but he really seemed to have underestimated his client. That is, if Antoine was telling the truth when he confessed to the murders. Despite the inadmissibility of confessions made under duress, and now that he thought about it, O'Halloran realized that Antoine's statement was made under the absolute textbook definition of duress, O'Halloran still believed "his boy" was telling the truth. Was this just a residual effect of his previous relationship, or was his feeling based on an objective assessment of all that he knew about the case? But if Antoine actually killed the three victims, why, and how could it be proved without the confession?

Back in his cubbyhole of an office, Crouse was on the phone with his cousin, "Motive, Farrell, we need to establish a motive. It has to come from some of Antoine's relationships, his sense of loyalty to people close to him. Otherwise, how do you explain these shootings?"

"Let me think about it. I will draw up a schematic. If we fill in the blanks with probables, we may find something. I'll get back to you later."

Chapter 33

"Mr. O'Halloran, it's Darla. I really need to see you. Can I come over now?"

"Huh?" O'Halloran was in a sleep induced fog and had not fully wakened. The clatter of the telephone had brought him somewhere near consciousness, but not enough to have any recollection of what was going on. Darla repeated her urgent request as Hamish slowly came around.

"Oh, it's you, Darla. Can't it wait until tomorrow? I'm in bed now. What time is it anyway?"

"It's only a little before ten. Do lawyers always go to bed that early?"

Ham had been reading the bible and suddenly was overcome with fatigue, as the difficulty he had in trying to understand the message of the three thousand year old parable from the Old Testament overwhelmed him. The bedside lamp was still on and the good book was resting open on his chest when the telephone on his nightstand woke him.

He wanted to go back to sleep but was intrigued in a prurient way by the insistence of the little beauty. "No, I was just exceptionally tired tonight, Darla. I usually go to bed after the weather report on the eleven o'clock news."

"Can you see me now?"

He gave in. There was some strange emotion behind his agreeing to see her at this late hour. Some of it was the rather unnatural attraction everyone seemed to have toward Darla, but there was something else. Could it have been something to do with that dormant primitive urge called a libido? Anyway, he caved when she assured him it would only take about fifteen minutes and was urgent, really important, imperative.

Darla must have called from Pine Ridge for she was at his house in five minutes, looking exotic, fetching even. She had on a shimmering blue dress, cut so that her tantalizing cleavage was emphasized, and royal blue satin high heels, like she was getting ready to go out to a ritzy restaurant on a dinner date for the evening. Her coif was perfect, made up just right, with enough but not too much rouge and lipstick. She looked so good he almost gasped.

Ham still had on his pajamas with the Mickey Mouse cartoons all over it and fuzzy slippers, and had just thought to put on his old plaid bathrobe in case anything was visible which shouldn't have been. He led her into the kitchen and started to brew a cup of tea. Sitting on one of the kitchen chairs with her feet resting on the top rung since they wouldn't come near to reaching the floor, she placed her oversized blue leather handbag on the table with a clunk. He turned and sat down while the water heated up, and said, "Now what is it, Darla, that was so important that my sacred nightly routine had to be invaded?"

"Well, I just wanted to tell you that I no longer need your services in the case against Butch. We are getting back together."

O'Halloran was stunned and a little angry, all that drama and anguish for nothing, plus he would be compelled to return part of the retainer. "Couldn't you have just called and told me that on the telephone?"

"Oh, no. That would have been rude." She was quiet as if she was weighing something heavily in her mind. Then she zipped open her purse and with some effort retrieved the menacing S & W .44 Magnum snub nosed. She handled it with some difficulty, as if she was uncertain with firearms, especially the forty one and a half ounce pistol.

"What's that?" O'Halloran was now in stall mode. He could clearly see what it was.

"Oh, this is Butch's. I went down to the magistrate's office yesterday and withdrew the Domestic Violence complaint. They gave the gun back to Butch a little while later. Apparently there was some confusion. The property clerk thought it might be the same one that Antoine had used to try to shoot you. Anyway, the cop at property kept looking at me instead of the paperwork and gave it back to Butch, and he stupidly signed for it. While Butch was gone, I had time to do a lot of thinking. You know, Mr. O'Halloran, I think you are a very smart man despite that sloppy exterior. I think you figured it out. Or if you haven't, you soon will." She pointed the pistol at him inexpertly, the gun shaking and waving around unsteadily as she tried to picture in her mind how to do the deed. "My problem is trying to figure out what to do with your body, but then I thought, maybe I won't do anything. Since this is Butch's gun and the one Antoine used to shoot those creeps, maybe I'll just leave it here along with your corpse. After I wipe off the fingerprints, of course. The paperwork will point to Butch." She giggled. Even her giggle had an evil sound to it. She reminded O'Halloran of a miniature witch.

It would be unnatural if O'Halloran had not been frightened out of his wits, so he was duly scared, a little tinkling going on, but he was also intrigued, as if he couldn't believe that little Darla was actually threatening to shoot him with that lethal .44 at point blank range.

"You are the one behind these killings? Why?"

"Well, sure. First, that creep Craddock, he hurt me, pinched me on the tit. I wasn't going to let him get away with

226

that kind of disrespect. And the second one, what's his name, Lethbridge? He told me about all the money he had squirreled away so his wife couldn't get her hands on it. He hated his wife and was planning to kill her when he found out about the pool guy. We planned it, Armand and me, especially when I found out that Mrs. Lethbridge's pool guy was my Armand, a regular at Mother Nature's. He's kind of cute, don't you think? We were going to split whatever he could cadge from the widow. And Sydney, poor Sydney, I loved Sydney, but she was so overbearing and possessive, and when she found out I was the one who killed Mother, she couldn't believe it. She threatened to tell, using the threat to keep me in line. She didn't think I would do anything about it. But she really underestimated me. I just hate it when I don't get the respect I deserve."

"You killed Mother Nature?"

"Don't call her that, Mr. O'Halloran. She was my mother. Sure, she was weird. Imagine a good looking woman, a little over six feet tall, marrying a midget. She even made me and Butch sleep together until he was twelve, and didn't think anything of it. We were a pretty precocious couple, well I was anyway, but when Mother found out what we were doing, she separated us for good. She walked in on us one night and caught us in the act. I always liked it. I think I must like sex too much, but Fred got screwed up, you know, sexually, and mentally, I guess. Maybe he was too young. I was a year and a half older than Fred, and already pretty experienced. I got these curves early but never grew any taller after I was ten when Daddy first porked me. When Mother found out that Daddy was regularly visiting me in my bedroom, she poisoned him. The coroner was a drunk and thought it was a heart attack. Little people like Daddy don't have very long life expectancies anyway, so he just wrote Daddy off. I worked at the club for a while until I met Butch. He can be a real jerk but he is great in the sack. You should see his schlong."

When Darla realized she was just happily babbling on and on, confessing way too much, she raised the gun unsteadily, apparently having difficulty holding it in her tiny hands. She seemed unsure of where she was aiming it because of the short barrel of the snubbie.

O'Halloran realized he had to stall for time, until he had a chance to grab the gun from her. "Have you ever shot that pistol, Darla?"

"No, but I think it's real easy. You just pull the trigger like this."

She tried to pull the trigger but didn't have the strength in just one hand, so she grabbed the gun with both hands and pulled as hard as she could. "Oh, the safety's on."

O'Halloran was frozen in place as she talked and wrestled with the menacing pistol, which was way too big for her tiny hands. He was shaking and felt the warm trickle down his leg again. Darla flipped the safety off, an almost diabolical expression on her face. O'Halloran suddenly had an inspiration.

"Look Darla, if you are going to shoot me, make sure you pull that trigger hard."

It was a desperate psychological ploy. He was banking on getting her to focus on 'pulling' the trigger with her right hand. Even at that close range, with that little barrel, he was hoping that she would have to tug the whole gun to her right as she pulled the trigger, causing the bullet to miss him, wide right, giving O'Halloran a chance to wrestle the gun from her. He was confident he could do that since she didn't look very strong.

Darla climbed down from the chair and stood, the gun waving wildly in her hands, making crazy circles. She pointed it in O'Halloran's general direction, holding the pistol with both hands, the unsteady aim because of the short barrel making it feel even more lethal to the sweating intended victim. She managed to squeeze the trigger, but concentrating on that action instead of aiming at Hamish, the barrel of the heavy gun dropped just as the gun erupted. The bullet went through his loose pajama pants just below his crotch, grazing his thigh. The powerful recoil caused the gun to fly out of Darla's hands, sailing over her head, and landing on the floor with a clatter. In a panicked reaction, they both frantically dove for the pistol, Hamish falling forward, precariously grabbing the .44 by the most tenuous hold on the short barrel just as Darla reached down to try to secure it.

Providently, even predictably, it was Officer Way North who happened to be on foot patrol near the house when the gun shot shattered the quiet of the peaceful neighborhood. Without giving a thought to any possible danger the sound might presage, he ran to O'Halloran's house and was on the scene in a minute. He burst in, and ran into the kitchen where he found Hamish and Darla frantically wrestling on the ground trying to gain control of the gun. It was quite a sight and North was momentarily stunned. The tiny beauty in her shimmering blue dress, one ample breast exposed, was sitting awkwardly on top of the hapless lawyer, as they wildly grappled for the pistol, while O'Halloran, lying on his back, one hand extended over his head, a tenuous hold on the short barrel of the gun in his extended right hand, his left desperately flailing in an attempt to keep Darla from getting a hold of it. His pajama bottoms had slid down, leaving him indelicately exposed. North grabbed the gun, jerking it away from both of them, ending the scrum.

As they stood, North got a good look at the extent of the wardrobe dishevelment. O'Halloran's pajama bottoms, his manhood exposed, were hanging haphazardly on an angle from his mid-thigh, slightly wet and with a streak of blood near a hole seared in them. Darla's fine blue dress was, well, revealing. She was breathing hard, her hair all mussed, and one of her elegant breasts showing in what has become commonly referred to as a wardrobe malfunction.

"He tried to kill me," said Darla, just a bit out of breath, with a touch of feigned sincerity, just a little too loud.

"No. It was Darla who tried to kill me," O'Halloran yelled.

"No way," Darla quickly responded, regaining her composure and correcting the malfunction while North gaped.

"Way."

"What?"

"Huh?"

They argued back and forth as to who tried to kill who.

The confused North called for backup. When backup quickly arrived, several neighbors having already dialed 911, it was the rookie reserve officer named Hank Platt. North took both of the disputants into custody, charging each of them with disorderly conduct, causing a public disturbance, assault, affray, firing a gun in an occupied dwelling, anything he could think of to place them in custody and restore the peace. Some of these charges obviously wouldn't fly since they were not in a public place, but right inside Hamish's home. North decided he would figure out what actually happened later, but had to do something to get the situation under control. He bagged the gun as evidence and intended to have forensics check for fingerprints, even though he knew they would at least get O'Halloran's prints off the barrel if they weren't too smudged.

He also wrote out a warrant charging O'Halloran with attempted sexual assault on a minor, figuring that any person as tiny as Darla had to be underage. He tenderly placed the would-be murderess in the back of his patrol car, apologizing for having to handcuff her, claiming it was Department policy, which it was, and subtly trying to sneak a peek. In the other cruiser, Hank Platt had to kneel down to attend to O'Halloran's bleeding thigh while he was handcuffed, sitting in the back seat. This caused the young cop no end of embarrassment.

Ultimately, Crouse figured it all out that night. The charges against O'Halloran were dismissed and he was freed that same evening. Darla, on the other hand, was not so lucky. Despite a cascade of pleas of innocence, blaming it all on the hapless O'Halloran, who she claimed with a straight face, was trying to rape her, when Patrolman North saved her from such an ignominious fate, she did not convince the officers. She even provided tears on call just to add a little color to her story. But the fact that it was Butch's gun, it occurred at O'Halloran's house, and he was in his pajamas didn't help her case at all. But then she did have that allure, so prurient suspicions in the department lingered.

Crouse would have none of it. He tossed her in the box and let her sweat for about five minutes while he fetched a cup of 211 degree machine coffee. It was still bubbling when he carefully placed it on the table, insulating his hand from being scalded by an ugly, used handkerchief. The diminutive suspect stared at the handkerchief with pure disgust. "Okay, Darla, if you still want to stick to that story, I'll let you write it down. But first, your rights. You know the drill, I'm sure." He read her Miranda rights straight from a plastic laminated card he pulled from his wallet, and then tossed a lined yellow pad and pen on the table. "Write," said he, all toothy grin.

She just stared at him. "Lawyer," was all she said.

"I thought so," the Detective said with a malevolent grin as he got up and left, shutting the door with an ominous click. After about five minutes, Darla began to panic, realizing she hadn't told Crouse just who to call, and he'd left her locked in this little room.

Darla started to panic, thinking she was trapped in the little room. She got up and tried to open the door none too gently. She sure was, and the metal door with the little window with wires running through the glass forming a diamond pattern, was too high for her too see out. She pulled the chair over and climbed up on it. Even standing on tip toes, she was barely tall enough to look through the little window, and started screaming, and pounding on the door with her tiny fists.

A deputy walked by, ignoring her. Crouse walked by and paid no heed to the muted racket coming from the room. She was nearing apoplexy when he returned, his coffee having cooled somewhat and being only half full now, still sheathed in the unsanitary handkerchief. He pretended not to notice the tears, the magenta red face, the running mascara, and the disheveled hair. "Okay, Darla. We don't really like people who conspire to murder our nice citizens here in quiet little Pine Ridge. That's why I'm charging you with several counts of conspiracy to commit first degree murder, one of attempted first degree murder, intimidation of a witness, assault with a deadly weapon with intent to kill, and maybe by the time we get to the magistrate's office, I'll think of twenty more charges to add to the book I'm throwing at you. Oh yeah, and discharging a firearm in an occupied dwelling, another felony worth a good ten years. It doesn't matter whether or not you were the actual shooter in the murders. The conspiracy charge puts you all in it together. Hanging together means you will all hang together." He snickered at this clever little remark.

She was quiet, wiping her tears and running her fingers through her hair. "Could you call Mr. Shapiro, please?" Nice and sweet now, puffing her chest in case it had any influence left.

"No, I don't think he can represent you, Darla. He's already signed up to represent your co-conspirator, James Matheson, aka Antoine al Aqwon, you know, the trigger man. I'll bet he will sing like a canary in order to avoid the needle. I am sure you are quite aware that the last man standing catches the heat. Right now, it's between you and Big Fred. Which one of you is it going to be, Darla, you or your brother? I'm dying to see where your loyalty lies."

"What?" She almost screamed it, throwing her hands up and grabbing the side of her head.

"I'll let you think about it for a few minutes," said Crouse, as he turned and walked out the door, a sly grin on his face.

Darla was faced with a Hobson's Choice of epic proportions. Actually, a Morton's Fork if you wanted to split metaphysical hairs. If she confessed, Darla would effectively be killing her beloved brother who would be the only one of the three who hadn't given up their role in the crimes. That is, if Detective Crouse was right about Antoine spilling his guts, or his statement about the death penalty. She couldn't be sure if it was just a major ploy or if he was telling the truth. She knew a little bit about human nature, but she realized it was the seamy sexual side with which she was really familiar.

This was really a terrible dilemma. If she didn't confess, she would be the one facing the ultimate punishment. And she could actually picture events unfolding so that it would really happen, and it would be her who got the needle. She shuddered, but kept swearing, a constant string of invectives, pacing in a circle, pulling her hair. She had no idea what to do, and finally sat down hard in the chair, her head in her hands. The release from all that physical movement caused her to start sobbing uncontrollably.

Her mind was spinning as Detective Crouse quietly came back into the room, observed the distraught woman, head in her hands, and leaned up against the door. When Darla showed some signs of awareness, he said, "Well? Who dies, you or Fred?"

Darla looked up at him, her face red with rage. "You know Detective Crouse, you are a real bastard. I hope you and yours rot in hell." She said that before making a complete statement, writing down everything, filled with the gory and often titillating details, reasons for the shootings, motives, everything except remorse. Darla apparently was not capable of that kind of emotion.

Crouse watched her with an almost intense curiosity as she quickly wrote out her formal confession. He had never met anyone with this kind of warped set of personal ethics or amorality, and he was intrigued by that. And even as disheveled and distraught as Darla was, she was nice to look at in a perverse sort of way. When she was finished, she tossed the yellow pad in his direction with a clear sense of irritation, even disgust.

Crouse looked over the statement in the meticulous manner of an experienced detective, and the thing that struck him the most was not the gory details, or the sexual sensationalism, but the ornate, childlike penmanship. He had never seen a written confession anything like it, with all the swirls, curlicues and decorations on the capital letters like the penmanship of a young child.

Out by the county line, Detective Francis X. Farrell walked into Mother Nature's alone. It was still early and the clientele from the netherworld of society had not yet shown up. Daylight shined in all its glory, so most of the troglodytes were still resting in their crypts waiting for the last rays of sunshine to fade and extinguish before they emerged. Fred had not been at the door, no one was, but after ordering a cup of coffee from the juvenile looking and scantily clad Tiffany, Farrell saw him emerge from the area where he imagined the kitchen to be. He motioned the big man over and asked him to sit down.

"Fred, I have some bad news for you. We picked up Antoine and charged him with the three shootings. He confessed to everything. We also sweated Darla and she gave you up rather than face the needle. I'm here to arrest you for your role in this sordid mess." He looked up into Fred's eyes. There was no sign of any emotion at first, but slowly a tear formed in the corner of each eye as the import of Farrell's statement sunk in. Big Fred merely nodded.

"I guess Antoine has already called Shapiro. I suppose that leaves me with a court appointed lawyer and an insanity plea." Big Fred looked blankly at Farrell, with the look of a man who had anticipated just such a fate and accepted it bravely. Farrell, who had gotten an understanding of the character of this suspect, was not the slightest bit surprised.

"It might just work, Fred, given your rather, uh, unusual upbringing."

"Darla gave me up, eh. You know about us, Detective Farrell, me and Darla?"

"Yeah, she gave us a pretty lurid account, Fred. I can just see the whole story on the front page of the *Philadelphia Enquirer.*"

Fred nodded, shaking his head a little, not thinking the crack was the slightest bit funny. Tears welled up in the corners of his eyes, which he quickly dabbed away with a napkin. "My whole world is coming apart, Mr. Farrell. Everybody I loved is turning on me, and yet I'm the only sensible factor in their lives. I'm the rock, the settled one that tries to make them do the right thing. But they are so impetuous, so flighty, so selfish and narcissistic. Both of them. Nothing is serious to Darla. Probable or even possible consequences mean nothing to her if she can have what she wants right now. And James, he's just as bad. On the outside he seems so stable, so in control, but under that calm exterior is a maelstrom." The welled up tears started to fall, cascade actually.

Calmly, Fred, the huge bull of a man, stood and turned around, clasping his hands behind his back in a submissive gesture, waiting to be cuffed. As Farrell applied the Zip-tie cuffs, Tiffany came up with a bill. "That'll be five bucks, Sir."

Fred said, "That's Okay, Tiffany. It's on me. I probably won't be back for a while, so I want you and Chef Randy to run the place while I'm gone. Keep a good clean set of books, Tiff. I'll audit them when I come back. You have just grown up a bunch, so run the place well and invest the profits wisely. Split them with Randy. And maybe leave me a little something for when I come back. If I do."

As they walked out, Fred as compliant and cooperative as a Buddhist priest, Farrell said, "That was a nice gesture, Fred. Do you think Tiffany can be trusted with that kind of responsibility?"

"It doesn't really matter now, does it Detective?"

Chapter 34

Judge Harley Martin scowled a serious moue as he looked over the plethora of motions filed by Shapiro, the Greeneburg lawyer representing Antoine al Aqwon aka James Matheson. "All right, I've read these motions. Let's start with the confession. Mr. Shapiro, I understand your position as you set out in your rather voluminous brief. I suspect you are charging him by the hour. Mr. Brown, let me hear what you have to say."

"Judge, er," Brown was as uncomfortable as a black man at a KKK rally. "Er. I don't think that knowing Mr. O'Halloran, the defendant could have possibly felt he was under duress."

"Mr. O'Halloran had the gun in his hand that Mr. Matheson had previously brandished, is that right?"

"Right, your Honor."

"And the Defendant posed no further threat to Mr. O'Halloran once the gun was in the old lawyer's hand, right?"

"Uh," he so knew where this was going. Brown was actually hanging his head as he spoke. "That's correct, your Honor."

"And Mr. O'Halloran's big wolf of a dog had its jaws around Mr. Matheson's neck, right?"

"Well, it is just a German shepherd, but yes sir, that's my understanding."

Shapiro couldn't stand it. He had to put his two cents in and stomp the man when he was down. "Judge, Judge..."

"Shut up, Mr. Shapiro. Okay, the confession is out, obviously made under duress, unless you have some earth shattering legal precedent that has just come down from on high, Mr. Brown." Brown looked like he had been struck by lightning, minus the smoke coming out of his ears.

"I didn't think so. Let's look at this marital privilege argument about Mr. Matheson, a man mind you, wanting to keep out testimony of his spouse, Mr. Darling, another man. Appropriate name, eh gentlemen?"

They both nodded nervously not knowing where the Judge was going with this, but Shapiro having an inkling. He was starting to sweat and get even more nervous. His brashness usually had the effect of intimidating judges, but this guy from this hick town, he sure knew how to control his courtroom. Again, Shapiro couldn't restrain himself. "They are legally married, Judge, according to the state of Maryland."

"You will agree, won't you Mr. Shapiro, that the legality of same sex marriages in North Carolina has been questioned and probably violates the Ninth and Tenth Amendments to the United States Constitution?"

"No, no," Shapiro's voice was almost a squeal. The United States Supreme Court recently legalized same sex marriages and made it applicable to all fifty states."

"Ah yes, the United States Supreme Court. Yes of course they would do that. But that ruling doesn't sit well with my own personal beliefs. I am sure you suspected that, didn't you, Mr. Shapiro?"

With a nervousness bordering on panic, Shapiro acknowledged the Judge's personal views. "But your Honor, the Supreme Court....full faith and credit....the law…"

"Oh, shut up Mr. Shapiro. Here's the problem as I see it. Perhaps these murders were committed before same sex marriage was legal in our state. Then you want me to make the Supreme Court ruling an ex post facto law right? Relating back?"

"Mr. Brown, what do you have to say?"

"I hate to do this Judge, but I will concede Mr. Shapiro's point about the same sex marriage privilege. But we don't need to use the testimony of the married couple even if they are both men and the privilege has only recently been granted. We have the testimony of one of the co-conspirators written out in her own hand and implicating all the conspirators in this plot."

Shapiro was trying to figure out how to counter the admissibility of co-conspirators, even if they were married which did present a rather dicey point, he knew, but the Judge just put his hand up a little. "What next, Mr. Shapiro?"

Shapiro, always on the top of his legal game, was confused. "Uh, your Honor, there is the matter of…" he looked down at his notes, a bit shaken. "Uh the failure of the state to make known to the defense exculpatory evidence. They had the murder weapon in their possession, a .44 caliber Smith and Wesson Model 29 Magnum snub nose pistol that belonged to one Arnold Fleming. They never told us they had it so we could have our own independent experts test it to corroborate or disavow their own expert."

"Hmmm. Mr. Brown, is that right?"

"We didn't know about that, your honor, until just recently, after we got the statements of one of the conspirators. The .44 which was used to kill the three victims was turned in by Mr. Fleming, who we don't think at this point was actually one of the co-conspirators. This was pursuant to a Domestic Violence order issued by Judge Sam Hill at the request of his wife, who was one of the co-conspirators."

"But not the co-conspirator represented by Mr. Shapiro, here?"

Shapiro was smirking, thinking he had this one and could roast the hapless prosecutor, but he had not taken into consideration Brown's prodigious memory.

"No, Judge, but the knowledge of one conspirator is presumed to be known by all conspirators. Thus, if Darla Fleming, one of the alleged co-conspirators, had knowledge that the murder weapon had been turned over to the police by her husband, who we don't think is a conspirator, then that knowledge is presumed to have been known by all co-conspirators, including Mr. Matheson, and legally attributed to him. In addition, Judge, the female conspirator secretly got the gun back from her husband without him knowing about it after she had the domestic violence complaint against him dismissed. She then tried to kill Mr. O'Halloran with it."

"You don't represent the female co-conspirator do you Mr. Shapiro? If not," said the Judge not giving Shapiro a chance to answer, "I guess it's not your argument to make. Anything else?"

Shapiro had filed a bunch more motions, maybe a dozen, but knew that most of them were frivolous, inventions of the most legalistic corner of his excellent but nefarious mind, and any residual esteem Judge Martin held for him would be gone if he seriously tried to argue them. So he just dolefully shook his head, and sat back down with a plop. As he did, a little air escaped from the faux leather seat cushion, making a *pfft* sound. Everyone looked at him with a slight grin. Shapiro was glad his client wasn't in court to witness his humiliation.

Chapter 35

A month later, the three defendants were standing meekly in front of Judge Martin, each clad in their jailhouse orange jumpsuits. Fred's was a couple of sizes too small and it looked like the Danskin on a fat ballet dancer that was about to burst at the seams. Darla's dwarfed her, the sleeves and legs of the jump suit extending way past the end of her limbs, no semblance of her curvaceous figure discernible. Judge Martin stifled a snicker as he looked at the motley trio. "So you three are the notorious alley murderers, eh?" He looked over at Prosecutor Brown, who was avoiding his stern glance by pretending to look down at the papers in front of him. Becoming aware of the silence, Brown looked up querulously. Judge Martin merely scowled.

"Uh, Judge, the defendants and the State have entered into a plea bargain. It's signed by the parties, their attorneys and the state and even countersigned by our own head DA. May I approach the bench?"

Judge Martin read the plea agreements carefully. Then he looked up, first at Brown and then at the Defendants and their lawyers. "This was originally supposed to be a death penalty case, am I right?" Nobody would have been far off if they thought the old Judge got a perverse sort of pleasure in handing down the death penalty, especially on psychopaths like this trio.

The lawyers nodded slowly, while the Defendants all became a shade whiter as the blood drained from their faces. Sitting behind Brown were Detectives Farrell and Crouse, and lost in the recesses of the courtroom was Hamish O'Halloran, curious, but unobtrusive as always.

"You three can consider yourselves lucky. Yes indeed, very fortunate indeed. If it was me that was prosecuting this case you'd be swinging by the neck." Some whispering caused the Judge to turn and pay heed to the clerk, who was standing and wanted to make something known to the Judge.

"I know that, Mr. Speedy, it's just a figure of speech. Now the liberals in our legislature have made it real nice and easy for murderers to die with their fancy new drugs and sleep medication, so they never feel any panic and pain like their victims did. Okay, I guess I'll have to live with this pap although I am seriously considering rejecting this plea deal and make the state go to trial with the death penalty option viable. Let me hear from each of the Defendants to make sure this is a voluntary admission of guilt."

As beads of sweat poured from the foreheads of the Defendants, the Judge heard from each of the three, the forked vein on the center of his own forehead becoming increasingly prominent as each allocuted, admitting their role in the sordid crimes.

"All right, let's take a twenty minute recess. I want to see the lawyers in my chambers. I'm not sure I will accept this plea arrangement and I want to get some input off the record." The Judge stood as the bailiff called for the recess. Each defendant, meanwhile showed their trepidation in various ways, none of which were particularly gracious, the most interesting being the wet spot that appeared on the front of Antoine's jumpsuit which looked kind of like a target.

The judge stormed off to his chambers followed by a trail of sheepish lawyers. Each one was concerned about the ramifications of the Judge's threat to reject the plea agreement. Brown was worried about a long and difficult murder trial interminably clogging the Superior Court Docket and the other three about the effect on their careers if their clients got the death penalty.

"Mr. Brown, tell me why you want to let these criminals off with life, especially after these psychopaths killed four people?"

Shapiro burst forth with an interruption in his usual arrogant, self-righteous manner. "Four? Judge, my client is only charged with three murders."

"Three, four, what difference does it make? They killed their own mother, Mr. Shapiro, or did that escape your notice?"

"Antoine al Aqwon did not have anything to do with killing Alberta Joralemon, your Honor. He's absolutely innocent of that."

"You know, Shapiro, you are so narrow minded you can look through a key hole with both eyes. If he didn't know about poisoning her before she died, he's certainly an accessory after the fact. He took her body across state lines to his own cousin's funeral parlor to have her embalmed with that hardening agent. His actions in that conspiracy can be legitimately claimed to revert back *ab initio*. Stop arguing with me. Take it up on appeal if you don't like my decisions. You are going a long way to helping me to decide to toss this plea agreement."

Shapiro must have come from a family fraught with bickering for he never knew when to shut up. Just as he was about to say something else, Darla's new lawyer, a heavy set woman named Jilly van Dyke, from Greeneburg, who had the unique habit of literally talking out of the side of her mouth, punched him hard on the upper arm.

"Oops, sorry, Mr. Shapiro. I hope that gentle reminder that it was my turn to say something didn't sting too much." The two stared at each other with absolute loathing as Shapiro rubbed his sore arm. The Judge smiled a little at this unofficial justice thinking Shapiro got what he deserved. "Judge, my client is very appreciative of the State's offer. She probably is a psychopath, you are right, but rather than go through months of psychological testing to get a forensic approval of what everybody with a little common sense knows, we would like to plead in according to the plea agreement, and let her spend the remainder of her years in some nice maximum security facility somewhere."

"I appreciate the candidness, Ms. Van Dyke. I wonder how long somebody that little would last in prison." It wasn't a question. The judge was making a rhetorical statement just to illustrate a point, leaving the real meaning up to the fertile imaginations of those in his chambers who understood the gruesome facts of America's prison system.

The judge stroked his chin for a minute and then decided. "You know, folks, Ms. Van Dyke makes a good point. If I don't accept this plea agreement, which does get a bunch of cold blooded murderers off the street permanently, this case will be kicking around the Court of Appeals until my unborn great-grandchildren are lawyers. Let's go back into Court and get the plea on the record."

The legal entourage trooped back into the courtroom, taking their appropriate places, his Honor pulling up the rear. All the chattering and whispering in the courtroom ceased immediately. The Judge began, "All right. According to this plea deal which spares the lives of these three reprobates and saves the Court months of time, I will sentence each individual separately. Mr. al Aqwon, also known as James Matheson, step forward. Based on your plea of guilty to three counts of murder in the first degree, and your allocution to the facts, you are hereby sentenced to ...."

Just then Antoine fainted, or appeared to. In a flash, Big Fred was virtually on top of him giving him mouth to mouth. That was quite a feat given that both men were handcuffed and shackled though the cuffs only bound their hands in front. A collective gasp arose from everyone in the courtroom. The entire audience stood up at once trying to get a better view of what was going on. The noise they created just in standing, was nothing compared to that created by the virtual stampede of all the courtroom personnel charged with security rushing forward, including the attorneys for the two, as it became apparent that there was a little more than mouth to mouth going on. Sort of a last gasp before life in prison, if you know what I mean. A half dozen brown uniformed bodies tore at the two defendants trying to separate them and restore order, but with all those hands pawing and pulling, and bailiffs and deputies shouting, it wasn't quickly restored. Judge Harley Martin was banging his gavel like a Metallica drummer and the old bailiff was calling out "Order, order," but it sounded more like "Water, water," so one of the other bailiffs, thinking there was a fire, grabbed a fire extinguisher and started spraying. Foam was flying everywhere, covering the defendants, court personnel, and some of the spectators, so that you couldn't tell who was who.

With the entire attention of the Courtroom focused on the two writhing bodies, the general chaos, the press of the audience rushing forward to get a better view of what was going on, and the foam spraying everywhere, little Darla quietly slipped out of her hand cuffs, which were a bit slack even though they were as tight as they could go. She left her cuffs, shackles and her orange jump suit in a pile on the floor. Now sporting a slightly wrinkled blue dress, the same one that was the cause of the wardrobe malfunction which so distracted Patrolman Way North, she joined the group of spectators pushing and shoving to the bar to get a closer look at the action, but losing ground on purpose, she let herself get pushed to the back. Or maybe she wangled her way to the back. In any event, she was out of the rear door of the courtroom in a few seconds, virtually unnoticed, and looking like any other kid in the courthouse accompanying their parents. Except for the remarkable physique, of course.

Hamish O'Halloran, though, was the only one not interested in what was happening up front, for he had his eyes on his former client. He was thinking about the dichotomy of how extraordinarily beautiful the tiny creature was, yet how thoroughly evil. He watched her wriggle out of her cuffs, the cuffs not able to be made small enough to effectively restrain her tiny wrists. He watched as she made her way out of the courtroom, and followed her, discreetly, trying to figure out what she would do. He lost sight of her as she got in an elevator packed with all sorts of defendants, spectators and witnesses just excused from the morning recess of traffic court.

O'Halloran was trying to think like Darla, figuring out what she would do, where she would go, how she would effect her escape. He realized that she would have no idea, for Darla was just not into planning ahead, and that made it that much harder to figure out. So he went out of the Courthouse, found his car in the parking garage, and decided to head for Butch's house. That would be the place she would instinctively head for, the one person she could talk into helping her out of this mess.

As soon as he was on the Greeneburg Road, he saw her, walking along the side of the road with long, purposeful angry strides, her left thumb pointed upwards away from her body, like a kid hitchhiking, the blue dress fluttering in the breeze as cars whizzed past. He passed her and stopped on the shoulder, waiting for her to catch up with him. As she opened the door she recognized Hamish and hesitated.

"You have to turn yourself in, Darla. You know that."

"Look, you dweeb. I'm not going to spend the rest of my life in prison being the sex slave of some big old smelly sociopath, with hair under her arms and unshaven legs. I'm going to get Butch to take me to Mexico. We can drink Coronas or Dos Equis, bask in the sun, have sex whenever we want, and live happily ever after. Take me home."

O'Halloran realized she was not only a psychopath, she was truly insane. Her immature mind matched her little physique, neither one quite developed. Not nearly so. "You know I can't do that, Darla. I'm not about to commit a felony for you or anyone else."

At the sound of the crunch of gravel behind her, Darla spun around. Another car had pulled up, a taupe colored Taurus, the kind almost all detectives drive. Fittingly, this one was driven by a cop they both knew well, Greeneburg's finest, Detective Frank X. Farrell.

"Saw you duck out, Ham, so I followed you," he called out as he hopped out of his car. "I see you have captured our most wanted murderess." He approached Darla, but hadn't pulled out his service revolver. Didn't think he needed it with this diminutive defendant.

She walked toward the detective, a seductive sway in her walk, accentuating her curves, throwing out a little sexuality. Without a word, she approached him, her hands extended, inviting the cuffs. As he reached behind his back to unbutton the cuff case and removed the standard issue handcuffs, in a lightning fast move she grabbed his service revolver. Backing up, she pointed it at the distracted detective. "You are way too slow, Farrell. All those doughnuts have gone to your head. Made you complacent and stupid."

As was her habit when holding a firearm, much too heavy for her, the gun was waving in lazy circles as she pointed the barrel somewhere in his direction. Farrell noticed the safety was on, and realized the little murderess was not a gun expert, or even adept. "Where are you going to go, Darla? To Butch? Didn't you even notice him in Court? Watching you, waiting to see what was going to happen to his beloved." He inched closer to the gun barrel, then stopped. If he got too close she might even hit him if she managed to get the safety off and pull the trigger.

Darla thought about that, the distraction fatal. From behind, O'Halloran reached over her shoulder and grabbed the gun. Déjà vu all over again. The gun went off, the bullet a through and through on the front tire of Farrell's ride, the powerful recoil causing the gun to go sailing over her head, smacking O'Halloran a good one right on the same wound caused by the falling tree limb and the hood of the Camaro. Falling backward, semi-conscious, he instinctively reached forward, grabbing the collar of the blue dress. It tore off like a breakaway in a comic skit. Farrell gawked staring at the completely bare, beautiful body, unbelieving.

But he retrieved the cuffs and had the presence of mind to make the arrest and cuff her. O'Halloran moaned as he came to, blood pooling in his eye socket, as he lay on his back on the gravel road shoulder. "I'm blind, I'm blind," he shouted. "Oh, God, I'm blind. She shot me in the eye! Oh, woe."

Farrell ignored his wailing as he secured the naked beauty, handcuffs behind her back, in the front seat of O'Halloran's car. "I'm commandeering your car and taking her in, Ham. Guard my cruiser. I've got paramedics and the police wrecker coming." By the way, just wipe the blood from your eyes and you'll be fine." And with that, Detective Farrell, with the seductively unclad defendant firmly seat belted with her hands secured behind her back, cautiously took off, merging into traffic.

Chapter 36

After wiping the blood from his eyes, smearing it all over his already not too pretty face, O'Halloran watched them drive off in his nondescript car, the sort of gray colored Japanese sedan, with the uninspired design nobody ever remembered. He had polished up the Camaro and was not about to take the chance of getting a dent in a parking lot at the courthouse, so he had driven the old gray whatever it was. As he heard a loud noise like *varrrroom*, he turned his head just in time to see a huge black Dodge Ram truck as it sped by his location. He had an inkling that he had seen that truck before somewhere, as it bore down on his own car, like a black cat about to pounce on a little gray mouse. The truck must have been doing at least sixty when it rammed into the back of his car. Ham had not fully returned to his senses watching the collision, and could only think, "So that's what Dodge Ram means."

Butch hopped out of the Dodge truck and ran up to the wrecked car. He tried to tear open the passenger side door, but the impact of the collision had wedged it shut. It took him a few minutes, but with something like superhuman strength, Butch was able to wrest it from its predicament, accompanied by a terrifying metallic screeching sound. He glanced over at the unconscious Detective swathed in the white deflated airbag. After whipping out a K-Bar knife he cut the seat belt restraining little Darla. Butch gingerly rescued his semi-conscious, gorgeously nude wife. Cradling her in his arms with the loving tenderness one might show a newborn baby, he ran back to the Dodge, and, after carefully wrapping her in a camouflaged poncho liner he just happened to have in the truck, and securing her in the passenger seat, he tore off on the highway at a high rate of speed.

A few minutes later, after his head had cleared, O'Halloran trotted over to his wrecked car to check on his friend. Detective Farrell had been slammed in the face by the impact of the airbag and no doubt had suffered severe whiplash, but he was starting to come around. Naturally, the first thing he said was, "What happened?"

O'Halloran, talking ninety miles a minute, spewing the words out like a sputtering volcano, gave him the whole story.

"Butch, huh? Let me call my cousin." Farrell was rubbing his temples, only about three quarters alert.

Ten minutes later an ambulance pulled up, sirens wailing. A tow truck followed, not more than a minute later virtually pushing some of the growing crowd of rubberneckers out of the way. Marsha Grainger jumped out of the ambulance while it was still moving, and immediately took care of O'Halloran's bloody head wound, while Mickey Mendenhall, the short armed heavy set guy, attended to the abrasions on Farrell's face. "It's just a minor concussion, Detective, but you probably will have a very sore neck tomorrow when you wake up. Whiplash is nothing to sneer at. Here, I'll give you this soft collar to wear, but you need to check with an orthopedic doc, ASAP, got it? In fact, why don't you get in the bus and we'll take you down to the ER for an x-ray. Let me check over there with my partner."

When she first looked at O'Halloran, Grainger was really worried. The bloody face looked like a hand grenade had gone off right in front of it, but after she wiped the still squeamish O'Halloran's head down with a saline solution and a couple of towels, she determined that all the blood had come from the same old newly opened head wound.

O'Halloran, in his dithering around, had just spread blood all over his face. After she had cleaned the wound and stanched the bleeding, Marsha swathed O'Halloran's head with a gauze bandage over his strenuous objection. "A simple bandage will do, Miss Grainger. You don't have to go overboard."

When she was done he looked like a voodoo zombie, or at least like the walking wounded at a triage center in Afghanistan, but still, a little blood did seep through the gauze. She wrapped it a few more times, snickering.

Just then Detective Crouse pulled up fast, skidding to a stop behind the ambulance, the gravel on the road shoulder flying, making a pockety-pock sound as the gravel his tires threw up peppered Farrell's Ford. He jammed it in park and was out of the door while his own big old Taurus was still rocking. He ran up to Farrell but before he could ask what happened, Farrell said, "Darla's gone. Butch took her. Let's go."

Both EMTs were protesting loudly as the two ran to the Taurus, hopped in and Crouse floored it. O'Halloran watched forlornly, looking from the big industrial strength wrecker, which was tending to Farrell's Taurus, while ignoring his own Japanese model which he was pretty sure would never be drivable again, to the EMTs. Marsha, figuring they really couldn't return to the ER empty handed, said, "Get in the bus, Mr. O'Halloran. Let's let a doctor look at you and see just what's wrong with your head." With a sardonic grin on her face resulting from her own little witticism, big ol' Marsha virtually perp walked the pathetic and meekly protesting O'Halloran into the ambulance, seat-belted him onto the gurney, and they took off, sirens and blue light on in full force, Code Three.

Meanwhile, it took Crouse about fifteen or twenty minutes to find Butch's house. They were originally dispatched to his mother's house, because that was his last known address according to the dispatcher, but after checking in with a totally flummoxed Mrs. Fleming, Farrell announced, "They probably went to Darla's."

The big black Dodge Ram truck, with some noticeable front end damage, but still as shiny and pristine as a new penny otherwise, was parked at an angle in front of the house. The two detectives rushed in without knocking, guns drawn, yelling, "Police, police," ready to shoot at the slightest provocation.

They stopped short. There was an eerie silence, a stillness that shouldn't have been there if the house was occupied. They quickly checked each room, guns drawn at the ready, and then, when they couldn't find any sign at all of Darla and Butch, ran up the stairs abandoning all caution. The more youthful and athletic Crouse was the first one to enter the master bedroom. "Oh, shit!" was all he said.

Farrell, wheezing a bit and still wearing the soft orthopedic collar, went in behind him a few seconds later. "What? Oh!"

They were lying on the bed, both of them stark naked, *in flagrante delicto*. Butch was lying supine, his head to one side, a little bluish green froth having dribbled from the corner of his mouth, his nose and mouth area very red, dead as a door nail.

"Cyanide, it looks like, Cuz. Darla killed him." He sniffed an open half empty beer bottle on the night stand, and nodded with an air of certainty. Meanwhile, Crouse checked out Darla. She was lying on top of Butch, her head on his massive chest, his huge dead hand still grasping her neck, the angle of which was unnatural. There was no pulse.

They looked at the two dead bodies with a sense of sadness for a few minutes, considering, evaluating, experiencing the emotions of all decent humans when they see premature death.

"What do you think, Cuz? One last romp before the serious shit started? Darla poisoned Butch as retribution for all the abuse, and when he realized what she had done, they were right in the middle of the act. Almost as a reflex, he just reached out and broke her neck with one hand, right? She was one sadistic little woman."

Farrell was silent for a minute. "Yeah, something like that." He shook his head, morosely.

Chapter 37

Neither policeman said a word as they slowly drove back to Pine Ridge after forensics processed the scene. The coroner took the bodies back to the morgue when he announced his preliminary findings. The first impression of the officers had been confirmed. If the coroner had been drinking, he sobered up in a hurry when he saw the two naked corpses. Farrell finally spoke as they approached Assistant District Attorney Brown's office. "Crouse, I have to find my car and get home after we finish here. Can I get a lift to the garage?" Not a word about the demise of the bizarre couple.

"No problem. Let's check in with the DA first."

Farrell merely nodded. A few minutes later, they knocked on Brown's door and went in without a sound from Brown. The veteran prosecutor was standing, looking out the window, his back to them. His hands were clasped tightly together, behind his back. He was rocking back and forth.

Farrell spoke, "Case is over, Billy. Darla poisoned Butch, and he broke her neck with one hand before he died. They're both gone. Down at the Greeneburg morgue now. We found their bodies, naked and dead at Darla's. You got anything for us before we go home? I don't know about Crouse, here, but I'm tired, really mentally fagged out."

At first Brown didn't answer, didn't turn around, just stood there, rigid. After a few moments, he turned to face them. "I heard." That was all.

They left and were surprised to see O'Halloran sitting on one of the wooden benches next to a stack of file boxes outside Brown's office. His head was still swathed in gauze, a little blood seeping through on his hairline or what would have been his hairline if he had hair there. He was bent over, his head in his hands, his elbows on his knees.

"Sorry about your car, Ham. Maybe you can get the big black Dodge Ram pickup if you sue Butch's estate. Worth a try."

He didn't want it. Too ostentatious for him. He knew the insurance company would eventually get around to paying him, although they would probably jack up his premiums. That meant he would have to write another indignant letter to the insurance commissioner. And, he thought with relief, he still had his snazzy old Camaro.

Later that afternoon, sitting on the tree stump in his back yard, idly stroking Caesar's big furry head, O'Halloran was thinking about his client, the late Darla Darling Fleming. She *was* really beautiful, that was for sure, but a miniature paragon of evil. Maybe that was why he never married, subliminally thinking all women had that evil streak. No, that was not it. He knew why he never married. In his entire life he never had a real relationship with a woman. He was too shy, too insecure, too aware of his own faults and shortcomings.

He thought of Doris at the Legal Lunch. And Honey, from Lefty's. Now that was more like it. Real women. Down to earth women. Decent women. Women without ambition, but not followers. No sir, they were their own women, for sure, confident and capable. They were his type of woman. Was he their type of man?

Chapter 38

After the furor had died down and Antoine and Fred had been sentenced to life without parole, the judge purposely not making a recommendation to house them separately, O'Halloran got a call from the insurance company. "Mr. O'Halloran, my name is Elvin Tweedy, the adjustor for Double Action Insurance. You remember, we talked about the fire at Lefty's Restaurant and Grill. Well, we have completed our investigation and.... He paused and then appeared to have just stopped. O'Halloran was thinking the connection or maybe Tweedy had died.

"You still alive, Mr. Tweedy? What did your investigators conclude?"

"Well, that's the problem, Mr. O'Halloran. They didn't conclude anything. They didn't find out who threw the flashbang, but they couldn't rule out Mr. Lefkowsky's involvement."

"So what are you telling me, Mr. Tweedy?" O'Halloran hated working with insurance adjustors. He knew the man was trying to figure out some way to justify not paying on the policy. The man was actually stuttering before he said, "We are prepared to pay your client half the policy proceeds as full and final settlement."

"Half?" O'Halloran almost shouted. He wanted to say, "You weasely, crooked cheapskate," and a whole bunch of other invectives, but instead he actually said, "All right, Mr. Tweedy, I'll just file this law suit, and by the way, I am amending it to include a request for treble damages for unfair and deceptive trade practices on the part of your company for denying this claim without any reason at all. You don't have a single even halfway legitimate basis for reducing this claim. I'll bet when we look into it through further discovery on the amended complaint we can find a distinct company practice where you shysters have a regular routine of refusing to pay valid claims. I just love discovery, especially in this electronic age." He was bluffing, but it sounded good.

"Well, uh. Well, I'll talk to my supervisor and see what I can do."

"You do that, Mr. Tweedy, and I bet on discovery I will actually find out you are the supervisor with all sorts of authority. And if I do, I'm adding you personally to my treble damages suit." He hung up and slammed the phone down, bruising his index finger in the process. "Ow, that hurt." He said as he stuck the swelling finger in his mouth.

A few moments later his phone rang again. "Mr. O'Halloran, you don't have to be so crotchety. I talked to my supervisor and he authorized a firm offer of eighty per cent of the policy limits. But I'm still suspicious. I have never had a claim so thoroughly documented by the claimant. I mean he even had the soda inventory itemized to the last bottle, and I consider this to be somewhat miraculous since none of the documents were burned up in the fire as they usually are in such cases."

O 'Halloran knew what he had to do legally, but he couldn't resist a dig on insurance company practices. "All right, Mr. Tweedy, I guess insurance companies kind of bank on people not being smart enough to keep their inventory records in places other than the ones insured against fire loss. Makes it tough to prove a case when all your records are burned up, eh Mr. Tweedy? I will talk to my client and see if he wants to settle or go forward with the suit. I'm actually looking forward to a little civil suit court time."

He could hear the adjustor sigh as he hung up the phone.

O'Halloran called Lefty's home phone but was surprised to find out the number had been disconnected — no longer in service. He called him on his cell but it just rang and rang. He let it go maybe twenty times but there was no answer. He sat there for a minute, frustrated, wondering what he would do if Lefty had moved without leaving any way to contact him. Why would he do that? With a little incipient suspicion, he wondered how to find Lefty. Inspired, he called Honey.

She had no idea but knew someone who might, and would call him back when she had some news. A half hour later, the phone rang in Ham's kitchen. It was Honey. "Ham, it looks like Lefty has moved to the Keys. I was told he sold everything he owned and moved in with his boyfriend in a condo in Key West. Here's his number."

O'Halloran was floored. After a few minutes he said, "Honey, do you think Lefty could have been behind the whole flashbang incident? Planned the fire from the very start?"

"I have no idea, Ham, but now that you mention it that thought does make some sense. Lefty was always complaining about the business, the hours he had to work. He hated that his gay friends were in such close contact with the super macho types like cops and bikers. He was petrified something bad would happen to them. Lefty was always as nervous as a bull at a milking machine."

Ham considered this development. That eighty per cent began to look pretty good just now, but it would be unethical to accept the payment without his client's knowledge or permission. And he would need Lefty's signature on the release in order to get the check. And where would he send the money?

He called the number Honey had given him. A professional voice like a radio announcer informed him of the number he had just dialed, which, of course, he already knew since he had dialed it, and invited him to leave a message. He did. O'Halloran could just picture Lefty on some whitewashed veranda in the tropical Keys, shaded by huge swaying palms, kicking back, wearing an undyed, embroidered linen guayabera shirt, drinking a mint julep. He had that picture fixed in his mind long enough to become jealous. Damn.

Chapter 39

He was still not sure how it could have possibly been Lefty behind the torching of the restaurant. He was sure Lefty had been in the bar, nervously checking to see if everything was copacetic, the patrons under control, everybody was getting along just fine, when the grenade went off. That, of course, started him thinking about the two women in his life, the steady Doris and the luscious Honey. Then he thought of the unparalleled beauty of his dead client. He could not concentrate on anything and his thoughts were racing. Attention Deficit Disorder is like that. Back to the competent Doris with her slight but intriguing curves and her unwavering competence. Doris represented family to him and he tried to put himself in that picture, being the man of the doublewide house, coming home from work and finding Doris at the stove, busy with dinner, dealing with the ornery, recalcitrant Maybelle.

Thinking of the defiant teenager caused him to think of the scantily clad young things at Mother Nature's, but he was repelled by that thought. He had no idea how to deal with young girls. He could remember when he was a boy, but girls were different. A different species even. The image at Mother Nature's was replaced with a more welcoming image. That of Honey and the dimly lit bar at Lefty's. That segued into the chaos following the flashbang and the soft erotic form as he lay on top of the unconscious Honey, experiencing her smell, her comfort, for just a second before reacting the way he should.

These thoughts disappeared and were replaced by the embarrassment of his dinner dates at the home of both women. He heaved a great sigh at these thoughts. He had to make amends.

Wrestling with these thoughts, he tried to think of what the ordinary man, that elusive standard in so many legal situations, would do.

He called Honey. He knew he wasn't an ordinary man. That was a much higher standard for him to try to achieve, but he would at least give it a try. He wasn't the most smooth talking guy, but after stammering and stuttering, she seemed glad to accept a dinner date for the next evening. He wondered for a minute just what was wrong with Honey that she would be interested in a klutz like him. He was excited as a puppy with a new squeaky toy when he hung up and then noticed that was not all that was excited.

He was fifteen minutes early for their date but decided to wait in the parking lot until it was time. Even though he definitely was, he didn't want to appear over anxious. He had stopped off at the local grocery store and gotten a couple of nice bouquets of flowers which he awkwardly thrust toward her when Honey opened the door, an ear to ear grin on his face. She was characteristically dressed in a clingy black dress with a set of large faux pearls decorating her revealing décolletage.

O'Halloran had thought long and hard about where he would take her. There was no restaurant in Pine Ridge that he thought would be suitable, that is, fine enough for such a wonderful woman, so in typical O'Halloran fashion, he left it up to Honey. They drove to Greeneburg, where she had made reservations at Luigi's. While perhaps not a five star eating establishment, the ambience at Luigi's Spaghetti House couldn't have been better. It was dark inside with most of what little light there was coming from the candles on each table. The little candles were stuck in Chianti bottles fulminating with a mélange of different colored hardened candle wax. Each table had red and white checkered slick oil cloth table covers, and a small bottle with a carnation in it. He was a little jealous when the maitre d,' a slender middle aged man with graying temples accentuating his shiny black hair and a pencil thin mustache, addressed Honey by name. O'Halloran was unsure whether the accent was genuine Italian or displaced Brooklynese.

They enjoyed the food, though, Northern Italian style veal with a side of angel hair pasta Bolognese, a bottle of Chianti, and a Caesar salad. There was something romantic about the Italian flavor, even as retro as the little restaurant was. O'Halloran had the feeling he was transported back in time to a safe and comfortable place.

There was nothing rushed about the dinner, the service impressive, and the conversation easy yet stimulating. They talked about Lefty, the interesting mix of customers at the bar and restaurant, the excellent food, and even speculated on who Lefty might have hired to toss the flashbang. O'Halloran was amazed at the range of things Honey could easily converse about, from politics to art, and even, surprisingly, an intelligent yet not self-righteous conversation about religion, the subject that most confounded O'Halloran.

They spent a couple of hours together in the restaurant, feeling as if they had known one another their whole lives. As they walked out of Luigi's, overwhelmed by a sense of contentment from the pleasant but not cloying meal and a few glasses of red wine, O'Halloran realized he had no idea what to do next. He supposed he had no choice but to take Honey back to her apartment, since he couldn't think of a single other thing to do, but as she was walking back to the car, holding his arm close to her but not, it seemed, for support, she made a suggestion.

"Ham, why don't we go over to Ridley's Drive-in, near the by-pass. It is just about dark, now, and they will soon be starting the main feature. I know, drive-in movies are passé, but they can be a lot fun. Ridley's usually features some old classic, sometimes even a black and white. It would be a perfect end to this wonderful evening."

Did he have a choice? He didn't object in the slightest, for it seemed like a great idea, especially when for the first time in forever he was feeling a romantic stirring in his loins.

They got there just before the feature started, a Bugs Bunny cartoon that was delighting the audience. The drive-in was not full but there were enough cars scattered about, O'Halloran thought, for Ridley to make profit. The feature film was *An Affair to Remember* starring Cary Grant, an old classic from the fifties. The nostalgic comfort of sliding back to an era when things were simple, the country was free of all the international and social crises to come, along with the wine, made O'Halloran feel euphoric, and, strangely, at peace.

As they settled down, parking in a spot near the middle of the drive-in, Honey suggested they put the top down on the old Camaro. It was a pleasant night, just an occasional breeze cooling the slight sweat that had begun to accumulate on O'Halloran's brow, and he readily acquiesced. He was surprised and delighted when she sidled over on the bench seat, and snuggled next to him as the movie began to play. He held her close, his arm around her like a reluctant teenager. He could feel her warmth, the sweet smell of her hair, familiar yet enticing, and her scent, redolent with an animal lure. He was filled with exhilaration, yet fearful that what he was experiencing was love. He just didn't know what to do, paralyzed in mind and body.

For twenty minutes he held her like that, his mind intermittently torn between thinking about the movie and sweet, sweet Honey, until his arm began to ache. He began to fidget and Honey looked up at him, querulously. He looked into her eyes. She wanted him to kiss her, he could just feel it. So he shifted a bit, stretching his legs as he did so, and leaned toward her, his lips puckered in anticipation, his mind racing. She closed her eyes, and…

AAAROOOGAH.

All eyes in the drive-in were on them. A couple of cars behind them even turned on their headlights to get a better look at what was going on in the Camaro. Honey started to laugh but O'Halloran was mortified.

Oh, the shame of it all!

CPSIA information can be obtained
at www.ICGtesting.com
Printed in the USA
LVOW03s2041050218
565347LV00004B/802/P